D1234125

Dear Reader,

Thank you for joining me on this journey. *Finding Home* is very close to my heart. Not only is our youngest daughter adopted from Korea—we have five daughters!—but my sister and her family also work with orphans in China, running summer camps there.

In *Finding Home* Anne's heart is tugged in the same way mine was when I came to see how wonderful these children are. There is nothing more satisfying than loving a child who needs a family. I hope you enjoy the story as Anne discovers just what it means to love "the least of these."

Warmly,
Traci DePree
writing as Emily Thomas

Finding Home

Secrets of the
BLUE HILL LIBRARY

EMILY THOMAS

Guideposts

New York

Secrets of the Blue Hill Library is a trademark of Guideposts.

Published by Guideposts Books & Inspirational Media
110 William Street
New York, NY 10038
Guideposts.org

Copyright © 2015 by Guideposts. All rights reserved.

This book, or parts thereof, may not be reproduced, stored in a retrieval system, or transmitted in any form or by any means, electronic, mechanical, photocopying, recording, or otherwise, without the written permission of the publisher.

The characters and events in this book are fictional, and any resemblance to actual persons or events is coincidental.

Every attempt has been made to credit the sources of copyrighted material used in this book. If any such acknowledgment has been inadvertently omitted or miscredited, receipt of such information would be appreciated.

Scripture references are from the following sources: The Holy Bible, King James Version (KJV). The Holy Bible, New International Version®, NIV®. Copyright © 1973, 1978, 1984 by International Bible Society. Used by permission of Zondervan.

"From the Guideposts Archives" is reprinted with permission from Guideposts magazine. Copyright © 2007 by Guideposts. All rights reserved.

Cover and interior design by Müllerhaus
Cover illustration by Ross Jones, represented by Deborah Wolfe, LTD
Typeset by Aptara, Inc.

Printed and bound in the United States of America
10 9 8 7 6 5 4 3 2 1

Finding Home

CHAPTER ONE

Anne Gibson felt her head jerk just a moment before realizing that she was still in church. She'd fallen asleep again. She opened her hazel eyes and saw her five-year-old daughter, Liddie, staring at her and shaking her head. Her little arms were crossed in front of herself and she raised a disapproving brow. Anne felt her face flame. She glanced around to see if anyone had noticed.

Lately, it seemed she was tired constantly. Why was that? She got plenty of sleep, yet her eyelids drooped as if weighted.

"Sorry," she mouthed, the adult apologizing to the child as Liddie returned her attention to the front where Reverend Tom Sloan was introducing the visiting missionary family to the Blue Hill Community Church.

"The Haydens have been a part of our extended church family for as long as I can remember," he was saying. "Your parents were from Blue Hill too as I recall," he said to Pam Hayden, the wife, who stood along with her husband and their seven children on the platform. The kids lined up like stair steps, ages five to seventeen. Three were biological, Caucasian like their parents, while the other four were of Indian descent with beautiful light brown skin and the black hair of South Asia.

"Yes, they were…originally," Pam said. "But my folks were missionaries in India for forty years, so that's really home to me.

That's where I grew up. In Mumbai." Pam nodded and turned to her husband.

The reverend followed her lead. "And you, Cory? Did you grow up in India as well?"

Cory shook his head. "No, sir, I grew up in Green Bay, Wisconsin. I went to Bible school just out of high school. That was where God gave me the vision of my future." Cory Hayden gave a wry smile, waiting a half beat. "Yes, that's where I met Pam."

The congregation chuckled. Anne remembered Pam's folks from the few furloughs they took in Blue Hill, Pennsylvania, when she was a girl. They were a quiet, unassuming couple with a heart for the poorest of the poor, friends of her great-aunt Edie's. Anne's parents invited them to the house for supper whenever they came home for visits as well, so she'd known Pam a bit growing up, though their visits were separated by years and Pam was a bit older than Anne.

Reverend Tom went on, "How long have the two of you been in India? Maybe you can tell us a little about your work there."

"We've lived in India since Pam and I got married." Cory reached for the mic, which the reverend relinquished. "We run an orphanage there, though our mission is to help needy children in whatever situation they find themselves. Many live on the streets, begging, hustling, doing all kinds of things just to survive. It is a tragic, tragic situation, where children suffer unimaginably." He glanced at Pam. "We identify these kids and, if they don't have families, bring them to our facility where we clothe and feed them, give them a good education." He turned, taking in the whole congregation as he went on. "Children who aren't adopted by the time they are ten or eleven years old aren't likely to ever have a mother or a father. So we train them, as best we can. Give them skills so that when they reach adulthood and are expected to survive on their own they're prepared. For example, we run a sewing school for young women. We don't want them to end up back on the streets." He shook his head, his gaze returning to his children and wife. "If you or anyone you know has room in your hearts, please consider adopting. There are so many children who need families." His gaze turned to his wife. "Pam and I have always loved children, as you can see. We've adopted four and, Lord willing, we'll adopt more. That's part of the danger of running an orphanage" — he chuckled — "you end up taking a few home with you."

Reverend Tom went down the line, introducing each of the seven children, asking their ages and their favorite subject in school.

Then he went on, lifting his gaze to the congregation, "The Haydens will be in Blue Hill for the next couple of weeks, so it's a great opportunity to get to know them better. They've offered to help with our new program, called Summer Fun, along with some of our regular members…" He pointed to Wendy Pyle who raised her hand. "That will culminate in the kids putting on a play for us about all that they'll be learning about life in India and other countries and what it's like to be missionaries." He smiled. "You're going to want your kids to participate in this awesome program. It's going to be special indeed. Who knows — maybe it'll inspire some of our kids to do the kinds of things that Pam and Cory do."

Anne glanced to the side. Liddie was swinging her legs as her wide eyes took in the family up front.

"Am I going to Summer Fun?" she asked in a too-loud whisper.

"Yes," Anne mouthed. She'd told Liddie that she'd signed her and Ben up for the two-week event a while ago, but that didn't seem to stop her from asking over and over again.

"I also wanted to thank all the families that signed up to host the Haydens for suppers while they're here," Reverend Tom went on. "We had enough families that Pam and Cory shouldn't have to cook at all while they're home."

Cory Hayden added, "Yes, thank you all for that. I want to add a thank you to the Pyle family for letting us bunk with them."

Wendy waved the comment aside. "Just wait till I put 'em to work," she said with a hand cupped around her mouth.

"We'll be praying for you!" Reverend Tom said, placing a hand on Cory's shoulder. Everyone laughed.

Then to the congregation, Reverend Tom said, "You're all invited downstairs for a lunch the ladies of the missions committee have put together." Even as he said it, Anne became aware of the scent of barbecued beef sandwiches in the air.

The organist played the final song of the service, and everyone rose to sing. Little feet shuffled, and the Haydens made their way to their seats in the front left pew, across from where Anne and her two children sat. Liddie gave a wave to a girl who looked to be about her age. She had dark-chocolate eyes and dimples in her plump cheeks when she smiled back at Liddie.

As the congregation moved out, Liddie went straight for the girl, with Anne and her nine-year-old son Ben following behind. "I'm Liddie," Anne's precocious five-year-old said. "You're gonna have supper at our house one night this week." She gave a toothless grin. "Which night is it, Mom?" Liddie lifted her face to Anne.

"I think tomorrow, but don't take my word for it," Anne said. "I need to check the sign-up sheet to be certain."

"We have a schedule that the church secretary gave us," Pam assured, placing a familiar warm hand on Anne's upper arm. "It's good to see you, Anne." She reached to give her old friend a hug.

"It's been a long time," Anne said.

Pam nodded. "Sure has. I know it's been since before Cory and I got married at least."

"My name is Natalie," the little girl Liddie's age said.

"I'm Liddie. How old are you?" Liddie asked. "I'm five."

Natalie smiled shyly and said, "Me too."

Anne reached to shake hands with Cory, but the father of the clan pulled her into a hug. He was a tall thin man with blond hair and a mischievous glint in his blue eyes. "Pam's told me about you. Anne Gibson, right?"

Anne nodded, instantly at ease with the gregarious man.

Each of their girls wore a traditional Indian sari, a long, elaborately decorated, brightly colored piece of fabric wrapped and draped around their bodies with a short T-shirt type top in a solid, equally vibrant color.

"How do you put that on?" Liddie asked Natalie, pointing to the girl's dress.

"Oh, it's easy," Natalie replied. "I can show you when we go to your house."

"Sweet!"

Ben had moved to talk to the boys in the Hayden family. There were three close in age to Ben, and two teenaged boys who wandered off, following the scent of food.

"So are you glad to be back in Blue Hill?" Pam Hayden asked Anne, pulling her attention back.

"I am. I like being the town librarian," Anne said, meeting the woman's pale blue eyes. She was a pretty thing, with honey-toned skin that complemented her dark brown hair. She was a bit older than Anne, in her late thirties. "It's so much different from the New York Public Library where I worked before," Anne said. "There were things I loved about working in the big city and there are things I love about small-town life." She shrugged. "I was just meant to be the custodian of Blue Hill's library."

Wendy Pyle moved into the circle. "Custodian?" She screwed up her face. "Don't let Anne act all modest. She's the best librarian in the state of Pennsylvania." Anne felt her face flame at the compliment.

"I just think it's pretty special, your aunt Edie doing that for you. And for Blue Hill. My folks always spoke so highly of your aunt Edie. I remember them getting letters from her." She glanced at her husband.

"Did your aunt ever visit India?" he asked.

Anne paused to think back. "I seem to remember a trip... I was a girl at the time, so I'm not sure. Do you remember, Pam?"

"Yes, I think there was some sort of visit...I went to boarding school during my high school years, so it's possible that she went when I wasn't around," Pam said. "Mom and Dad passed years ago or I'd ask them."

"I was so sorry to hear that," Anne said. "Aunt Edie told me at the time."

"Were Edie and your folks close friends?" Wendy asked.

Pam pursed her lips. "I think maybe they were high school friends...? Edie Summers was someone they talked of often." She finally shrugged and said to Liddie who was whispering with Natalie, "Are you excited about Summer Fun, Liddie?"

The girl's eyes lit up. "I am! I want to wear a dress like Natalie's!"

"It's called a *sari*—pronounced like 'I'm sorry.' We're going to have some Indian food too," Pam went on. "Have you ever had Kachumbar?"

Liddie shook her head.

"Oh, you'll like it. It's an onion cucumber salad—we have it with almost every meal."

"Onions and cucumbers?"

Anne could tell that Liddie wanted to twist up her face but was resisting the urge. She'd never really loved cucumbers. Anne gave her a little shake of the head. And Liddie said politely, "That sounds...good."

Pam laughed and said, "I won't make you eat everything, deal? Just try it and if you don't like it, you can pass."

"Deal!" Liddie grinned.

* * *

A few minutes later, members of the Blue Hill Community Church chatted, eating lunch around long folding tables in the basement of the late nineteenth-century church as ladies from the kitchen peddled coffee. There was something familiar about having a noon meal here with people Anne saw every week, many of whom were frequent patrons at the library. They'd become family. People whom Anne treasured and prayed for. That connection had started soon after her return from New York, where she'd lived with her husband and children for several years. Then after the deaths of her husband, Eric, and her great-aunt Edie Summers she'd moved back here, and these people had filled in that hollow by small spoonfuls. Unintentionally at first. Just by being neighborly. Then as her connection to them grew, she came to love them as her own family.

Chad and Wendy Pyle rose from their seats at the long tables to head home, along with their tribe of children. "We'll see you back at the house," Chad Pyle said to Cory Hayden who was talking to Mildred Farley.

"Sure will," the missionary said.

As Anne studied them, she could see that Cory and Pam had an easy way about them. They were natural with children and adults alike. She could picture them working at an orphanage in India, caring for little ones who would likely never know the love of a mother or father.

She wondered about Aunt Edie and Cory's question of whether or not she'd visited the Stiebs, Pam's parents, in India. Where had that friendship grown from? Anne was curious. She seemed to recall that Aunt Edie had gone to India when Anne was in her early teens, remembered seeing some mementos from a trip to that region of the world somewhere in the attic when she'd first moved into her great-aunt's house. Maybe she could find out a bit more. Dig a little, just to see if there was more there.

Anne was curious, and when Anne was curious it always led to action.

* * *

It was a quiet Sunday afternoon. The kids were playing in the yard behind the big Victorian while Anne sat on the front porch with a glass of iced tea and a good mystery novel opened on her lap.

As she read, she kept thinking about Aunt Edie's trip to India. What had she done there? Where exactly had she gone? Had she traveled alone or had someone gone with her? In all the years she'd known her great-aunt she couldn't recall much about it. Of course Anne had been young still, barely a teenager. Perhaps the older woman thought she wasn't old enough to hear about her adventures or she thought that Anne wouldn't be interested.

Well, she was interested now. If only her great-aunt were still around to tell the stories. Anne missed the vivacious woman who could never seem to pass up the opportunity to tell a good tale.

The children's voices mixed with the sound of lawn mowers buzzing across the neighborhood. Birds sang in the lilac bushes that lined the backyard of the old Victorian house, which housed the town library and Anne and her children, who lived in its second- and third-story apartment.

Ryan Slater had come over after lunch to play with Ben. The two boys had become almost inseparable since the Gibsons had moved to Blue Hill. Ryan had lost both of his parents in a car accident four years ago. He was being raised by his uncle Alex Ochs, Anne's former high school sweetheart. His loss and Ben's loss of his father seemed to be the very thing that bound the boys, made them understand each other like no one else could. To lose a parent or both parents was incomprehensible to Anne, especially when the children were still so young.

Hershey, Ben's chocolate Lab, was in the middle of the boys' play, wanting attention. He climbed on the old refrigerator box the boys had picked up on the curb at one of the neighbors' houses and were using as a fort. "Hershey, get down!" Ben hollered at the dog.

Hershey bounded off the wobbly box, then circled around and jumped right back up. "I said *down!*" Ben repeated.

"Ben," Anne called across the yard. She waited until he looked her way to continue. "I'm going to head inside to look for something in the attic. Is that okay?"

"Sure, Mom," Ben shouted back. "Can you take Hershey upstairs? He's driving me crazy."

"Okay." She called the dog who came running.

"Keep an eye on Liddie," she added.

"I will."

The five-year-old was holding one side of the fort in place with one hand. In her other hand, she held a big roll of shipping tape, at the ready for the boys to fix the "additions" — other, smaller boxes they'd scavenged — into position.

Anne led the large dog up the steps and into their darkened apartment. Then she moved to the attic door on the third floor. The attic was dark as Anne's eyes adjusted. Dust motes floated in the sticky air through the shaft of light that followed Anne. The hot June air felt stifling in the dank, musty space.

Aunt Edie sure liked to collect things. Old hatboxes were stacked in a haphazard pile next to several trunks. A spinning wheel was visible amid cobweb-laced wooden chairs, tables, file cabinets, and an ancient metal crib frame. Lamps, books, crates, tchotchkes of all kinds, as well as box after box of who-knew-what that formed a maze through the cramped space.

Anne knew that Aunt Edie had traveled to many exotic locations in her lifetime as a travel writer. The woman enjoyed adventure almost as much as she treasured small-town life. So perhaps Anne was making too much of this. Perhaps Aunt Edie's trip to India had been like so many others, merely work. Yet something told Anne to dig deeper.

She moved to the boxes near the back wall of the attic where she felt certain she'd seen some of Aunt Edie's correspondence from the early '90s, the time period when she'd visited India.

She pulled out the first box. A musty smell met her nose when she lifted the lid. Inside were income tax returns from ten years prior to her great-aunt's death. She set them aside to toss, then moved to the next box. Photographs of Aunt Edie's childhood, ancient black-and-whites with shots of Anne's extended family members were nestled inside. Anne recognized many of the photos as duplicates from the albums she had downstairs. She moved through the bundles of photos, all labeled with the year and important events captured. There was nothing in the box as recent as the 1990s.

She moved through several more boxes, each tempting her to linger in long-forgotten days. But she reminded herself that she was on a mission. Finally, after the sixth box, she hit pay dirt. She found bangles in a small ornate cardboard box. Anne tried to slip them on her wrist, but they were too small to fit over her hand. There was a doll that looked Indian. A postcard of the Taj Mahal in Agra, India. Its pristine white façade and long, majestic walkway were unmistakable. Anne read the back of it:

Dear Edie,

    Thanks for all your help! I can't wait to see what you do. Come back to India soon.

Lance and Laura Stieb

Anne sat back on her haunches. She glanced at the postmark—June 4, 1993. Anne had been a young teen. What did Mrs. Stieb mean? Was she simply being kind or had Aunt Edie done something in particular? *I can't wait to see what you do.* That comment in particular seemed pointed.

Setting the card down, she turned back to the box and shuffled through the assortment of papers and photographs, some tourism brochures from Aunt Edie's trip, as well as personal notes from those she'd met along the way, all people Anne had never met.

Reaching for an envelope of photographs, Anne found pictures of people in dress much like the Haydens had worn that very morning, brightly colored saris; crowded marketplaces with large baskets overflowing with produce, baked goods, and stalls where thin Indian men sold steaming food on skewers. Aunt Edie was a good photographer with an eye for finding a depth in her subjects. One photo was of a young boy, with black hair, bangs cut straight across his dark forehead. Hazel eyes gazed deeply as if searching for something beyond the photographer, perhaps hope, the thought struck. The background was squalor—a city of tin shacks, miles, it seemed, of shanties built all together on a hillside with low-hanging electrical wires in a tangled web against a dull gray sky. Water flowed through the crowded alleys, a stream of muck under the child's bare feet. Anne could imagine the stench that accompanied it. Something about the boy pulled at her.

He had a noticeable scar on his chin. She wished she knew his name. She turned the photograph over and read: Thomas Gee. Who was he? Just a child on the street?

She flipped through several more photos, similar shots of the desperation that was India. Trash everywhere, filth. There were a few shots of Nepal as well, Mt. Everest looming in the background as prayer flags flapped in the foreground's breeze. Anne vaguely recalled that Aunt Edie had stopped at the nearby country on that journey though she hadn't climbed the famed mountain, only sojourned in its shadow. While Aunt Edie had been adventurous she wasn't quite that athletic other than her skill at archery.

Then there was another photo of the same boy, and this time a man and a woman flanked him. His parents? There was no writing on the back of this shot. Anne lifted the next photo. For a moment her mind couldn't adjust to what she saw in the shot—she immediately recognized Aunt Edie, though she didn't know the man who had his arm around her. But it was the other woman next to them who stunned Anne. Mother Teresa! Her smile was beatific, eyes crinkling at the corners, and though she looked younger in the early 1990s, she was still a tiny woman, a spitfire of generosity.

Anne turned the photo over. "Me with Mother Teresa at Missionaries of Charity in Calcutta."

Underneath that was an envelope with an onionskin sheet of paper inside. Anne gently pulled it out.

Dear Edie,

I am so thankful that we met. I can see that you have a heart for the people of India as I do. I'm excited to see where our conversations will lead, what God will make of our meager ideas. I am contacting people here about getting things set up. I'll be in touch. You let me know what you need from your end, and I'll let you know what we need from mine.

There were a few more lines in closing, but it was signed *Mother Teresa.*

Anne turned the sheet over. It was blank.

Aunt Edie met Mother Teresa? Why had she never mentioned that to Anne? Anne looked at the photo again. It was definitely her great-aunt. Who was the man? He was clean shaven and handsome, with a light-colored suit that contrasted with his dark features. He had a protective arm around Aunt Edie's back. Anne shook her head and placed the photo back on the stack of items she'd found from Aunt Edie's trip to India.

Anne whispered to her deceased aunt, "I wish you could tell me what this was all about."

CHAPTER TWO

When Anne got downstairs she went straight to her laptop and searched for images of Mother Teresa's signature. She needed to make sure this wasn't some sort of hoax, someone being funny writing a letter to Aunt Edie, pretending to be Mother Teresa although the tone of the letter seemed to contradict that idea anyway. Within a minute a search page popped up and Anne clicked on "Images." There were several photographs of documents written by the famed nun, all signed with the same careful script as the page in Anne's hand.

Anne sat back and stared. If she'd been curious before, now she was beyond curious.

Mother Teresa! Anne couldn't get over it. They'd clearly been planning something. But what?

* * *

Anne made taco soup for supper. It was an easy meal that she'd tossed into the Crock-Pot before church. Betty Bultman had given her the recipe after she'd made it for a Cinco de Mayo celebration at the library. Anne had decorated the place in a Mexican theme, even a piñata for the children to swing at. The event had been a big hit and Anne's kids had raved about the soup and had begged for seconds, so it had become a regular on their rotation of go-to meals.

"Mom," Liddie said as she ladled herself a second bowlful, adding a heaping pile of shredded cheese and sour cream.

"Yes, honey," Anne waited for the girl to go on.

Liddie reached for a tortilla chip from the bag on the table and scooped the soup and toppings up like a dip, plopping it into her mouth. "Do you like the Haydens?" she talked around the food.

"Of course I do," Anne said. "Can you chew with your mouth closed, please?"

Liddie nodded as she finished chewing. She swallowed and said, "Do you think they have too many kids?"

"Too many kids? What makes you say that?" Anne took a spoonful of soup too.

"I heard one of the boys at church say that to Ben." Liddie glanced at her brother, who immediately frowned at her. "He said that the Haydens couldn't give the kids the attention they need because they have so many."

"Well, I don't know about that," Anne said. "Do you think the Pyles have too many children? They have seven too…"

"No!" Liddie said. "They love their children."

"The Haydens love their children also. I think a lot depends on the parents, don't you?" Anne asked. "I mean, some parents are overwhelmed with one baby while others have no problem at all with a dozen." She watched Ben consider the comment. He seemed thoughtful, quiet.

She could tell he was a bit irked that his little sister had tattled on one of his friends.

Liddie, however, wasn't done. "Do *you* like a lot of kids?"

"I don't know," Anne said, sensing that this was leading somewhere else. "I've never had a lot of kids of my own—just you and Ben. I don't know how I'd handle being a mother to that many."

"Well, I think you are a great mom." Liddie nodded as if that settled it, her light brown curls bouncing. "I think you are *very* good with children."

Anne leaned forward and met her daughter's chocolate-brown eyes. "Why are you saying all this?"

"I know why," Ben put in. "She wants us to adopt a bunch of kids from India."

"What's wrong with that?" Liddie practically shouted at her brother. Then turning back to her mother she added, "I need a baby sister, Mommy. Every little girl should have at least one baby sister and maybe a brother too. Though I don't know what I'd do with a brother...but any kind of baby would do! She could sleep in my room with me. I can get rid of some toys to make room for her. Natalie told me her family had to leave their baby behind in India. We should adopt her!"

"Leave a baby behind?" Anne's brow furrowed.

Ben chimed in, "It's their foster sister. Isaac told me about her too. There's some reason they can't adopt her and they couldn't take her out of the country since she isn't theirs so they left her with a friend in India."

"Oh," Anne said. She couldn't imagine leaving a child behind for months at a time when the baby had known only her as mom. The poor thing must be so upset.

"But I could take care of her...," Liddie insisted.

"Honey," Anne interrupted.

Liddie looked at her expectantly, hopefully. The expression reminded her of little Thomas Gee in the photograph she'd found from Aunt Edie's trip to India. Hope was so clearly etched across Liddie's trusting eyes. Anne reached for her hand on the top of the table.

"I love that you want a baby sister," Anne said. "And adopting is a wonderful thing to do. But…"

The girl's shoulders slumped before Anne said another word. Anne went on, "It's just that I'm a single mother. It's really hard for single mothers to adopt. Many countries don't even allow it."

"But why?"

Anne wished there were an easy explanation. "Most adoptions are by couples, though there are some single people who adopt. Being a parent is hard work, especially alone. It's one thing to have a parent die like your daddy did, but to take on being a single parent intentionally…" She shook her head.

"But you're a *good* mom." Liddie's brow furrowed. She was still unwilling to concede the point.

"Thank you for that, sweetie. But can you imagine taking care of a new baby and running the summer reading program at the same time?"

Liddie twisted her lips. Anne glanced at Ben. Even he seemed to resent the harsh reality.

"I guess…," the five-year-old finally said.

Anne smiled and tousled her daughter's hair. "There are other ways to help kids in need," Anne said.

"The Haydens had cards on the table in back of church that talked about stuff that they were doing at the orphanage…Maybe we could do that," Ben said.

"You mean support them financially?" Anne said.

"It wasn't really about the Haydens... It was about the kids at the orphanage... They need money for food and school and stuff. They don't come to live with you or anything."

"Okay," Anne said, "so a sponsorship."

Ben nodded.

"Let me think about it, okay?"

"Okay," Ben said.

Liddie nodded too, adding, "It'd be *kind* of like having a baby sister, wouldn't it?"

Anne smiled into her eyes. "Kind of," she agreed.

* * *

Anne didn't have to wake Ben or Liddie on Monday morning. They were up even before she was, dressed and eager to head out to the first day of Summer Fun. Anne glanced at the clock.

"It's only six thirty," she said to Ben as she made her way into the kitchen, still wearing her pajamas. She caught a glimpse of herself in the hall mirror. Her hair stuck up in the front, and the back was matted flat. Flattering. She finger-combed it to try to tame it.

Bright sunlight filtered in from the open window, and a faint breeze fluttered the curtains.

Ben stood in front of the coffeepot, filling it with water. The container of coffee grounds sat on the counter next to him. Hershey was already busily chomping away on his breakfast near the back door.

"I thought I'd get the coffee going," Ben said, sounding oddly more like a forty-year-old man than a nine-year-old boy.

Anne pulled out a chair at the kitchen table and watched him work. He scooped the grounds into the filter and turned the machine on. "Summer Fun doesn't start till nine," she reminded him.

"I promised Isaac Hayden that we would go early," Ben informed her. "He told me they needed help setting up some of the activities."

"Oh, he did, did he?" Anne gave him a wry smile. She shook her head, and suddenly a lump formed in her throat as she thought of a real fortysomething man that Ben reminded her of, her deceased husband Eric. He was just like that, getting up to make coffee for his wife, offering his own time to help anyone he met.

Generous to a fault. Just like his son. She studied Ben for a moment longer, comforted by the realization that a part of Eric lingered in him.

* * *

By seven thirty they were out the door. As Ben had predicted, the Haydens were already setting up stations on the church lawn. Each station offered a glimpse into life in a different region—there were six, one for each of the inhabited continents in the world, with foods to sample from countries within those continents, as well as local clothes for the children to play dress-up. There were also games children around the world liked to play set up on the lawn in front.

Anne glanced at a booth that depicted South and Central America. It was brightly colored with embroidered fabrics and woven baskets. Photographs of equally vibrant looking nationals lined the back of the booth, some dirt smudged and poor looking yet with beautiful smiles and shining eyes. "Where did you get all this?" Anne said, drawing Pam Hayden's attention.

The dark-haired woman lifted her head from cutting out construction paper crafts at one of the folding tables. She smiled. "Oh, here and there. The main mission office has a box of these kinds of things for us to use. All the different missionaries donate to it and we can all check it out for weeks like this one."

"The kids are going to adore this," Anne said.

"I hope so."

"Want some help?"

Pam held out the scissors and several sheets of construction paper on which boats and fish were outlined. "I never turn down help." She smiled. "Just cut along the lines. The older kids will be able to do it themselves so we don't need to cut them all out."

Anne took to the task. They worked in comfortable silence for a few moments, then Anne said, "Say, yesterday I found some photos of my aunt Edie in India."

"You did?"

Anne nodded, reaching into her pocket to pull them out. She handed the shots to Pam.

The woman's eyes crinkled, like an old friend seeing a familiar face. "Aaniya and Bakool Gupta," she said as she gazed at the photo of the couple flanking Thomas Gee. She looked up at Anne. "They worked with my parents in Mumbai. Bakool was the schoolmaster."

"And the boy in the middle is Thomas Gee?"

Pam nodded, her eyes clouding. "He was one of our kids at the orphanage. He was never adopted. He still comes around sometimes but now, as a man, I can see that he struggles..." She shook her head. "He drinks. His wife died in childbirth, and it's hard for him to care for his daughter alone..."

"That's so sad."

Pam nodded. "I worry that she'll end up on the streets, or worse, stolen...sold."

"Sold?" Anne couldn't even imagine living in a world like that.

"Thomas does his best to protect her. He's talked to us about putting her in the orphanage, giving up his parental rights, but he just can't bring himself to do that. He's a good man but..." She shrugged. "What can he do?"

She turned to the next photograph. "What's this?" Her eyes widened. "Mother Teresa?" She held the picture of Edie with the famous nun and the unknown man up for Anne to see.

"I thought you might know the story behind that one," Anne said.

"My parents—and Cory and I—lived in Mumbai. We rarely get to Kolkata where Mother Teresa's mission is. We never met her. Did you?"

"Heavens, no," Anne said. "Do you think your folks had anything to do with their meeting? That's what I've been wondering."

"I doubt it," Pam said. "The orphanage tied them down pretty much 24-7 unless we got volunteers, which we did on occasion. Kolkata is on the opposite end of the country from Mumbai. Of course India is a lot smaller than America, but it's still quite a trip. A full day's drive, and that's not taking into account India's crazy traffic."

Anne glanced at the picture in Pam's hand again. Aunt Edie looked so young, with a 1990s short hairstyle that created a sleek frame for her pretty face. "I was wondering when Aunt Edie would've seen her..." She pulled out the letter she'd brought along with the photos and held it out for Pam to read.

Pam took it in hand, her mouth opening in astonishment when she saw that it was from Mother Teresa.

"Wow" — she handed the letter back — "that's a good question. You know someone who might have an idea? Joy and Chris Ochs were good friends of my folks. They trained Cory and me for the mission field. They might've had something to do with Edie meeting Mother Teresa."

"I didn't know that they trained you."

"Oh yes," Pam said, "they taught us everything we know." She gave Anne a wink.

"I wanted to ask if you know who that man is in the photo with Edie and Mother Teresa." Anne pointed to the shot again.

Pam studied it for a long minute, then placed it back on the stack of photos. "I have never seen him before. If he worked with Mother Teresa, he was probably from Kolkata. Or perhaps he was traveling with your great-aunt?"

"I was wondering that myself," Anne said as she laid the scissors down, having cut out the last of the construction paper shapes. "Ben mentioned something I wanted to ask you about." She paused. "He said that you had to leave a baby behind in India...?"

"Yes we did — Klara. The kids were pretty upset about it. So was I, to be honest. A friend of ours from Big Lake, Minnesota, is taking care of her while we're on furlough."

"Have you had to do that before? Leave a foster child behind while you were on furlough?"

Pam shook her head. "This is our first furlough since we got Klara. We've adopted all the other foster children we've gotten! She's fourteen months old, born with spina bifida..." She broke off for a moment. "She had the initial surgery to enclose her spine, but she'll need several more operations. We love her. She's a normal, beautiful little girl. Sweet too. Her smile lights up a room. But with all her special needs, Cory and I simply can't afford the surgeries, and India isn't exactly known for its stellar medical facilities. She needs a family that has good insurance. Someone who can bring her to the States or another more advanced country for her surgeries and therapies..." She shook her head. "It'll kill me to have to give her up." Finally she added, "It's one of the dangers of this job, I'm afraid."

Anne studied the woman as she gathered up the cutouts and moved to her next task. Clearly she loved the little girl, yet she spoke of giving Klara to another family so matter-of-factly, as if the hard realities of needing to hand her to another if it meant her greater good was something that simply must be endured. Such selfless love.

Yet the little boy in the photo—Thomas Gee had never found that, a family to love him so selflessly when he was a child. Was that why he struggled now as an adult because he'd never known that kind of deep love?

CHAPTER THREE

A nne was back at the library by nine o'clock that morning, getting ready to open up. The old Victorian which housed the Blue Hill Library was a creaky yet magnificent structure, filled with charm and mystery. There were numerous nooks, perfect for playing hide-and-seek, and hand-carved mahogany banisters along the grand staircase to the second floor. Built in 1896, it was a house Anne knew better than any other. It was here that she spent many lazy days, learning to love books in the sunny alcoves while her great-aunt read to her.

The front windows were open on this glorious June day. Anne could hear birds singing from the tall trees in the front of the house and an occasional car meander past the quiet library. With many of Blue Hill's children caught up at Summer Fun she knew the morning would be fairly slow for a summer day, but those same children would swarm her doors come one o'clock.

Mildred Farley walked in, sending a wave in Anne's direction. In her mid-seventies, the longtime friend of Anne's great-aunt was famous for her polyester pantsuits and stunning white hair, but today she wore a bright red shirt with a bold floral print and white dress slacks.

"What are you up to?" Anne asked.

"And why would you ask that?" Mildred smirked and motioned up and down her outfit like a model highlighting a new offering on *The Price Is Right*.

"Are you going on a trip?" Anne guessed.

"I sure am! My sister booked surprise tickets to Hawaii. Can you imagine that? Two old ladies heading to Hawaii all by our lonesomes!" Mildred was beaming.

"That sounds wonderful."

"We're going on a jungle safari and touring a volcano...I don't know how I'll manage! But I can hardly wait."

"When do you leave?"

"Saturday. I barely have time to pack! But my sister said I had to do it with her. She'd never have the courage to go alone."

"So you're just doing your part," Anne said. "Helping your sister out."

"Exactly! It's the charitable thing." She winked at Anne, then glanced around the library. "Oh, enough about me," she said as if she couldn't tolerate another minute of gloating. "The kids are already out and about for the day?" she asked, referring to Summer Fun.

"Sure are," Anne said.

"I was so excited I almost forgot these." Mildred lifted the tote bag she'd set on the counter and dropped several tomes into the checkout desk's book drop. "It's a pretty wonderful thing those missionaries are doing," she said as the books fell into the cart, "coming all this way to teach our kids like that. They could just visit, use their time here as vacation time. They must really love children."

"I think they do..." Anne paused.

Mildred lifted a wondering eyebrow when her gaze met Anne's. "You look like you have something else to say."

"I do," Anne said. "I was going to call you this morning."

"That sounds ominous."

"Nothing ominous at all." Anne smiled. "I found some old photos of Aunt Edie's and I was hoping you could tell me the story behind them." She reached into her purse where she'd stashed them after showing them to Pam Hayden. "They're from her trip to India. It says on the back that it was taken in 1993."

"India...Edie went on so many trips." Her brow furrowed. "I recall that one vaguely. 1993—I believe that's correct," Mildred said, taking the photos from Anne's hand.

"Pam Hayden was able to tell me who these people were." Anne pointed to the shots of young Thomas Gee, as well as the one with the schoolmaster and his wife. When Mildred got to the photo of Edie with the unknown man and Mother Teresa, Anne said, "It's this one that I'm most curious about."

"That's Mother Teresa," Mildred said. She seemed as dumbfounded as Anne had been upon first seeing the photograph.

"I was pretty amazed by it too. So you don't know anything about it? Do you know who the man was?"

"No. I think I would remember if she told me she'd met Mother Teresa."

"I was just curious about what prompted their meeting, if Aunt Edie was there to visit Mother Teresa specifically...?"

"That would be just like Edie." Mildred pursed her lips, then she said, "That woman still amazes me! Why wouldn't she mention something like meeting Mother Teresa? I can assure you I would mention it if it were me!" Mildred shook her head. She lifted her head, chin in palm as she tried to remember. "Oh, I remember now."

"You remember Edie meeting Mother Teresa?"

Mildred shook her head. "No, I remember why I don't remember. 1993. That was the year my mother was diagnosed with Lou Gehrig's disease. I took care of her till she passed that December. I was pretty preoccupied during that time."

"That's such a devastating disease. It must've been difficult." Anne's heart went out to her dear friend.

Mildred sighed. "Indeed it was." She shook her head. "But God was truly there with us, like a warm hand on my back when I needed encouragement." She sighed. "I miss her. Twenty some years after the fact and I still miss her."

"I know how that is. It's been three years since Eric's passing and some days it feels like yesterday." Anne placed a hand on her friend's forearm.

Then a wave of weariness came over Anne, a tide of sleepiness. It had been happening more and more lately—getting so tired she could barely open her eyes once the afternoon hit. It even happened in church again yesterday. She'd wondered if her blood sugar levels were somehow affected—she knew that hypoglycemia could affect a person that way. Yet she had never had any kind of issues like that before. Perhaps she'd simply been staying up too late and getting up too early. That was probably all it was. She needed to catch up on her sleep.

* * *

Liddie and Ben were spending the afternoon at the Pyles', playing with their many children and the Haydens' large clan, so they hadn't come home after their morning at Summer Fun.

Anne was just dozing off when Alex Ochs came into the library at two o'clock. Her eyes were droopy as she stared at the computer's screen.

"You should put a cot back there," Alex teased as he leaned his tanned frame against the checkout desk.

Anne jerked awake and slapped at her own cheeks.

"It's that obvious?" she complained. "I'm so tired!"

Muscular with broad shoulders and piercing blue eyes, Alex was a local contractor. The two had been friends since they were children and had dated for much of high school before Anne left for college and met Eric. That had changed everything. She'd fallen in love with the older man and married him. Anne knew she'd broken Alex's heart all those years before, so when she and the children moved back to Blue Hill their re-acquaintance was awkward at first. Yet they'd managed to form a new friendship, a stronger friendship as adults who shared the grief of loss and the trials of parenting as singles.

Alex's brow quirked at Anne. "Stop slapping yourself," he scolded, laughing.

"I need a coffee," Anne admitted. She rose from her seat and motioned for him to follow her to the break room where she put on a pot of the heavenly scented brew.

"You want some?" she asked.

Alex nodded.

As Anne got out two mugs from the cupboard, Alex pulled an envelope from the back pocket of his jeans. "I have a bit of a mystery for you." He held up the envelope, which looked like a bank statement.

"What's so mysterious about a bank statement?"

"Look at the addressee."

He laid the envelope on the desk between them. It was addressed to Marla Slater, Alex's sister. She and her husband had died in a car accident four years earlier.

"Okay…," Anne said. "That is curious."

"I thought I'd closed all of their accounts right after they passed. Then today I got this overdraft notice and a statement of account."

"Overdraft? So someone has been drawing money out of your sister's account?"

"I don't know." He pulled the documents out of the envelope, the first a letter with "Insufficient Funds" stamped across the top in red ink, the second a monthly statement. There was a lot of activity on the account, both deposits and deductions. Who would be making deposits on an account in Marla's name so many years after her death?

Had someone been stealing money from this account? Anne turned the statement over. There was nothing on the back.

"Why wouldn't the bank have closed this account when you went in? Do you have any idea how much money was in there when they passed? Who's taking funds now?"

Alex crossed his arms over his chest. Clearly, he'd already wondered all these same things. "I have no idea, but I'd hate to think that someone might be stealing money that rightfully belongs to Ryan."

Ryan, the Slaters' only child, left parentless. Raised by Alex ever since his sister's passing. Ben's best friend.

"You clearly have something in mind," Anne said. She sat back in her chair waiting for Alex to voice what she sensed was coming.

"You'll help me unravel this thing, right, Annie?"

"*Annie?*" She quirked a brow. "You haven't called me that since we were in third grade."

"I thought it might butter you up."

"I only use butter on my toast." She was definitely waking up. "And of course I'll help you. Isn't that what friends do?"

CHAPTER FOUR

A lex handed the phone to Anne as it began to ring. She handed it right back.

"The bank won't talk to me," she said. "My name wasn't on the account."

"Mine wasn't either," he said.

"Well, at least you're the executor of the will. You'll have a better chance than I will."

The line rang a second time and someone said, "Blue Hill Bank and Trust."

"Hello. This is Alex Ochs. I'm calling in regard to an overdraft notice I received on an account that my sister had." He explained the situation, that she had died four years prior and he had closed all her accounts. Then he waited while the person on the other end rattled off rules regarding privacy that Anne had already warned him about.

Finally, Alex hung up with a groan. "They said I have to go in with a death certificate and a will stating that I'm executor."

"You still have those documents, right?"

Alex nodded. "I'll have to dig them out of a file, but yeah, I have them."

"Well, I need to wake up anyway…I'll let Betty Bultman know I'm heading out and meet you at the bank in half an hour."

* * *

Rita Sloan sat erect in the leather chair across the desk from Alex and Anne. The bank manager's brow furrowed as she studied the letter that Alex laid on her desk. There was nothing else on the hardwood surface save a cup that held several pens bearing the bank's logo and a small stack of business cards. Not even a family photograph or a blotter. The back counter that ran the length of the tan wall held a computer and keyboard, but it too was Spartan. The only artwork in the room was a painting of ducks flying across a lonely marsh.

"I'm sorry about all this," Rita said when she finally lifted her face. The thirtysomething had a cute pixie haircut and pale green eyes. "I remember your coming in not long after your sister's death to close her accounts." She shook her head. "It was such a sad thing, when she and her husband died." She met Alex's gaze. "I just can't understand why this one wasn't closed. Or why you'd get this notice now, after so much time has passed."

"Well, I'm glad we aren't alone on that," Alex said good-naturedly. Anne sensed he was trying to ease the tension in the room, yet ever since the bank manager had first seen the note she'd seemed upset.

She abruptly rose to her feet. "Excuse me," she said. "I need to show this to Eldon." Eldon Martin was the bank's president. "I'm hoping he can help us figure this out."

She quickly exited the office and made her way down the hall toward the more lavish office of the president. Anne could see her walk down the carpeted hallway as tellers chatted with customers in the main section of the bank.

Anne exchanged a glance with Alex. "She seems nervous, doesn't she?" Anne whispered.

"Yeah," he said. He rubbed his chin thoughtfully.

Blue Hill's bank had been a cornerstone for the small town for as long as Anne could recall. When people needed a new car or a tractor or a house, it was where they came. She knew all the tellers by name, and they knew everyone in town, as well as whether their children liked suckers or their dogs liked Milk-Bones.

Within a few minutes Eldon Martin returned with Rita. He was a member of the library board, so Anne was acquainted with him from their regular meetings to discuss library funding and programming. He was a level-headed man, outgoing. He offered a hand first to her and then to Alex.

"This is curious," he said to Alex before letting go of his hand. "Curious indeed."

"I agree," Alex said.

"What do you make of it?" Anne cut to the chase. "Do you think someone is stealing from this account?"

Rita's hand moved nervously to her throat where it splayed just south of her collarbone.

"Oh no, I'm sure that's not the case," the banker answered. Anne could see concern immediately enter his gaze at the possibility. "I see no reason to think that."

Eldon had a second sheet of paper in his hand. He lifted it. "Here's the thing," he said. "That notice shouldn't have even gone to you. The management of the account was transferred." He mentioned the date of the change.

"That was the same week Marla and my brother-in-law died," Alex said.

"Near as I can figure, the overdraft notice hadn't been set to the new owner of the account when it was transferred. An oversight. That's why you received the duplicate overdraft notice."

"To whom was it transferred?" Anne said.

Eldon cleared his throat and said, "I realize you were executor of the will, but this is something else. These funds weren't part of the estate, so it really isn't something that I can divulge to you."

"Wait," Alex said. "What do you mean they weren't part of the estate?"

"This was a fund your sister *managed*, but it wasn't her money. It was a nonprofit. The name of it was Heaven's Child."

Alex sat back. "I know about Heaven's Child, but you're telling me it's still in existence?" His gaze was suddenly tense. "I thought Heaven's Child was closed shortly after my sister passed away." He looked to Anne, then back at the bank president. "Can you tell me anything about who's running Heaven's Child now? Is it still part of Bring Them Home adoption agency?"

"I'm afraid I can't say," Eldon said.

CHAPTER FIVE

I don't get it," Alex said as he and Anne made their way through the quiet streets of Blue Hill to the library. "Why would I be told it was closed if it wasn't?"

"Beats me," Anne said.

Betty Bultman was at the checkout desk, helping a few kids with their summer reading sheets. She lifted her head in acknowledgment of their return before taking the three little girls into the back room to collect their prizes.

Anne moved behind the checkout desk, taking her seat at the computer. Keys clicked on the keyboard.

"What are you doing?" Alex asked.

"Looking up Heaven's Child."

Alex stood behind her, reading over her shoulder. Several links came up with the name Heaven's Child in their content—one a music video on Youtube, another some astrology site. Finally, Anne found a site that looked promising. She clicked on it.

Imagine living in a third-world country where there are few choices, few chances for changing your circumstances, it read. *Poverty surrounds you. Your parents are deceased or have simply abandoned you. There is no school, no way to better your situation. What choices do you have? What hope for the future? Heaven's Child is a relief organization that offers a way out of this cycle of poverty offering scholarships for adoptive families and job training for children who never find permanent families.*

There were several other pages attached to the Home page—a "Donate Now" page and one labeled "I Want to Adopt," as well as a contact page.

"That's my sister's foundation," Alex said. He shook his head. "I don't get it."

Anne clicked on the "Contact Us" page and reached for the phone. She dialed the number and waited for an answer, but it went to voice mail, "You've reached Heaven's Child," the recorded female voice said, "Please leave a message at the tone." It added their hours of operation before beeping. Anne disconnected the call without leaving a message.

Alex sighed, and Anne turned to study him. "What is it that bothers you about this? No one's stealing from an account meant for Ryan, so...what is it?"

He crossed his tanned arms over his chest. "What bothers me"—his eyes met Anne's as he paused to give her question thought—"is that Marla isn't here to ask."

Anne nodded. "I was just thinking the same thing about Edie's visit with Mother Teresa."

Alex quirked a brow. "Mother Teresa?"

She told him about her discovery, then said, "Now, back to this." She pointed to the statement that lay between them on the desk. "Maybe your folks would know something," she offered, remembering that Pam had suggested them in connection to Edie's trip as well.

"Maybe."

"Why don't we head over there after work?" Anne suggested. "Perhaps they can put both our mysteries to rest."

* * *

The Ochses' home was modest. It was a rambler on a half-acre lot shaded by tall pine trees and a live oak that spread its gnarled fingers toward heaven. Anne knew the place well. Alex and his sister, Marla, had grown up here. Anne had been in this home countless times, eating banana splits after football games, watching movies in the den, playing Scrabble with Alex's mother and sister. Good memories.

Alex's folks reclined on the front porch that reached across the front of their home, two wicker rockers in rhythm with the songbirds that chirped from the treetops.

Mr. Ochs rose to his feet when Anne and Alex climbed out of Alex's pickup and made their way up the front walkway. He shaded his eyes with one hand and said, "Well, this is a treat."

Christopher, who preferred to be called plain "Chris," was an older version of Alex, tall like his son but lankier, not quite as muscular. His eyes were the same blue, though the older man had a dimple in his left cheek.

He bent to give Anne a kiss on the cheek, then hugged his son.

"Ryan's watching a TV show," he said. "Should I go get him?"

"No, actually," Alex said. "We were hoping for a chance to talk to you."

Joy Ochs waved Anne to the padded white wicker couch. Anne took a seat next to her. "You came at a good time," the older woman said. "We just finished packing for Kenya."

"Kenya?" Anne said. "It seems everyone is headed off on an adventure these days." She told them of Mildred's surprise trip to Hawaii.

"Good for her," Joy Ochs said.

"When do you head out?" Anne asked, adding, "How long will you be gone?"

Chris said, "We leave first thing in the morning for two months. Doing some field work, encouraging some of our missionaries..."

The couple's work often took them to foreign places for long periods of time. It was part of the reason Alex had taken custody of his nephew Ryan when Ryan's parents had died, though they were a huge help to him whenever they were in town.

"What brings you out?" Joy said, looking at her son. She had a knack for drawing people in, making them feel welcome, wanted. Anne hadn't always felt that way growing up. She'd often wondered if the woman thought she had been too bookish, but now that she was an adult Anne understood her better. Anne could see that when she was younger, she had been so absorbed in her fictional world when there was a world outside in need of her special gifts. They'd had many heart-to-hearts on this porch over sweet tea and cinnamon cookies in the past months.

Anne and Alex had discussed how to broach the subject of the Heaven's Child account on the way over—Alex had been concerned at how the topic would affect his mother, who still suffered bouts of sadness over the loss. She would never say she was depressed, and truthfully she wasn't. Hers wasn't a sadness without hope. She simply missed her daughter and was looking forward to the time when they would be reunited in heaven.

Anne said simply, "We have a few questions for you." She looked to Alex, eyeing him for permission to ask about Edie's photographs. He nodded.

"I was told by Pam Hayden that you were good friends with her parents before they went to India."

Joy Ochs's face split into a grin. "We were. The Stiebs are the reason we do what we do. They were mentors to us of a sort—God rest their souls."

"How did you get started training missionaries?" Anne asked. While she had learned bits and pieces of this story over the years she'd never heard it in one telling. She turned to Chris Ochs, knowing he would tell the story. He loved a good story, and Anne was truly interested even as that familiar sense of exhaustion tugged at her eyelids.

Mr. Ochs leaned forward, folding his fingers together. He glanced between Alex and Anne, then dove in, "Back in 1973 I graduated from Bible school with a head full of learning. Bible, linguistics, cultural studies, you name it. I thought the Lord would take us to the mission field to put all that good information to work, but He had different plans. Seems to be the way He works—we make a plan then He vetoes it with a plan we never would conceive." He sat back and took a sip of his iced tea.

"Oh, excuse me," Joy interrupted as she rose. "I forgot to get you two something to drink." She disappeared through the front door without giving them a moment to decline.

"So after graduation," Mr. Ochs went on once the screen door slammed shut, "we visited Port Au Prince, Haiti. Worked for two months with Laura and Lance Stieb—Pam's folks. It was before we had any children. Before they did too. Our time there showed us a real need. Those poor missionaries were ill equipped for all that they faced—they didn't have a strong knowledge of the Word, so when those voodoo witch doctors came around they didn't know what to do. They didn't know diddly about culture shock so they were constantly trying to figure out why they were struggling so much, or what they'd done to offend the nationals." He shook his head. "It was difficult. They cared about the Haitians, but they needed more tools to reach them. And they needed resources to get the relief aid that is so critical in that poor country—so many hungry, with illnesses… I remember seeing a little boy playing with a tin can that had been cut up and reshaped into a toy car. Can you imagine all the sharp edges on that thing? But it was all they had. They needed medical intervention, good hygiene, and the like. Simple things. Joy and I saw that if we could help the missionaries by giving them those kinds of tools they could better serve the people of Haiti. The rest kind of grew from there. We started the Missionary Assistance Network. Now we serve in twenty-eight countries, and we work with eight different sending agencies."

Anne knew that Joy and Chris Ochs cared deeply for the needs of missionaries and provided solid training in the Bible and in cultural studies, as well as ongoing support once their missionaries were on the field. Theirs had been a vital ministry for over thirty years. She glanced at Chris. Though he was well into his sixties, he was a long way from retired. The older man had the energy of a man twenty years his junior.

Chris went on, "Of course, that was before learning English as a Second Language became such a foray into the undeveloped world. Now we teach that as well. Many missionaries use that route to connect with the nationals, as well as Business as

Missions—starting businesses in closed countries to provide jobs and opportunities for locals. Of course we still do a lot of relief work in areas hard hit by hurricanes, tsunamis, and other natural disasters. Much of that work is through short-term missions. We help prep folks for that too. You'd be surprised at how many people get a vision for full-time work by going on those shorter trips."

"Pam Hayden told me that you trained her and Cory before they went to India," Anne said.

Joy Ochs returned then with a tray holding a pitcher of iced tea and glasses, as well as her famous cinnamon cookies. She passed the glasses to Anne and Alex, then set the tray on a side table and offered them each a cookie before taking her own seat next to Alex.

"Oh yes," Chris Ochs continued. "Good students, those two. Same desire to help the poor as her folks."

Anne took a bite of the cookie. The taste filled her with long-lost memories and reminded her of how much she cared for these people who had given their lives so beautifully for others.

"The Haydens and Stiebs are like family to us," Mrs. Ochs said. "The Stiebs were the first missionaries we started visiting on the field."

"They were our guinea pigs. We worked out the kinks in our program on them." Chris laughed. "When they moved to India, we saw them at least once a year, up till the year he passed and she went to live with Pam and Cory. He died of pneumonia back in 1995 and she went about a decade later. Cancer." He shook his head. "Good, good folks."

"Do you recall my aunt Edie visiting them in India?"

"Oh yes," Joy said.

"They were thrilled to have a good friend from Blue Hill travel all that way to see their work."

"We helped Edie make her itinerary for that trip," Joy added. "She went to Nepal too. That was part of her travel writing work. I believe she was able to write the trip off because of that. I don't recall if she wrote about India too." She tapped a finger on her chin. "In any case she wanted to visit the Stiebs and see their work for herself. Edie was always such a blessing."

"Did she say anything about meeting Mother Teresa while she was there? Did you help her get to Kolkata?"

"She met Mother Teresa?" Joy said, her mouth dropping open. "I never heard anything about that."

Chris scratched his head. "I know she went to Kolkata. Though I don't know that she ever said why she wanted to stop there, or that she met Mother Teresa. That's remarkable."

Anne took a sip of her tea and set it back on the wicker coffee table in front of her. Didn't anyone know the circumstances behind her great-aunt's trip? The thought frustrated her. Yet she pushed it back. It was hardly Joy's and Chris's fault that Edie hadn't shared her reasons for the stop.

There was a long pause as everyone took long draughts of their iced tea.

Then Alex cleared his throat and said, "I got this in the mail." He held out the bank statement with the letter stamped "Insufficient Funds." He waited while his father read it and handed it to his mother. Then he added in a low voice as Joy took it, "It's a statement from the account for Heaven's Child."

"Heaven's Child?" Joy's face crumpled. "But..." Her words fell away. Alex reached for her hand, enveloping it.

Chris took over. "You told us Heaven's Child was closed."

"That's what I thought," Alex said. "But the bank tells me it's been in existence ever since Marla died. Anne looked it up online. It still has a Web site. She even called the number and got an active voice mail."

"I don't understand," Chris said. The news was upsetting him too, Anne saw. Dredging up old memories. Painful memories. "Marla had closed it. That was what you said."

"No, it wasn't Marla," Alex said. "You know..." He turned to Anne. "I just remembered the reason I thought it had been closed."

"Oh?

"Bring Them Home called to tell me that *they'd* closed Heaven's Child shortly after the funeral."

"Bring Them Home?" Anne said. "You mentioned that earlier. What is it?"

"It was an adoption agency out of Deshler that managed the fund. Those connections are all pretty fuzzy now. Marla didn't talk about it all that much—there were privacy issues, people's financial situations, that kind of thing."

"The adoption agency called to tell *you* that they'd closed it?" Anne asked. "Something doesn't seem right about that. Does it? Why would they feel you needed to be informed?"

Alex paused, thinking. "It was right after the funeral. I had so much to do...and taking Ryan on...it never crossed my mind that the person on the phone might not have been legitimate." His eyes were a shadow. "Who do you think that was?"

"I have no idea," Anne admitted. "But it sounds awfully suspicious."

* * *

Anne finally went to pick her children up from the Pyles' around eight o'clock. With fifteen kids to play with after a morning at Summer Fun, Liddie was exhausted. She fell asleep in the car on the way home. Her little mouth hung open as her head moved with the motion of the car.

"Did you have a good time?" Anne asked Ben, glancing at him in the rearview mirror.

"Yeah."

"What did you learn about this morning?"

"We talked about Sunday school—how we're so used to going to church and having a Bible and how there are kids in other places that don't get to go to church. They don't even have Bibles. Mrs. Hayden read to us in some strange language."

"Sounds good."

He nodded. Then he said, "I feel bad for them. We are so used to being able to read the Bible and stuff..."

"We take it for granted," Anne finished.

"Yeah." He paused. "It makes me feel bad."

"Why's that?"

Ben shrugged.

"It's okay to feel bad for other people—if it encourages you to help them."

"I suppose." After a long pause he said, "There are so many children who don't have enough to eat. We can't feed them all. It seems like too much."

"But we can help a *few*," Anne reminded. "At least the ones that come across our path. We can make a difference for some, and if other people do the same...before you know it the world is better."

That seemed to ease the worry on his face.

"Thanks, Mom," he said.

CHAPTER SIX

After Anne carried Liddie up to her bed and tucked Ben in with a book, his bedside light casting an orange glow, she moved to her own room. The old house creaked with her footfalls. Hershey lifted his head from a spot near the back door. He'd amble into Ben's bedroom soon, she knew, to settle at the foot of his bed for the night.

The house sighed as Anne turned off lights. A lone lamp lit her modest bedroom, giving it an amber hue. Anne loved this room. This was the same bedroom Anne had often stayed in as a child when she visited her great-aunt. On one side was a large leaded glass window that looked out over the valley. She could see Cooper's Pond in the distance, named for the family that had farmed the land a century ago. So much remained the same since that time in this little town.

She moved toward the bed and pulled down the blankets to climb in. Her body sank into the mattress, easing the tension of the day. It was no wonder she was exhausted. Getting up with the kids early. Talking to Pam Hayden about the little girl they'd had to leave behind in India—Klara, Pam had called her.

Anne hadn't really discovered much about her great-aunt's trip, other than that the Ochses had helped her plan it and she'd visited Pam's folks, making a stop in Kolkata where she'd met Mother Teresa.

But it was Alex's discovery that troubled her. Why would someone have called to tell him the account for Heaven's Child was closed? Why was it important that he think that? She'd seen how that knowledge troubled him, how it brought back hard memories of losing his sister and brother-in-law. Memories better left dormant.

Anne knew all too well how that felt. How many times in the past few years did memories of Eric do the same thing to her? Undo her completely. Make her think all the progress she'd made was simply an illusion. There were times that she missed Eric so terribly she was tempted to crawl back into that hole of self-pity. To linger there, though it hurt, if it meant a glimpse of what she'd had before with him. The man she'd loved like none other.

Alex. His name accompanied the image of his face, pained. She'd cared about him in high school. She still cared. Like a sister cared for a brother.

She lay there for a good hour as thoughts sped by one by one. When she finally decided sleep would not be soon in coming, she got up to spend some time in the Word. The Bible never failed to ease the tensions that swirled, refocused her on the things of life that mattered.

The pages fell open to Matthew 25 where she read, "For I was hungry and you gave me something to eat." She'd read the passage before, of course, yet with the events of the past couple of days they seemed to take on a deeper meaning. She thought of the Haydens with their children and the orphanages in India.

She sat back when she'd read the whole section. Wasn't that exactly what Ben had been struggling with? Seeing the need of children around the world and wanting to do something about it? That same desire burned in His heart that pushed the Haydens and the Stiebs to do the things they did.

Getting up, she retrieved her purse where she'd left the photos of Mother Teresa and Aunt Edie along with the letter. She read the note again.

One line in particular stood out to her: *I'm excited to see where our conversations will lead, what God will make of our meager ideas.*

What meager ideas? Had anything come of those conversations? It was next to impossible to think that nothing would have followed, knowing both her great-aunt and the reputation of the force-to-be-reckoned-with nun.

What had the little woman been like? What did the note mean? Would Anne ever know? She looked at the date of the letter. 1993. Over twenty years ago.

She sat back, thinking. Twenty years ago the idea of booking tickets online, especially for international travel, had still been very new. Joy and Chris said they'd arranged much of her itinerary — had they used a travel agent? She glanced at the clock — too late to call to ask them.

On a hunch Anne got out her laptop to look up the names of former travel agents in the area from that time period. There were no longer any travel agencies in Blue Hill, but perhaps there had been one or two in 1993…

Within a few moments a list of agencies popped on to the screen. Only one had a Blue Hill address. The name of the agent was Virginia Olson.

* * *

Ben and Liddie headed out to the church the next morning for the second day of Summer Fun.

Liddie had carried two pieces of paper around all morning. When Anne asked her what they were, she said, "My lines." She closed her eyes and held the sheets to her chest, an actress working her performance through in her head. Her little lips moved ever so slightly as she rehearsed.

The children would perform their play, including musical productions with choreography, entailing all that they'd learned during their two weeks of Summer Fun. Anne was impressed at the undertaking with so many children.

"Can we stay to play with the Haydens and Pyles again afterward?" Ben asked as they climbed out of Anne's car in the church parking lot.

"I don't want you to be a burden to Pam and Wendy," Anne said.

"They *want* us to come, Mom," Liddie said, her puppy dog eyes wide. "Natalie showed me how to tie a sari yesterday. Who knows what kind of fun we can have today—I'm *learning* new things!" She knew that would hit Anne in the soft spot.

"Okay, fine," Anne agreed with a smirk. "But not every day this week, 'kay? We need to have them over to our place too."

"You mean to play at the library?"

"You know what I mean." She smiled at her daughter, then waved good-bye as they ambled into the church building.

Anne returned to the library. All was still and quiet before the day's rush. This was her favorite time, before the mayhem, when the world was silent. Morning light floated across honeyed hardwood, strained by lace curtains and a faint breeze through the open front windows.

Anne went about her morning routine—gathering books for the courier to deliver to the other libraries in the system, checking the mail, answering urgent e-mails, opening several packages of new books she'd ordered for the library and getting them entered into the system, placing them on the cart to be shelved. She moved to the overnight return bin and pulled the many books from there, taking them to the checkout desk where she would check them back in.

By the time she finally unlocked the front doors for the day and sat back at her desk, a steady calm had fallen on her. She felt her eyelids droop. *Oh no, you don't,* she thought. *I am not falling asleep this early in the day.* She gave her head a shake, determined to wake up.

Anne glanced through the previous day's Internet history and revisited the site for Heaven's Child. She hoped she could help Alex figure out what had happened.

Clicking on the tab for the "contact us" page, Anne found the phone number of the foundation. She dialed it, and a woman's voice came on the line. "Heaven's Child," the woman said.

"Hello. My name is Anne Gibson," Anne began. "I'm a friend of Alex Ochs. His sister was Marla Slater. I believe she was the founder of Heaven's Child..."

"I think you have the wrong organization, ma'am."

"Why do you say that?"

"Heaven's Child was created in 2008 by Edie Summers from Blue Hill."

CHAPTER SEVEN

For several long moments Anne couldn't speak. Heaven's Child was created by Aunt Edie? Anne couldn't seem to wrap her mind around it.

"Edie Summers?" she repeated. "Of Blue Hill, Pennsylvania?"

"Are you having a hard time hearing me?" The woman didn't sound like she was trying to be snarky. Anne was sure she herself must sound like she'd lost her marbles.

"Edie was my great-aunt." She wasn't sure what she'd hoped the woman would say. Silence was what she got. "Are you sure she was the creator?"

"I am."

Finally Anne cleared her throat and went on, "I was wondering a few things about Heaven's Child. Maybe you can answer those questions for me."

The woman said, "Okay," on the other end of the line.

Anne went on, "I was told that the foundation closed a few years ago."

"Who told you that?"

"I'm not exactly sure. You see, Alex—Marla Slater's brother—received a phone call from someone at your organization. You're part of Bring Them Home adoption agency, aren't you?"

"Heaven's Child is run as a separate entity, but yes, the two are associated. Many of our scholarships go to adoptive families through Bring Them Home adoption agency."

"Marla Slater did work there, didn't she?" Anne said.

"Yes," the woman confirmed. "But I don't know much beyond that."

"Why would someone want her brother to think that fund was closed?"

"Closed? When?"

"Right after Marla's death."

"Well"—she cleared her throat—"that is peculiar. I have no idea."

Anne thanked the woman, then hung up.

She stared at the receiver blankly. Edie founded Heaven's Child? Another secret! She wondered if Alex knew that detail. Or did he too think that Marla founded the charity? Not that it mattered all that much now with both of them gone.

Anne ran her fingers through her hair, frustration welling. She opened a new tab and searched for Virginia Olson, the travel agent she'd read about the prior night on the Internet. Maybe she'd get further on her own mystery, find out if the longtime agent recalled Edie's trip to India. Yet after several clicks, that also led to nothing.

* * *

That evening the Haydens came to Anne's for supper. Anne had hoped for sunshine so the crew could spread out across her large backyard, maybe throw a ball or a Frisbee. Instead she got rain.

Her little apartment was more than full with the Haydens' seven children. The kids found spots in the living room, eating off of paper plates heaped with coleslaw and pulled pork sandwiches.

Anne, Pam, and Cory sat around the little table in the kitchen of the small third-story apartment. Hershey moved between the groups, hoping for handouts.

"I talked to Joy and Chris Ochs about my aunt's visit to India," Anne said as she took a bite of her barbecued pork.

"You did?" Pam said.

"It sounded like my aunt wasn't there for pleasure. She was there to write about it."

"Even if she had been vacationing," Cory said, "I'm sure Pam's folks would've put her to work. They believed in showing visitors what the missionary life was like in full color. Plus, Pam's dad always needed more help than he got."

"That's not a bad thing, I don't think," Anne said. "Edie probably loved it."

Cory chuckled. "If Pam's dad hadn't been so good at recruiting help, Pam and I might've settled in suburbia. I visited Mumbai with Pam while we were engaged. Pam's folks gave me two little boys to take care of, 'round the clock, while I was there. Mind you, I'd never been around kids, didn't particularly like them either. But that youngest one…" He shook his head. "Well, those two just changed my heart. I couldn't really come back to the States and get on with my life after that." He turned to look his wife in the eyes. "It totally wrecked me. I'm sure that was your dad's plan all along."

Pam shrugged. "More than likely he was just overworked and you were a pair of hands."

Ben came past, carrying a pile of plates to throw into the trash can. Hershey trailed behind him. "We're going to go play in my room, Mom," he said.

"That sounds good, honey."

Ben disappeared with Isaac Hayden in the lead and two of the Hayden boys trailing behind.

"The kids seem to really enjoy Summer Fun," Anne said.

"We do too," Pam said. "It's actually the same program we do with the kids in the orphanage in the summer."

Anne finished her sandwich, then reached for Pam's and Cory's empty plates. "Would you like some coffee?" she asked. "I have decaf." That sensation of feeling tired was back, tugging at her eyelids.

"I'll take some," Pam said.

"Me too," Cory added, "though it looks like you could use the caffeine."

Anne laughed the comment off. "You caught me," she said. "I've been feeling so tired lately." She got up to make coffee.

"Are you sure there isn't something wrong with you?" Pam asked, motherly concern in her tone.

"Oh, I'm fine," Anne said. "It's just part of being a single, working mother. Sleep is always the thing that gets squeezed."

Liddie scooted past her mother and picked up a half-empty bag of potato chips.

"What are you doing with that?" Anne asked.

"Oh, nothing!" Liddie said, motioning Natalie to follow her into her room. The two girls closed the door. Anne could hear their giggles from the other side.

"Kids." Pam smiled as the coffeemaker began to make its rumbling gurgle.

"I'm surprised that you would do the same program there as here," Anne returned to their prior conversation.

"Why?" Cory said.

"That's the mission field. It seems to me kids *here* need to understand how the rest of the world lives more than those kids would need it."

"The mission field is everywhere," Pam said. "Just because children here have money and food doesn't mean that there aren't other things they need. The children in India need to care about others too."

There was a long moment of comfortable silence. "What was Klara's situation?" Anne asked. "I mean, how did she come to be in your orphanage?"

Pam shook her head. "We don't really know what Klara's situation was. She was left at the orphanage gates in a duffel bag."

"Just *left*?" Anne shook her head. "What if no one came around to find her? I can't imagine..."

"Likely her mother was watching from somewhere," Cory said. "It's pretty common, especially in China where people are penalized for having more than one child. We just pray for her mother, that she'll have peace, knowing she made the best decision she could."

"We Skype with Klara whenever we can," Pam said. "Our friend who's taking care of her says she's doing okay. It is hard for her, though, when she sees us on Skype—she cries and says she wants Mama." She pointed to herself. "If only I could be Mama for her." Then she sighed. "It is what it is."

"She is standing by herself," Cory said. "Soon she'll be walking. We weren't sure she was going to be able to do that with her spina bifida."

"Of course it happens while we're away!" Pam said. She shook her head. "Little stinker waited for us to leave just so she could walk."

"She sounds like a special girl," Anne said.

"She is," Cory said, "It doesn't take much time with her to forget about her physical challenges and just enjoy the sweetness of that girl. We've adopted children with minor health issues before. But they've all been issues that we can manage without a lot of medical intervention. Klara needs many surgeries, depending on how she develops, what challenges she might have…We could probably swing the adoption costs…but with all the rest we just don't see a way clear to make her a Hayden."

Cory reached for the billfold in his back pocket and pulled out a photograph of the child. She had a brilliant smile that tugged at Anne's heart. Sweetness itself, Eric would've called it.

"Could she come to the States periodically for surgeries?" Anne asked when Cory put the photo away.

"If there was a way to pay for them, maybe…," Cory confided. "But with the physical therapy she would need afterward, that's hard. We've taken her to doctors in India, but the care there isn't the best. We simply don't have the funds to travel to the States that often. Plus, the private healthcare we have won't cover what we'd need."

"We love her," Pam said simply. "But sometimes it takes more than love to make things come together."

CHAPTER EIGHT

The Haydens left around nine o'clock. To Anne it felt more like midnight. She glanced at the clock as she told Ben and Liddie to get ready for bed. She'd asked Pam if she remembered Edie using a travel agent for her trip. Since Pam could barely remember the trip in the first place, her answer was no, as Anne had suspected. She'd called Joy and Chris Ochs to ask them the same question, forgetting that they were already on their way to Kenya and wouldn't have phones while they were gone. The line went straight to voice mail. Anne hung up without leaving a message.

She went into the kitchen to empty the dishwasher that Pam had helped her load after supper. Dish clanked against dish as she stacked and placed them in their spots in the cupboard.

Hershey was patiently sitting by the back door, watching Anne, then turning again. He gave a cry in his throat.

Anne groaned. "Ben, did you forget to put Hershey out earlier?" she called into the hallway.

"Sorry, Mom." Ben stepped out of his room, already in his Superman pajamas.

"I'll take him," she conceded.

Anne hooked the leash on to the big chocolate Lab's collar and moved down to the first floor, where she waited on Hershey. Although she sometimes resented the animal's demands she realized the joy he brought to them all too. Especially to Ben. Missing his father but able to pour that love on to the dog.

What was it like for children who didn't have such luxuries? A pet to call their own? Pajamas with a Superman insignia on the chest?

Her children weren't spoiled. These were the basics. Love in tangible tidbits, offered by a mother who couldn't give them what they really needed—a father. But at least they had her.

She supposed other mothers did the same for their children. Offered what they could to make up what they lacked. She thought of Chris Ochs's story about the little boy playing with a truck formed from a cut-up tin can. The thought that the child could be hurt, then the realization that it was all his parents had to offer. A gift of play. She couldn't judge that. She understood. She was a mother too.

When Anne returned upstairs, she could hear Liddie crying in her room. She unhooked Hershey, then made her way to the little girl's room.

"What's wrong, honey?" Anne asked. She sat next to the five-year-old in her twin bed, the covers pulled up under her chin. Her chin quivered and she closed her eyes for a long moment before lifting them to look at her mother.

"I feel bad for Klara."

"The Haydens' foster child?"

Liddie nodded. "I heard them talking about finding her in a bag in front of their orphanage. Why would someone do that?"

Anne smoothed Liddie's hair as she thought how to answer. "I don't know for sure. Klara's mother probably thought it was the best way for Klara to get the kind of care she needed, because she couldn't provide it herself."

"But she'll never see her again."

"That's true," Anne conceded. The comment seemed to go straight through Liddie—her brow knit together, her eyes glistening.

"But what if something happened to me and you couldn't pay to help me? Would you give me away?"

Anne smoothed the lines of Liddie's face with a gentle hand. "Never," Anne assured. "India is very different from America. Besides, we have insurance to take care of those kinds of things."

That seemed to settle her a bit. "What about Klara? Will God take care of her?"

"He's already given her a foster family that loves her...He'll take care of the rest."

Finally, the tension in Liddie's face eased, though sadness lingered. Empathy for a little girl she would likely never know.

"Are you going to be okay?" Anne asked.

Liddie gave a little nod.

Anne bent to kiss her forehead, then turned out the bedside light. "I love you," she said and Liddie gave her a fierce hug.

"I love you too, Mommy."

* * *

Why was it always so much easier to tell her children to trust God than it was to trust Him herself?

That thought stuck with her for the rest of the evening. She'd felt out of sorts, and sleepiness clung to her even though it was only nine thirty. Yesterday she'd gotten up early, but today she had no such excuse.

She thought of Liddie's tears—so worried about facing the same kind of fate so many other children faced daily. The world was indeed unjust. How could a mother explain that to a child?

She scoffed. How could she explain it to herself? Yet she knew God. Knew that He loved her. That was enough.

She didn't want to try to go to bed, though her body pushed her that way. She knew she'd sleep for an hour or two, then be awake again. Rising from her chair and flicking off the TV, she moved to the kitchen. Hershey lifted his head and tilted it at her. "Hey, boy." He laid his head back on the kitchen floor.

Nothing to do there. So she moved to the hallway and descended the stairs to the library. The place was deadly silent, the windows black portals into the darkness beyond. Sitting at her desk, she fingered a few chores she could do. Order some new titles, see what was coming up on her schedule of Summer Reading events... but that didn't interest her either.

Her thoughts turned to Alex. Why would someone want him to think Heaven's Child had shut its doors? She knew it bothered him. She could see it in his tense form, the way his brow furrowed deep over his eyes. He needed the answer to that question. Not for himself but for his sister. Marla had been the caretaker for that ministry. She'd believed in what she'd done there. She'd loved children so.

Anne sighed and glanced at the newspaper she'd tossed onto her desk earlier in the day. She hadn't had a chance to read the headlines, but the top story caught her eye now— "Deshler Town Celebration Begins." She read the list of coming activities in the neighboring town. A parade that weekend might prove fun for the kids. Perhaps they could invite the Haydens along. She read for a while, glancing through the other articles in the weekly paper.

When Anne checked the time she realized it was going on eleven o'clock. How had it gotten to be so late?

Climbing the stairs back to her apartment, she flicked on the bathroom light. It was a small bathroom with a claw-foot tub and hardwood floors that creaked when Anne crossed in front of the mirror.

Her eyes were sunken with dark hollows underneath, attesting to her weariness. Picking up a brush, she stroked through her hair. Then she grabbed her toothbrush and gave her teeth a quick scrubbing. As she brushed, a glob of toothpaste landed on her collarbone.

"Nice, Anne," she said into the mirror, then grabbed a washcloth to wipe it away. But as she did she felt something she hadn't felt before. A lump. In the space between where her two collarbones met. The little hollow that was usually there was filled with a hard nodule.

Anne pressed against it. The spot was tender. Pain shot up her neck and radiated down her chest. Why hadn't she noticed it before?

She turned sideways. Could she see it in the mirror? Yes. There it was. About the size of a large marble. But this was no marble.

Sudden panic came over her at the thought of what that lump could be, what it could represent.

Her mind flashed a memory of Eric in a coffin. Then herself in the mirror — those sunken, tired eyes. The lump. Liddie and Ben in bed, sleeping restfully.

"Anne," she spoke to her own image, "you have to stop it."

But her mind roiled on.

Without thinking, she called Alex. A drowsy voice answered.

"I'm sorry!" she said, realizing the time and instantly regretting the call.

"No, it's okay. What's going on?"

Anne drew in a deep breath, not sure if she should voice her fear. She was making too much of it.

"Anne," he prompted.

"I found a lump…in my neck."

"A lump?" She heard the instant concern in his voice. It tugged at her. She didn't want him worrying. Not when it was probably nothing.

"I was getting ready for bed. It's at the base of my throat in the hollow spot. Only it's not hollow."

"You've been so tired lately too," he said, filling in what she'd already thought. Had everyone noticed it? "You need to see a doctor."

Since Eric's passing Anne had avoided doctors as much as she could. She'd brought the children into the clinic here and there when they had colds or sore throats, but for herself…she hadn't wanted the reminder of those sterile halls, the antiseptic smell, the sounds of monitors, the deep ache that invaded her chest.

"Anne, you heard me, right?" Alex said.

"Yeah, I heard. I'll go in."

"Promise? Go tomorrow morning, first thing. I can take the kids to church."

"It's not like I'm sick, Alex. I can take Liddie and Ben to Summer Fun."

"Okay," he agreed. "But right after that, okay?"

"Okay."

"Do you want me to come along?"

"No, that's silly. I can go by myself."

"Well," he paused, "tell me what they say."

They finally hung up.

She stared at the phone for a long moment. Why had she chosen Alex of all people to call? She could've chosen any number of friends—Wendy, Grace, Mildred. Yet in her panic she hadn't even considered it—she'd instantly chosen him.

She brushed the thought aside. He'd comforted her and told her what she needed to hear, what she knew to be right even in the midst of her fear. That was all. Alex had a level head. He was a friend.

Suddenly that old longing returned. *Eric.* "Why aren't you here? You promised me you'd never leave me," she spoke into the quiet of the bathroom.

Just like you promised Liddie, the thought echoed. Some promises weren't possible to keep. "I don't want to think about that," she argued with herself.

Hadn't she and the children just been talking about orphans? Fear—real fear—traced her arms and back.

What would happen to Liddie and Ben if they discovered Anne had some life-threatening illness? They'd already lost their father. They couldn't withstand losing her too.

Anne closed her eyes and inhaled deeply. She couldn't allow herself to think about this.

The thought was simply too terrifying.

* * *

As soon as the clinic opened the next morning, she dialed the number. The earliest they could get her in was Friday morning.

"Are you sure there isn't an opening sooner?" Anne said. Then, realizing two days wouldn't make any difference, she said that would be fine and hung up.

Dead ends and waiting. That seemed to be the way of things lately. Unconsciously her hand slipped back to the lump between her collarbones, lightly touching, checking to see if it was still there.

Anne sighed, closing her eyes. She shouldn't dwell on what she couldn't control. She knew that. Worry would only crumble her.

* * *

Anne stopped in at the *Gazette* office during her morning break. Grace Hawkins was bent over her computer keyboard, her blonde hair a cascade framing her pretty face as she typed away, too distracted to notice that Anne had come in. Anne moved toward her desk behind the front counter. Grace lifted her head, a smile dimpling her cheeks, her blue eyes alight.

"What brings you here?" she said.

"I was hoping to do a little digging."

"And what are we researching today?"

She told her about Aunt Edie's photo with Mother Teresa and her curiosity to know what their meeting had sparked.

"Why so curious about a meeting that happened so many years ago?" Grace probed. Grace had become a friend since Anne had moved back to Blue Hill. The two women shared a love of the written word and a deep curiosity to learn. Anne was often found in the newspaper's archives room, looking up long forgotten stories as she researched one thing or another.

"Let's just call it a diversion," Anne said with a smile. Grace lifted an eyebrow, clearly intrigued by the comment, but she didn't explore it.

"Is it okay for me to head back?" Anne pointed toward the archive room.

"Always," Grace said.

The archive room housed the microfiche machine, the oversized screen that magnified old newspapers immortalized on film. Anne pulled out the file for 1993 and found a bit about Edie's trip in the "Out and About" section of the paper. The "Out and About" section detailed comings and goings of folks throughout Blue Hill, from Aunt Agnes's gallbladder surgery to Grandpa Bill visiting his grandchildren in Tucson.

Edie Summers is taking an extended trip to India with stops in Mumbai and Calcutta and a jaunt in Nepal.

That was the extent of the mention. Nothing new there.

Anne scanned through several films before she decided to look through the films for the following year. It wasn't likely there would be anything about her trip, but it was a hunch. After several minutes she came across another article that mentioned Aunt Edie, this one a bit longer.

Blue Hill native Edie Summers has always had a heart for children. Last summer that heart grew a little bit bigger when Summers traveled to Calcutta, India. It was there, she says, that she saw firsthand the devastation of that poorest country's children. "It's just heartbreaking to see so many orphans left to fend for themselves on the streets." Those who are lucky enough to live in the orphanages often aren't adopted by the time they reach eighteen. When Summers returned to the States she began looking for solutions. Bring Them Home is just such a solution. An adoption agency in Deshler especially for international adoptions, their goal is to help connect children with adoptive families. Summers hopes to launch the international adoption agency next month. If you are interested in volunteering please contact Summers. There is still a need for people to paint and construct the facility in Deshler. Or, if you are serious about adopting and want to begin the home study process, she welcomes inquiries.

Edie founded Bring Them Home *and* Heaven's Child? Was Bring Them Home what Mother Teresa had been referring to in her note? The project that her time with Edie had birthed—an international adoption agency? It would seem so. Anne wondered how many families had found their children through the agency.

Anne pressed further, searching through page after page. There seemed to be nothing else about Bring Them Home. If only the microfiche weren't so random. It wasn't searchable like an article on the Internet. If she happened to come across a subject it was pure serendipity.

She glanced at the clock. Three hours had passed. She needed to be getting back.

Her hand slipped to her throat, feeling the lump. It had become an unconscious habit since its discovery the night before. Anne pushed down the worry that went with the action.

She stretched her back. It had grown stiff from sitting so long. She glanced at the stack of films next to the microfiche. So many.

At least she'd discovered that Edie's trip to Calcutta had birthed Bring Them Home in response to the impossible need for international adoptions.

But something tugged at her. A sense that there was more.

"Well, Lord, You need to show me what it is," she whispered into the paper-scented air.

Taking the stack of blue-colored films to the files, she put each back in its place. She could hear someone chatting with Grace in the outer office.

She slipped the last one into its spot and went to push the cabinet closed. But the year 2008 caught her eye. Something about it tugged at her. Why 2008? She paused, staring at the number. Finally, she lifted the blue sheets for that year from their spot and took them to the microfiche.

"There's no good reason to believe that there will be anything of importance in this file," she said to herself. "But here goes."

She scanned through headline after headline, then finally she saw one: *Heaven's Child Created, an Offering of Bring Them Home Adoption Agency.*

She read the article.

Bring Them Home, an adoption agency founded by Edie Summers out of Deshler, Pennsylvania, has been helping families and orphaned children from around the world find their adoptive families since 1994. Heaven's Child, also a brainchild of Edie Summers, is a scholarship foundation that helps adoptive families afford the staggering costs of international adoption. Bring Them Home manager Merle Meyer said, "This is the perfect combination — an agency with the mission of bringing families together and a foundation offering the resources to accomplish it."

Some adoptions cost as much as twenty thousand dollars. "With rising costs," fund administrator Marla Slater said in a recent interview, "fewer and fewer people can afford to adopt. It is our goal through Heaven's Child to ease this burden." Set up as a separate fund, and managed by Slater, Heaven's Child can be found online. Learn more there about how to give or if you are a family wanting to adopt, fill out the scholarship application.

Merle Meyer. Anne wrote the name down. She wondered if he was still connected to Bring Them Home. Maybe he'd have the answers both she and Alex sought.

As soon as she finished reading the article she punched Alex's phone number into her cell phone.

"Wait," he said when she told him that Aunt Edie had founded both the adoption agency and his sister's foundation, "you're telling me my sister worked for your great-aunt?"

"No, Aunt Edie didn't manage the agency. A man named Merle Meyer did."

"So maybe he'll know something about this overdraft notice."

"Exactly."

CHAPTER NINE

A little after nine o'clock the next morning, Mildred Farley came into the library. She had a library bag in hand. "I'm not too early to return a few DVDs, am I? For some reason I always forget that I have them and end up getting late charges."

"You know I can take those off your account."

"I don't want special favors," the older woman insisted.

"As much as you donate to the library, it's hardly a favor." She studied the woman who had been her great-aunt's dearest friend. "Did you know that Aunt Edie created an adoption agency?"

"Is that what her talks with Mother Teresa were about?"

"From what I've read, yes."

Mildred shook her head. "That woman," she said, "she sure was something else." Anne couldn't help but agree.

"I still don't know who the man was in that photo or the details surrounding her trip to Kolkata. I'd like to know more…"

Then that weariness started in again. Anne rubbed at her forehead, wishing she could make it stop, wondering if it was caused by that lump.

"What's wrong?" Mildred asked, meeting her gaze.

The story came out. Finding the lump, calling Alex. Her fears for her children.

"Oh dear." Mildred moved behind the checkout desk to give Anne a hug. "Don't you fret," she said when they finally pulled apart. "You're going to be okay. You just are." Mildred watched her for a long while. "Are you okay?" Her look was dead serious. "You need me to cancel my trip to Hawaii?"

"Of course not," Anne said, chuckling at her friend's kind offer yet thankful for it too. "That time with your sister is important."

At first Anne didn't think Mildred would relent. Her brow furrowed hard, her gaze insistent. Then finally she said, "Just speak the word and I'll stay here. You know that, right?"

"I do." Anne nodded. "You're very sweet to say so. I want you to go. There's nothing you can do here."

Mildred sighed, then gave Anne's arm a squeeze.

"I did wonder something else," Anne said, wanting to return to their prior conversation. "In regard to who that man could've been. Could Edie have used a travel agent? I was able to find a Virginia Olson who would've been here in town at the time. Do you know her?"

"Of course I know her. Virginia was everyone's travel agent back before the Internet practically shut down that industry. She's at the Blue Hill Retirement Center."

"Do you think she'll remember Aunt Edie?"

"I don't know. I haven't seen her since she went into the home."

"Could you come with me?"

Anne glanced at the clock. Betty Bultman would be in to help out at the library in half an hour.

"Of course."

"I can get away for a little bit," she said. "Once Betty's here."

Just then the front door opened and Betty came in.

"Well," Mildred said, "go get your purse."

* * *

Virginia Olson's gray eyes cut through Anne, measuring her. Or perhaps trying to assess if she should know her visitor. Anne held out a hand to the rail-thin woman in the wheelchair as she introduced herself.

"Well, you can't be all bad. You brought Mildred Farley out of hiding," Virginia said.

Mildred laughed as if the former travel agent were the opening act of a comedy routine. "Oh, Virginia, what makes you think I've been in hiding?"

"Well, you don't come around here all that much. Aren't you getting old enough to join us in this home anyway?"

"I'll join you when I'm good and ready," Mildred said, "and not a minute sooner!"

"*Pfft!*" Virginia dismissed her with a wave of her hand. "Why don't you take a load off?" She motioned to the stuffed chairs in the corner of her room. The floors were a vinyl made to look like hardwood. A bland dresser and nightstand lined the wall nearest the hospital bed. A corkboard above the nightstand held photos of children and grandchildren surrounding the petite woman.

"So what brings you out?" Virginia said when they had each taken a chair. "Or were you going to sing me a lullaby and put me to bed?" She laughed at her own joke.

Mildred exchanged a look with Anne.

"I'm just teasing, Mildred. Don't look so serious." Virginia turned her gaze to Anne.

"I wanted to ask you a few questions about my great-aunt Edie," Anne began.

"Edie?" Her face twisted as if she were confused for a moment. "Edie who?"

"Summers?"

That seemed to spark something in the elderly woman. "Oh yeah. She's deceased now, isn't she?"

"Yes," Anne said.

"I'm sorry." The shift in her demeanor was so abrupt that Anne wasn't sure what to make of it.

Finally, she said, "Thank you."

"So what do you want to know about Edie?"

"You were a travel agent here in Blue Hill in the early nineties."

"And the sixties and seventies and eighties. Your great-aunt was a regular customer with all her travel writing." Virginia lifted a tissue to her nose and gave it a swipe.

"I'm wondering about a trip she took to India in 1993. I believe she made a stop in Nepal as well. It was because of that trip that she founded an adoption agency in Deshler."

Virginia nodded. "Well, sure, I remember that. She stopped in Mumbai, Pune and Nagpur, then Agra and Calcutta. She was excited to see the Taj Mahal."

"It is beautiful architecture," Mildred said.

Virginia glanced at her. "I suppose."

"What do you remember about her trip?" Anne said, leaning forward in her chair.

"She was going to visit Laura and Lance Stieb in Mumbai, only back then it was called Bombay, then she was going to meet a friend on the way to Calcutta."

"Was that Merle Meyer?"

"No, that name's not familiar. It was a gentleman friend. I believe his name was Wayne Wilchel. He was from Deshler. Worked with kids a lot, I think."

Anne pulled the photograph from her purse. "Is this him?"

"Yeah," Virginia said. "I think so. He came by the travel agency to ask me about flights for the both of them. Oh yes!" She shook her head. "Edie went to India to pick up her baby boy with him."

"With this Wayne Wilchel? She was adopting a baby boy?" That bit of information was new. Anne couldn't seem to wrap her mind around it.

Virginia took her time thinking about Anne's question. "Yes...I don't know. I can't remember what their connection was exactly, just that he did a lot of work in India."

For several long seconds Anne couldn't speak. Edie went to adopt a baby? Her mind flashed to the crib she'd seen in the attic just a few short days ago.

"I remember her going on and on about a little boy—Thomas something," Virginia began. Anne kept quiet, not wanting to feed her a name that might not fit with her memory. "I think it was something like Guy or, no, Gee. With a *J* sound. Thomas Gee."

The boy in the photo. The one Pam knew, the one who'd never been adopted.

* * *

"She would've told us if she'd wanted to adopt a little boy," Mildred insisted as they made their way back to the library.

"Are you sure?" Anne said. "Or did she know that everyone would try to talk her out of it? She didn't say anything about creating Bring Them Home either, but she did that too."

"I don't know…," Mildred confessed. "She wasn't big on tooting her own horn when it came to charities — that's all I can think. I can't believe she would attempt to adopt a child and not tell me…or her family. That simply wasn't like her."

Anne had to agree, yet the coincidence of the boy's name was too much to ignore. Perhaps it had been a passing thought that had simply fallen through before she'd had a chance to make it a reality. Yet the fact that the boy had never found a family to call his own as a child was still sad. How would his life have been different if Aunt Edie had indeed brought him home as her son?

I wouldn't be living in Blue Hill, Anne realized. Not if he'd inherited the house instead of her.

* * *

Wayne Wilchel was the name Virginia Olson had given Anne. Anne couldn't recall ever hearing the name before, though she'd been just a young teen at the time of Edie's trip, so she could have easily forgotten. But the article she'd found in the newspaper archive had mentioned a Merle Meyer. She jotted a note to herself to look him up a bit later.

A little past noon there was a lull in library visits, so Anne took advantage of it to look up Wayne.

There were several Wayne Wilchels listed in the computer search. Two in Seattle, one in Lincoln, Nebraska, and a fourth in

Altoona, Pennsylvania. Anne clicked on that name to find a link to a genealogy site.

Apparently there had been eight Wilchels who emigrated to the western part of Pennsylvania in 1850, Wayne's great-great grandfather among them. They'd had a slew of kids, many who took off for the South during the Civil War. Wayne's grandfather fought in World War I and died a week before the end of the war. Wayne's father had been a boy at the time, the eldest of five. Anne scanned down the page, looking for more about Wayne. There was a marriage record to a Lucia Harmon. Then a death certificate for her in 1982. So Wayne Wilchel had been widowed at the time of Edie's trip to India. He and Lucia had had two children in 1964 and 1966—Teresa and Amelia. Wayne had died in 1998 from a stroke.

Anne sighed and sat back. Perhaps his daughters would know about the trip. She punched in their names. Only Amelia lived nearby. Her married name was St. James. The site gave a rural address, halfway between Deshler and Blue Hill. Anne tried the number, only to get a message that the line was no longer in service.

Anne glanced at the clock. Wendy wasn't due to bring the kids home for another hour. Picking up the phone again, Anne dialed Alex.

He answered immediately. "Have you heard anything?"

For a moment she didn't understand what he was talking about, then she realized he thought she'd seen the doctor already.

"No, the clinic couldn't fit me in till Friday."

"You'll let me know, right?"

"Of course." She appreciated his concern. She told him about her visit with Virginia Olson and what she'd learned of

Wayne Wilchel. "I was thinking about heading over to meet his daughter Amelia St. James. Would you like to come with me?"

"You mean now?"

"No, after work. I'll see if Wendy can keep the kids a bit longer."

"Sounds good. I'll be over then."

* * *

Alex buckled his seat belt as Anne pulled out toward the street. She'd explained what she'd learned from Virginia Olson—that a man named Wayne Wilchel had traveled with Edie to India and the surprising possibility that she might've tried to adopt a boy — Thomas Gee—when she'd been there. Alex was as amazed by the revelation as Anne had been.

"That's an awful lot for one trip, isn't it?" Alex said when she'd finished. "I mean, travel writing, adopting a child, and coordinating an adoption agency with Mother Teresa..."

"It is," Anne agreed. "I don't know if Virginia is right in her recollections. But it can't be coincidence. She pulled up the same name as that photo!"

Alex nodded agreement. "And how this all connects to my sister, and finding out who wanted me to think the account had been closed..."

"*If* it's connected," Anne added.

"True."

There was a long pause. Anne touched the lump in her throat. She didn't want to talk about the discovery of the lump again, not until she knew something from the doctor. Thankfully, Alex didn't bring it up.

"How are the kids liking Summer Fun?" he finally asked.

"They love it. They've been playing with the Haydens and Pyles all week too. It'll be hard when the Haydens have to go back to India. How about Ryan?"

"He loves it."

There was another long silence. They passed fields of crops a vibrant green in the summer sun. Anne made a turn onto a dirt road that led north along a steep ravine. Through the trees she could see glimpses of Foster Joseph Sayers Lake shimmering in the distance. Several more turns led them down into the valley.

A prim little house sat alone alongside a meandering creek. The yard must've been several acres, mowed grass without a shrub or tree to break up the expanse. Surrounding the property was a deep woods, dark in contrast to the sunny meadow where the house sat.

Anne pulled up alongside the house and killed the engine. There were several vehicles parked off to the right, all trucks and a couple four-wheelers.

Anne and Alex got out and glanced around. No one was in sight. They made their way to the front porch, knocking on the screen door.

Anne could hear footfalls inside, then a woman answered the door. She looked about the right age, in her fifties or so. She had dark brown hair with touches of gray and pale blue eyes.

"Can I help you?" she asked.

Anne introduced herself and Alex, then said, "I'm Edie Summers's great-niece."

"Edie Summers? I remember her. She was a friend of my father's."

Anne was relieved that she'd found the right Wilchel.

"I was hoping we could ask you a few questions about a trip your father and Edie took to India in 1993."

"Oh, I remember that." She pushed the screen open. "Come on in."

The house was sunny, with white furniture and bright fabrics for the cushions and curtains. An enormous photograph of Audrey Hepburn hung over the modern couch where Anne and Alex took seats.

Amelia sat in a birch rocker that creaked when she settled. "How is your aunt?"

When Anne told her that Edie had passed, the woman offered her condolences. Then Anne went on telling her a bit about what she'd discovered—the trip, Aunt Edie meeting Mother Teresa, the possibility that her great-aunt had been adopting. She showed Amelia the photograph of Aunt Edie with Mother Teresa and Wayne.

Amelia gazed at the shot. "I've seen this before."

"You have?" Alex said, clearly as interested as Anne.

"It was a few years before Dad passed." Amelia rose and went to a bookcase on the far side of the room, returning after a few moments with a photo album in hand. She turned the pages, looking for something, tucking her long dark hair behind her ear. "Here it is," she finally said, pulling a photograph from its plastic sleeve. She handed the shot to Anne. It was the exact same photo that Anne held in her hand.

Anne turned it over and read the lines on the back written in a masculine hand. *The start of something new.*

"Bring Them Home adoption agency," Anne said.

Amelia nodded.

"What role did your father play in that?" Anne asked.

"My father was very active with Mother Teresa after my mother passed. He was a liaison of sorts, helping get the word out about Mother Teresa's work, connecting her with speaking opportunities in Pennsylvania and the East Coast. She had other staff, of course, who worked with her full time. But Dad really believed in what she was doing..." She met Anne's eyes. "It gave him a sense of purpose during that time of his life."

"Of course."

"He spoke in a lot of the local churches, did fund-raising. That kind of thing."

"That was how Edie was able to meet with Mother Teresa?" Anne asked. "Because of him?"

"It was."

"So what do you know about the formation of Bring Them Home? Do you know Merle Meyer?"

"No. I've heard of him—he's the manager, right? But that's really all I know about him. My dad introduced Edie to Mother Teresa, and your great-aunt took the ball from there. I'm not sure who she met with or exactly how she did it, but this picture..." She held it up again. "That's what they were working on here."

"Do you know anything about my aunt trying to adopt a little boy?"

Amelia shook her head. "No. I don't know anything about that."

Anne exchanged a look with Alex. Was she chasing a reality or an old woman's delusion?

Chapter Ten

Dappled sunlight floated across the hood of the car. Both Alex and Anne were lost in thought as they made their way back to Blue Hill.

"So Mother Teresa helped Aunt Edie form Bring Them Home." Anne looked at Alex. "I don't understand why Aunt Edie didn't tell me about the adoption agency. What's so secretive about that?"

Alex shrugged. "Hard to say."

"No doubt she had something to do with Marla becoming the manager of Heaven's Child too."

"Knowing your great-aunt, I'd lay money on it."

"We need to talk to Merle Meyer," Anne said.

"That's what I was going to say."

* * *

Wendy Pyle brought Ben and Liddie home just before suppertime. Anne was finishing chopping up a salad and setting the hot Crock-Pot in the middle of the table.

"Go wash up," Anne told the kids. Ben had dirt smudged across his cheeks and his hair had that sweat-laden look of long play.

"You are wearing my children out," Anne said to her good friend.

Wendy quirked a brow and said, "Isn't that the goal? I think he ate several bugs on a dare too."

"What?" Anne's eyes grew large.

"Isaac Hayden told him real missionaries eat bugs." She shrugged. "You know boys. Besides, it's protein."

Anne chuckled. "As long as he didn't bring home any parasites…"

"I can't guarantee that."

Anne sighed as that familiar exhaustion passed over her, like a shadow falling across a meadow. It often came on suddenly, the urge to lie down nearly impossible to refuse.

"What's wrong?" Wendy said, noting the sudden shift, her brow furrowing.

"I'm just tired."

"You've been tired a lot." Her head tilted and she had the look of a school marm about to scold. "There's something else," she added.

"I found a lump," Anne admitted. Her hand touched it again.

Wendy squinted, her gaze following the movement. "Have you seen a doctor?"

"Tomorrow."

Wendy nodded. "Good. Then you'll know what it is." She reached for Anne's hand, studying her. "You're afraid."

"I am." Anne sighed. "I have too much to lose."

"You think God isn't in control of this? That He's off the clock? 'Cause He's not. He's still taking care of the universe, and of you."

It was so like Wendy, pragmatic and to the point. Just hearing it eased Anne.

"I know He is in control."

"Honey, He loves you. Don't underestimate how much. We can't comprehend His kind of love."

The warmth of those words brought a tear to Anne's eyes.

Wendy touched her arm. "Do you want me to come along tomorrow?"

"No," Anne said, "I'll be fine. It's just a consultation."

"I will come if you want me to—you know that, right?"

"I do."

"That's what friends do."

Anne was learning that more and more. She followed Wendy to the back stairs.

"Call me when you hear back from the doc?" Wendy said as she gave Anne a hug.

"I will."

* * *

The squat building that housed the Blue Hill Medical Clinic had been a bank when Anne lived in Blue Hill as a child. Now ivy crept up the faded brick walls and wound around the corner pillars.

The clinic was run by a rotation of four doctors and two nurse practitioners. Anne had made an appointment with one of the doctors, a woman named Jones whom she'd never met.

As Anne sat in the waiting room, a TV droned mindlessly in the corner. Anne wished she had the remote to turn it off. It irritated her. She needed to focus, to hear God's whisper that everything would be all right. Instead she got the latest from CNN. She closed her eyes.

Stop letting your imagination roam, she scolded herself.

A heavyset elderly woman took a seat across from Anne. She used a walker and huffed loudly as she plopped down, her breaths labored. She picked up a magazine and thumbed through it. A woman with a baby tucked into a carrier came from the back, offering thanks to a nurse who followed behind.

The nurse moved to the front desk and grabbed the next file, then called Anne's name. The nurse led her to an exam room and motioned to a chair nearest the minimal desk, then took her blood pressure and temperature, asking the basic questions.

"So what brings you here today?" she finally asked. Anne noted the smile in the corners of her light gray eyes.

"There's a nodule at the base of my throat," Anne said. The words scratched out. Her hand moved to the spot unconsciously.

The nurse wrote something into her notes, then told her the doctor would be in shortly and left her alone. A clock ticked nervously on the wall. Anne sighed. Maybe CNN wouldn't be so bad—at least it was a distraction.

The doctor came in a few minutes later, a youngish woman who shook hands and introduced herself as Dr. Jones. She was tall, a good six feet, with short-cropped, no-nonsense hair.

"So you found a lump," she said, scooting the wheeled stool a bit closer.

"Yes. Here." Anne pointed.

The doctor rubbed her hands together to warm them before touching the spot. Her gaze traveled somewhere behind Anne as she felt it, the touch sending shards of pain up and down Anne's chest and neck.

"When did you notice it?" The fingers were still probing. Anne braced herself against the pain.

"Just a few nights ago, as I was getting ready for bed."

The doctor turned to scribble into the file. "Any other symptoms?"

"I'm tired. A lot. Afternoons especially. I can barely keep my eyes open. I'm in a fog till suppertime, then it seems to lift."

"Do you nap?"

"When I can. I work, so that's difficult."

The doctor nodded, then tapped her pen on the desk. "Let's run a few tests to narrow this down." The corners of her eyes crinkled into a calming smile. "We'll start with a blood calcium, check your blood sugar. Did you eat anything this morning?"

"No."

"Perfect. Once we get those results we'll see what we have to do from there."

Anne nodded mutely. This wasn't like her, being so paranoid, so worried about herself. What was wrong with her?

Liddie and Ben, the answer came. She wasn't worried for herself. She was worried for them. Because she knew how desperately they needed her.

"You okay?" The doctor met her gaze.

Anne nodded. "I'm fine."

* * *

When Anne returned to the library she saw the concerned looks from Betty. Remi Miller and her sister Bella, who worked at the library, seemed unusually attentive too. Anne found it unsettling how quickly word got around. Why had she told anyone? The last thing she wanted was pity and concern. She knew they meant well, but it only served as reminders when she wanted mostly to forget.

She took her purse up to her apartment, then returned downstairs to the library to take over at the front desk. There was a line of children cashing in their reading hours for prizes from the Summer Reading program's stash.

Mildred was in the Nonfiction Room perusing the travel books about Hawaii. Anne made her way to the older woman once the children had all left.

Mildred lifted her gaze. "Hey." There was no hint of concern or worry in her gaze, and for that Anne was grateful.

"I wanted to tell you," Anne began, "I found out about Aunt Edie's trip. The man in the photo was Wayne Wilchel. His daughter told me about the trip." She went on to recount the visit and the discovery that Wayne had been Edie's connection to Mother Teresa.

Mildred closed the book in her lap. "Did you find out if she tried to adopt Thomas Gee?"

Anne shook her head. "No. I still don't know what to make of that."

"It would be completely believable that Edie wouldn't be intimidated by taking on the stigma of being a single parent. But I don't remember her filling out home study papers or going through any of that…"

"So you don't think she did?"

"No, I don't. But if Virginia remembers it, I wouldn't discount it either."

"I want to head to Bring Them Home to talk to Merle Meyer," Anne said. "When do you leave for Hawaii?"

"Tomorrow," Mildred said.

Anne thought through her schedule. There was no way she could get away by the next day. The earliest she could get to the agency would be the following Monday.

"Okay. I'll see if Alex wants to come to the agency with me."

"Of course he will."

* * *

That afternoon the library was dead. Not a soul searched for books or sat at the computers. It was no wonder, the way the sunshine outside called.

Anne remained inside. She had plenty of work to do. There was always more than enough work to keep her busy as town librarian and as a mother.

Liddie and Ben were playing with the Haydens once again, though this time at the library. Natalie and Isaac Hayden had come home with them from Summer Fun. She could hear their peals of laughter ring through the open window that overlooked the backyard.

She glanced at the clock. It was four o'clock. Not quite closing time, but she doubted very many people would come by with such a stunning day to distract them.

Standing, she stretched, allowing her aching muscles some reprieve from sitting. The exhaustion was coming over her again, filling her head with a hazy sensation, her eyelids heavy. Perhaps if she moved around a bit she could push it away. Picking up a dusting rag, she moved from shelf to shelf, wiping, moving books backward then forward as she cleaned. She climbed the stairs to the second story of the old Victorian and did the same on that floor. She glanced at the staircase that led to the third floor and saw the attic access.

Surely Aunt Edie had left more clues up there — more evidence of what her trip had been about, especially if she'd tried to adopt Thomas Gee, if that was indeed the truth. Anne had called Alex earlier, asking about the two of them taking a trip to Bring Them Home adoption agency. He'd said he could get away on Monday to head to Deshler. In the meantime, perhaps she could learn more in the attic.

Returning her dustrag to the cleaning closet on the first floor, Anne glanced at the clock again. Closing time. She turned the lock on the front library door, then returned to the attic, climbing the folding stairs to the hot, muggy darkness.

She tugged on the string to the overhead light, glanced around, and noticed the metal crib. She'd seen it the last time she came up here. Why would a single woman with no children have a crib? Had she ever put it up? Anne couldn't recall seeing it in any rooms of the house, and she'd practically lived here when she was a girl. She lightly touched the white-painted metal.

Unless Aunt Edie had bought it for Thomas Gee. Though judging from the photograph, Thomas would have been too old to need a crib.

She made her way to the section where she'd found the photos of the boy with the schoolmaster and his wife along with the shot of Edie, Wayne Wilchel, and Mother Teresa.

Could Aunt Edie truly have wanted to adopt him? What had prevented her?

Bending down, Anne opened a box of correspondence. There were several large packets of it. She doubted Edie had ever thrown away a letter in her life. Glancing at the postmarks, she could see that they were from the correct decade at least. Realizing the light to read would be better downstairs, she lifted the box and headed for the stairs.

Anne settled on the porch where she could watch the kids and enjoy the afternoon sunshine while she searched. There were many letters from relatives, thank you notes from Anne's own parents for this gift or that. It was such a lost art, letter writing, taking the time to think of another person, writing down happenings as well as deeper thoughts, struggles, insights. It was so intimate, caring.

The sheer number of people represented here was stunning. These weren't letters all from the same person. These were letters from a multitude of people, some Anne knew from Blue Hill and family, but many of them were strangers, and according to a few she read, many had been strangers to Edie as well. And everyone who wrote to Edie seemed to thank her for some goodness she'd shown—a meal delivered, a ride here or there, time spent at a bedside.

One read,

Dear Edie,

I can't begin to thank you for the car you gave us. Because of it, we have been able to visit our family out East without worries of breaking down on the side of the road. I don't know how I could possibly repay you . . .

And another said,

The food you brought to my daughter when she was ill was deeply appreciated. So many have forgotten about her. When she first got sick there were many cards and visitors. But as the months wore on those people drifted away. Only you have remained faithful, coming to call, bringing your delicious meals. Thank you from the bottom of my heart. I wish I could be there myself, but my own poor health keeps me away. It is good to know that someone like you is there to fill in the gaps.

She scanned through the next box, but there was nothing there that looked like a home study. No collection of papers profiling Edie's life so she could apply to adopt a little boy from India.

Anne was about to take the boxes back inside when she reached several thick envelopes. She noted the foreign looking stamps in the corner and *Airmail* in red ink. They were from Calcutta, India. She opened one.

There were several brochures in the first, each with photos of children glued to the front and profiles describing their lives in the orphanages of India. A few were from the orphanage where the Stiebs had worked and where Pam and Cory Hayden now worked. The others were in cities around India. The back side held information on how to support the children financially, through Heaven's Child — Marla's foundation. Folded inside the brochure was a handwritten letter dated not long before Marla's death, sent from Blue Hill. It was still sealed, as if it had never been opened.

Anne opened it. The handwriting looked vaguely familiar. She turned it over and saw that it was signed "Marla Slater." Alex's sister had written to Aunt Edie. And judging from the date it was just before Marla's death.

Anne began to read.

Dear Edie,

I am writing to you because I don't know who else to turn to. I've tried calling you, but it seems you've been out and about with your travel writing and since I needed to get my worries off my chest and on to paper I decided to send a letter. There's something about seeing it on paper that helps me know this isn't all in my head. Though in my heart of hearts I hope it is in my head.

I know that you share my love for children and for the causes that Bring Them Home and Heaven's Child stand for. I also know that you are a discreet person and can advise me without causing undo embarrassment or unneedful concern. I would hate for anything to diminish the wonderful work that goes on there.

I have, however, become suspicious over the past few months that something is going on at Heaven's Child, something wrong. I don't have proof, at least nothing that I can point my finger at. But I have a sense that someone there has been taking money. Or perhaps more than one person is behind this.

But to steal money from children! I am appalled if it's true. Yet I don't know how I can prove it. When I go through my records everything seems to be in order. Yet I've gotten calls from several donors whom I have no record of. They show me cancelled checks made out to Heaven's Child, even receipts they've gotten for those same funds, and I haven't been able to reconcile the two.

I'm not asking you to solve this for me. I know you have a lot on your plate and I don't want to burden you. But since Heaven's Child works so closely with Bring Them Home I can't help but wonder if someone from that adoption agency is involved. They are the ones who deposit donations that come into Deshler. But who could it be? You know the staff at Bring Them Home better than I do. I'm hoping you can advise me, offer your wisdom. Because I deeply need it.

I hope I am wrong here. That this sense I have that someone is stealing is wrong. Yet I can't seem to let it go. Any words of wisdom you can offer will be greatly appreciated.

Yours truly,
Marla Slater

Anne read the note again. The thought that someone had been stealing was deeply troubling.

Given the fact that the letter had never been opened it would seem that Edie had never read it, never knew of Marla's concerns. How was it the letter had gotten placed in this box without ever being read? Anne wasn't sure if she'd ever know the answer to that question. She shook her head. Had Marla ever figured out who the thief was? Or perhaps that individual had been the very same person who'd called Alex to tell him Heaven's Child had closed, Anne realized. Concealing theft would surely be motive enough for someone to keep Alex from taking up the digging his sister had been doing.

She called Alex right away, knowing he'd want to hear about the letter, but her call went straight to voice mail. She left a message asking him to call her as soon as possible.

Moving back to the front desk of the library, she typed in Bring Them Home and Deshler into the search engine of her computer.

Anne clicked on the link and read the adoption agency's tag line: "Bringing children to their adoptive families since 1994."

Anne clicked on the "Contact Us" page. There were several photos there of staff members, including Merle Meyer who was still the managing director, with phone numbers and e-mail addresses. Anne picked up her cell and dialed the main number. While she and Alex were planning on stopping by the following Monday she couldn't help but see if he was around now to answer a few questions.

"Hello. Is Merle Meyer available?" Anne asked.

"I'm afraid he's not in. Would you like his voice mail?"

"No, that's okay," Anne said.

Anne wasn't ready for the woman to hang up just yet, but she couldn't very well ask about the theft without first meeting the people on staff and finding out who was who. She opted for a more indirect route. "I'm wondering if you can help me. I'm trying to find out about Heaven's Child. Can you tell me about it?"

"Let me connect you with the person who runs that fund," she said.

A few moments later a woman's voice said, "Hello. This is Karina. I understand you're interested in learning about Heaven's Child?"

"Yes," Anne said. "It's an adoption grant?"

"It is. We have certain qualifications. Are you looking to apply for a grant or to donate to the fund?" She went on to tell Anne about the application process and income qualifications. "The fund is really for many different needs for families, support as well as adoption, and it also supports several girls' vocational schools in India. They train young women in the garment industry so that if they aren't adopted by the time they reach maturity they can find viable employment." She rattled off the names of the cities in India where the schools were based—all cities Virginia Olson had mentioned Edie visiting.

When she was finished, Anne said, "That's really impressive. I'm not really looking to adopt, though I am interested in donating." She paused, then said, "To be honest, there's something else I'm curious about. Is it possible to find out about an adoption?"

"What do you mean?"

"My great-aunt—she's deceased now—but I'm wondering if she tried to adopt a little boy from India by the name of Thomas Gee."

"Adoption records are private. Once they are sealed..."

"Of course," Anne said.

The woman apologized, then asked if there was anything else she could do for Anne. Anne simply thanked her, then hung up.

Alex returned her call a few minutes later. When Anne told him about the letter she'd found from Marla to Aunt Edie, he was dead silent.

"Alex?" she said. "Are you okay?"

"I *knew* there was something wrong, something fishy..."

"But other than that phone call telling you that the fund was closed, what do we have?"

Alex let out a heavy sigh. "Nothing."

CHAPTER ELEVEN

Alex asked Anne and the kids to come over after supper. He was eager to find out the truth about Heaven's Child, and he wasn't about to lose another minute.

"I've already lost four years," he said. Anne knew he was referring to the time since his sister and brother-in-law had died.

"Where's Ryan?" Ben asked, holding up his baseball glove as they entered the front door of the ultra modern one-level house. "I thought we'd play a little catch."

"He's in his room." Alex tilted his head toward the back of the house, a long hallway off the main living room.

Liddie too had a baseball glove in hand. Anne hoped the boys would throw her the ball every now and again. Brother and sister moved down the hall and within a few minutes the three of them were outside.

Anne and Alex went into the inviting living room with its large picture window overlooking a ravine. The backyard was open with several large Linden trees lining the border. A swing hung from the lowest branch of one. Anne saw Liddie drop her glove on the ground and head straight for the swing.

"That kid is something else, isn't she?" Alex said, pulling Anne's gaze. He was smiling as he watched Anne's youngest, the corners of his eyes crinkling up.

"She is," Anne agreed. "At least she won't be bothering the boys."

"She's never a bother."

Anne watched him and let the comment pass. She could see in the way he studied Liddie that he cared for her. Liddie swung high then leaned back hard to get the swing moving.

"And how are you?" Alex's look wasn't lost on Anne.

"I'm fine. Waiting on test results."

"Any idea how long?"

"No. They always seem to be vague when it comes to that question."

He scoffed and shook his head. "Can I see the letter?" he asked, referring to the note his sister had written to Edie.

Anne handed it to him. She watched as his face darkened. He blew out a breath.

"Why didn't she tell me?" he said.

"She was trying to be discreet," Anne offered. "She didn't really want to believe it herself."

"I suppose…" He sighed and met her gaze. "I did a little digging after I talked to you."

"Oh?" Anne said.

"I looked through some bins of paperwork—my sister's stuff that got shoved into boxes after the funeral. Stuff I never looked at. I found a folder on Heaven's Child."

"Can I see it?"

Alex led the way to the long oatmeal-colored couch. Anne took a seat next to him and he reached for a thick file folder on the boomerang-shaped coffee table.

"What is all this?" Anne asked.

"Bank statements."

She reached for it. Inside were months of bank statements, arranged by date. "What am I looking for?"

"These are from the very beginning, when my sister opened this bank account."

Anne paged through them, noting that someone had written on many of the sheets, she assumed Marla. Next to several withdrawals were names with addresses. Some had asterisks but others did not.

"What do you think these are about?" Alex pointed to the names.

"I'm not sure." Anne paused to give it thought. "Maybe the couples designated to receive that money?"

"That makes sense. Take a look at that last sheet." He pointed to the stack in her right hand.

Anne turned it over. A sticky note was stuck on to the back with these words scribbled in the same handwriting: "Not a real account."

"It's on the last statement," Anne observed. "So Marla thought that transaction was theft."

"The month she and Rick died. It was shortly after that that I got the call that the account had been closed."

"You don't think there was some connection?" Anne asked, sudden anxiety rising.

"No," Alex assured. "The accident was just that—icy roads. No foul play."

Anne exhaled a breath of relief. But still, the fact that they had died so soon after Marla's realization meant that someone had likely gotten away with theft. And for how long? Anne thought of the overdraft notice. Was that person still stealing money from the fund?

"There's a reason someone called to tell you the account was closed," Anne reminded Alex. "Someone wanted you to believe it."

"Don't you think I know that?" He shook his head. "What gets me is that they've been getting away with it all this time."

Anne flipped back to the first months of Heaven's Child's existence, then slowly paged through, hoping to see some sort of trend. Her brow furrowed as she studied the sheets.

"Look at this." She pointed to the withdrawals. "All of the withdrawals were checks. See the check numbers? But here." She pointed to the more recent bank statements. "We start seeing ATM withdrawals. Not all of them, but some..." She lifted her face to look at Alex.

He nodded and shuffled through another pile on the table before handing her a statement.

"Look at that," she said. On the back of the statement was an odd code. It read: C.B.—?; J.H.—30; G.S.—35; R.F.—?; L.K.—5; M.M.—?

"What do you think these are?" Alex asked, motioning toward the code.

"I'm not sure," Anne said, "but it has to be connected."

* * *

Saturday dawned sunny and hot. The parade in Deshler was due to start at ten o'clock. Anne had invited Alex and Ryan, as well as the Haydens and Pyles.

"I've never been to an American parade," Isaac Hayden said as he unfolded his chair and set it up alongside Ben at the curb.

"Never?" Ben said, astonished. Ryan seemed equally amazed.

The dark-haired missionary kid shook his head. "No. We have festivals that we go to sometimes with the children from the orphanage, but our parades are very different."

"Do you have fireworks?" Ryan asked.

"Yeah. I've seen fireworks in the States. They're wimpy compared to the ones they have in India. Lots of people get hurt from them though."

Natalie was talking animatedly to Liddie as they set up their chairs on the far side of the Haydens.

Anne sat between Alex and Pam Hayden. "Thank you for inviting us," Pam said. She looked as excited about the event as her son.

They talked for a little while about the parade and the first week of Summer Fun.

Finally, Pam said, "So what did you find out about your aunt's trip?"

"Actually," Anne said, "I was going to ask you if you think Aunt Edie might've tried to adopt Thomas Gee." Anne had wanted to ask Pam the question ever since she'd spoken with Virginia Olson.

"Adopt Thomas Gee?" She shook her head. "I never heard anything about that. I know she cared about him and wrote to him often."

"She did?"

Pam nodded. "He talked about her."

"I suppose it doesn't matter now that she's gone and he's a grown man."

"I don't know. Maybe you could help him."

"How so?"

Pam shrugged. "It's just a thought."

Anne thought of the kids' prayers asking to help the needy children of India. But how could she help a man on the other side of the world?

"I just thought of someone who might be able to answer some of your questions though," Pam said. "A retired missionary from Bellefonte. Mona Robinson. She worked at the orphanage during that time. She and Edie became good friends. She's been retired for quite a while so I'd forgotten that she'd lived there then, but I remember her talking about Edie."

"Can you write down her contact information?" Anne reached for her purse to pull out a pen and paper. Pam jotted down the information and handed it to Anne.

Soon the police cars came past followed by military veterans carrying flags. The crowd stood in reverence as they passed, then broke into applause.

The Deshler marching band followed, crisply marching as they played a John Phillips Sousa ditty. Then the Shriners with their swift-moving mini cars flying past feet lined up along the street. Pam Hayden shrieked and pulled her youngest up off the curb. "They come close!" she said with a huge grin on her face as the cars screeched by, then did a quick turn and came past again in perfect V formation. "Wow," she mouthed to the boy in her arms. He was pointing at them and clapping his hands. "If only Klara could see this," Pam said into Anne's ear.

Another Shriner entry passed, a Chinese dragon that wove back and forth across the street, spitting white smoke at unsuspecting children. The crowd erupted in laughter.

The sign on the car that followed them caught Anne's attention—*We ride so kids can walk,* it read.

She'd never really thought about the Shriners before, though she had a vague recollection that their activities funded health care for children. As she watched them ride away and the next parade attraction came past, a thought began to form.

Maybe Klara had been here, in a way. Or at least something intended for her.

* * *

Anne hadn't been able to get little Klara out of her mind. As soon as she got home from the parade, she kicked off her shoes and reached for her laptop computer. She had an idea that wanted attention.

Once the machine booted up she found the site for the Shriners. Theirs was an extensive mission, offering surgeries, physical therapy, and top-notch medical care for children from low-income homes around the country and Canada. They specialized in spinal cord injury, burn recovery, cleft lip and palate repair, and orthopedics. Klara's spina bifida would surely qualify as a spinal cord injury.

Anne pulled up several pages on their services and locations, printing each one to take to the Haydens when she saw them in church the next day.

From what Anne could tell, if Klara qualified, all of her surgeries and therapy would be free, as long as the Haydens could get to the States often enough. It was worth a try, anyway. If the Shriners took Klara's case, perhaps the Haydens would be able to adopt her after all. Anne only hoped.

Maybe this was the answer to prayer they'd been looking for.

* * *

On Sunday, the kids who were participating in Summer Fun gave a preview of their upcoming play, a song about children around the world, with a solo sung in perfect tune by Natalie Hayden. The kids clapped in rhythm and swayed when the song kicked up a beat, taking on an African flair. Liddie was in the middle, her face beaming, while Ben was off to the side, a bit more sheepish in his performance.

When they finished, the congregation clapped wildly and the children returned to their seats.

Reverend Tom stepped to the podium. "After that, I can't wait for the full play," he said, with a smile on his face.

He gave the announcements—the list of those in the hospital having surgeries or who were ill and in need of prayer, as well as upcoming events—then he asked the ushers to come forward to take the offering.

After he dismissed the congregation and people began filing toward the back, Anne went to find Pam and Cory Hayden.

"I looked up something yesterday after the parade that I thought might be of interest to you," Anne began. She tugged the sheets she'd printed out of her purse.

Pam turned and watched as she unfolded them. "What's this?"

"Do you know much about the Shriners?" Anne asked.

"You mean the men in the parade?" Cory asked.

Anne nodded.

"Not really. Other than their funny hats," Pam said.

"Cities pay for them to perform in parades—that money in turn pays for hospitals, medical care for children."

Pam and Cory leaned forward, clearly interested.

"All their hospitals are free. If the child qualifies and is accepted into the program, they can have the surgeries or therapies they need for as long as they need them." She handed Cory the pages she'd printed and he bent his head to read.

"So someone like Klara could get free surgeries..." he finished the thought Anne had begun. "But we live in India. How would that work? Do the Shriners have hospitals in India?"

"From what I saw online, no, they don't. But maybe you could bring her back whenever she needs those procedures."

The idea seemed to spark something in Pam. Anne could see it: hope.

Pam turned to Cory. "We could adopt her then," she said, "couldn't we? If we didn't have to pay for the surgeries. A few flights aren't so much, but..."

Cory was nodding. He looked up at Anne. "Thanks for this." He pointed to the papers in his hand. "Really. Thanks. We'd always assumed God wanted Klara to go to another family, but this might be the answer we're looking for."

Chapter Twelve

The kids had begged to play with the Haydens again, and Anne finally relented when Pam said, "We really love having them."

Anne called Mona Robinson's number after lunch. There was no answer, but the drive to Bellefonte wasn't long, so she decided to hop in the car and see if she could drop in on the retired missionary.

A light rain began to fall on the drive over and left a sheen on the road surface. She pulled on to the street that led to the missionary's home, a quiet neighborhood of smallish houses on cul-de-sacs. A boy on a bicycle rode past her slow-moving car as she tried to make out the house numbers. He looked at her curiously, then pedaled away.

Mona's home was a two-story Cape Cod, white with black shutters. Anne parked on the street, then made her way to the front door where she pushed the doorbell. She could hear its ding inside.

Mona was a tiny finch of a woman. Too thin, though her posture was erect despite her eighty years. She peered at Anne with a no-nonsense gaze when Anne took her seat in the tall wicker rocker that overlooked the postage stamp-sized front yard that was one solid flower bed.

Mona got right to the point after Anne made introductions. "Pam told me you have questions about your aunt Edie's time in India."

"Yes, ma'am, I do," Anne said.

"I had a great affection for your great-aunt. That Edie..." She shook her head. "She had a way of making friends wherever she went. She cared about people. Would've made a good missionary."

"She *was* a missionary, in her own way."

"I suppose that's true. She cared about things like justice and mercy. Some people don't see how those two things can coexist, but she did. She lived it out every day."

Anne smiled as memories of her great-aunt filled her. She remembered Aunt Edie taking her to volunteer at the food shelf in Deshler and visiting shut-ins, yet Aunt Edie was quick to protest unjust political issues of the times too.

Mona leaned forward, her rocking chair screeching with the motion. "What was it you wanted to know about her trip to India?"

"It was 1993, right?"

"Indeed. A year before I retired."

Anne pulled out the photographs she'd found and handed them to Mona, whose eyes crinkled.

"Ah, Thomas Gee with Aaniya and Bakool Gupta." She flipped to the next, then stopped on the shot of Edie with Mother Teresa and Wayne Wilchel. "I took this shot." She sighed. "She wanted to visit Mother Teresa, though we had no idea if she'd be able to get a hearing. That woman was busy! But Wayne arranged it, got her in."

Mona sat back and Anne waited for the full story to come out. "Those two talked long into the night. They were both so passionate about the needy. Mother Teresa in her ministry to the dying of Calcutta, though by then her ministry had spread far and wide. She was getting pretty old. This was just four years before her death. Edie had seen so much suffering in India, especially in Mumbai. We called it Bombay in the early days. When she was with the Stiebs, she was deeply impressed by the kids who were aging out of the system. Those kids would never know the love of a mother and a father. She wanted to give them opportunities, help get them set up so they wouldn't fall into temptations of lesser professions once they were on their own." Mona shook her head. "So many suffer greatly once they leave the orphanages. Edie established schools to teach skills, and of course she started talking about helping more families adopt. There are many who want to but simply don't have the money."

"So she created Bring Them Home and then later Heaven's Child," Anne finished for her.

The older woman nodded.

"Did you know Marla Slater?"

Mona shook her head. "Who's that?"

"She was the fund administrator for Heaven's Child."

"Sorry. I don't know her."

Anne told her of the woman's passing but nothing more. Since Mona hadn't known Alex's sister she wouldn't be able to offer any information about the thefts.

"Do you know if Edie tried to adopt Thomas Gee?" Anne asked.

"Who told you that?"

"Virginia Olson from the travel agency in Blue Hill said that Edie went to India to adopt him."

"I don't think she did. At least she didn't take him home with her on that trip. Was he ever adopted? I can't recall."

"No," Anne said. "Pam Hayden said that he aged out of the system."

"I'm sorry to hear that." She frowned. "We tried our best to equip the older kids, to give them skills to support themselves. But the caste system is stacked against them. They are untouchables — the lowest caste. Treated with disdain. It's not like here in America where anyone can make something of themselves. Not like here at all."

Mona sat back, her gaze taking on a distant look. "So many children like him. I wished I could take them all myself. But after my husband passed — he was just fifty-four when he had his heart attack — I simply couldn't do it."

She studied Anne. "I just remembered something." She stood up and moved toward the front door. "Wait right here."

She moved inside. Anne could hear her climb the stairs just inside the door. A few minutes later she returned with a small book. She handed it to Anne. "Your great-aunt sent me this after she got home."

Anne turned the brown leather journal over in her hands. It had yellowed some over the years, but the distinctive handwriting was Edie's. Anne could see that right away.

"It's the journal she kept when she was in India. I think she wrote in it a bit after she got back to the States too. You can keep it."

"But she gave it to you."

"What will I do with it?" Mona said. "I've read it already. You're the one who needs it now."

* * *

As Anne drove the few miles back to Blue Hill, she wondered about her aunt's life—she had truly left a legacy for others to follow. Not in children or grandchildren, but in lives touched by love and generosity. Would others be able to say the same of Anne? That she'd left a trail of kindness across the globe?

Her hand moved to the lump.

Was that what was causing all this angst, this sudden urge to do something bigger than herself? She thought of Thomas Gee. Who would Liddie and Ben live with if something happened to her? The thought rose and along with it the answer—her parents, Eric's parents, her brother and sister-in-law. They had deep roots in those people. Thomas Gee had only his daughter.

She passed the turn for the Blue Hill Retirement Center and on a whim turned into the parking lot. Perhaps another talk with Virginia Olson could settle her questions once and for all.

She parked in the nearly empty lot and made her way into the antiseptic smelling halls. A caregiver wheeled a man toward the dining hall. Anne said hello.

She knocked on the doorframe of Virginia's open door. "You again," the woman said when she met Anne's gaze.

"I hope you don't mind my intruding," Anne said.

Virginia didn't reply, simply shrugged. Anne went in and took a seat on the wing in the corner. Virginia seemed very different.

Agitated. Morose. Hardly the lucid and sharp woman she'd talked to a few short days before.

"I wanted to talk to you again," Anne began. "Do you remember me?"

Virginia didn't answer. Just turned to look at her, her eyes rheumy.

"You mentioned that my aunt was going to adopt a little boy, Thomas Gee, when she went to India. Do you remember?"

"Thomas Gee," Virginia said. "Wasn't that the name of an actor in the 1930s? I think he was in silent films."

Anne studied her for a moment. What was she talking about?

"No, he was an orphan at the Stiebs' orphanage in Mumbai," Anne reminded. "Pam Hayden works there now."

"I don't know those people." Virginia's brow furrowed deep.

"A few days ago you said you did. You even mentioned Thomas Gee by name."

"I don't know what you're talking about." Virginia turned away from her and turned on the TV, its volume set to high the moment it flared on.

"I…" Anne broke off. She watched the older woman for a moment.

Rising, she moved back to the hallway and made her way to the nurse's station. The nurse lifted her face and said, "Can I help you?"

"Yes. I'm wondering about Virginia Olson. Does she have memory issues?"

"Honey, this is the memory care wing—all the residents in this hallway have memory issues. Is she acting peculiar?"

"I guess I don't know her well enough to answer that," Anne admitted. Then she thanked the nurse and moved through the heavy doors back to the main wing and out to her car.

The only proof she had that Aunt Edie had tried to adopt Thomas Gee was the word of a woman who had dementia. That wasn't proof at all.

She had been chasing an illusion.

* * *

The drive to Deshler wasn't long on Monday morning. Wendy had offered to cover the morning at the library while Anne and Alex headed out to talk to the staff at Bring Them Home, especially Merle Meyer. The kids were at Summer Fun and would head to the Pyles' afterward with the Haydens.

Heat rose in waves from the blacktop. Alex cranked up the air conditioning.

"It was pointless," Anne said of her search to find out if Aunt Edie had tried to adopt Thomas Gee. "A waste of time."

"But you learned about her heart, the things she loved. Was that pointless?"

Anne didn't respond. She supposed Alex was right. Yet she'd felt such an urgency. At least she could help Alex find out what had happened with Heaven's Child, if someone had been stealing from the fund as Marla had suspected.

"What do we know about this Merle Meyer so far?" Alex asked as he drove his pickup through the quiet streets of Deshler.

"Only what the newspaper article said, that he's the managing director of Bring Them Home. I don't even know if he's connected to Heaven's Child."

Alex turned on to Euclid Avenue where Bring Them Home was located. The adoption agency was an impressive place on the edge of Deshler, two stories high with a red tile roof and a brick exterior. White shutters flanked the many windows, and a cobblestone walkway led to the bright red front door.

A woman who looked to be in her thirties got out of her car as they walked up. She had long, dark hair and a flowing, hippie-style dress, with leather-strapped sandals completing the ensemble. She gave a wave. "Hey, I'm Ginny," she greeted. "One of the social workers here. Welcome."

Anne and Alex shook hands with her.

"Are you here for the adoption seminar?"

They answered no in unison. Then Anne added, "We're here to see Merle Meyer."

"Oh, good, because I was going to tell you that you're a half hour early for the seminar! Or I'm late." She laughed good-naturedly and led the way to the front door, holding it open for them.

A sign over the door read, *Where Children Come Home.*

Why hadn't Aunt Edie told Anne about this place? She would ask her folks if they'd known about it.

A woman with crazy-curly carrot-red hair greeted them at the front desk. Her smile was broad, her teeth almost too white. "Welcome to Bring Them Home. I'm Karina."

Anne recognized her voice from the phone call she'd made earlier asking about Heaven's Child. She noted the lineup of photos on the wall behind her, pictures of families with their adoptive children. Happy smiles and tears of joy, mothers holding dark-skinned babies, fathers with almond-eyed sons.

"I'm Anne Gibson," Anne began. "We spoke on the phone last week."

"I see."

Anne went on, "My great-aunt was Edie Summers."

Recognition filled Karina's face at the mention of Edie. "Oh yes, the woman who founded this agency."

Anne nodded. "So you told me."

"I never met her, but Merle talks about her all the time. Her vision for kids."

"We were hoping to see Merle, actually," Anne said.

"I'll see if he's free." Karina smiled as she rose from her seat and moved to a closed office door behind her. "Could you sign the guestbook, please? It's for our mailing list and for security reasons," she said over her shoulder and motioned to the tall counter that overlooked her desk. Anne and Alex complied, writing the date and time of their visit and their contact information.

A man walked by with a name tag on that read "Jinx." He wore a wool hat despite the warm day. Dark sunglasses covered his eyes. He offered a wave, then moved up the staircase to the left that swept to the second story, his black wingtip shoes tapping a beat on the tile risers.

Merle Meyer came out of his office, followed by Karina, a few minutes later. He was a mountain of a man. Anne noticed his warm gray eyes and honey-toned skin. When he saw Anne he held out a giant paw to shake with her. "Edie Summers's niece, huh?"

"Great-niece, actually."

"All the better!" He reached to shake with Alex. "And this is the husband?"

"Um…" Anne cleared her throat, feeling suddenly embarrassed. "Actually, no. This is a friend. Alex Ochs."

"Nice to meet you," Alex said, seeming to take no note of the faux pas. "My sister was Marla Slater."

"I'm happy to meet you. Marla was a wonderful, wonderful gal. We were so sad to lose her."

Alex offered his thanks.

"We just found out that Edie was the founder of this place," Anne said.

"Just found out?" He seemed puzzled. "Come on in." Leading the way, he directed them to his open office door.

The room was cozy with floor-to-ceiling bookcases. Behind the large oak desk was a massive framed photo of Merle with his family. He was at the center of the shot next to a trim, petite wife, surrounded by a dozen children of many racial backgrounds.

"Edie's great-niece. I'm so glad to meet you," he said, taking the leather chair. Anne and Alex sat opposite him in matching plaid wing chairs. "So what brings you out?"

Anne told him of her conversation with the Haydens.

"I found this last week." Anne pulled out the pictures she'd unearthed of Edie's time in India and handed them to him.

"Ah, Wayne Wilchel and Edie, and of course, Mother Teresa." He handed the pictures back. "That was the year before we opened Bring Them Home."

"Can you tell me about that time?"

"Of course I can." He sat back, his hands behind his head as he spoke. "Your great-aunt called me after her trip. She'd heard from Mona Robinson that I knew about international adoption." He pointed to the photograph on the wall. "As you can see!" He laughed heartily, a deep rumbling sound of warmth and ease. "Edie worked with Mother Teresa all that year, connecting us with orphanages in India and around the world, helping smooth out relations with local governments, finding funding, and placing children, especially kids older than five. It's so much harder to place those kids." He shook his head. "She was a starter, that aunt of yours."

"Starter?" Alex said.

"She'd get a vision for something and get it going, then move on. I knew that when I first met her. We collaborated on vision and mission. I took over leadership of the agency, me and Ron Fields, and she moved on." He told her about his chief financial officer. "Ron and I went to high school together, best friends since then."

"He's here at the agency too?" Anne asked.

Merle nodded. "Just down the hall."

"Did you work directly with my sister too?" Alex asked.

"I did work with Marla. Sweetheart of a woman." Merle turned to him. "I am so sorry for your loss. So hard to lose both her and Rick like that. How's their son? I was so sorry I missed that funeral. I was in Malaysia when I heard the news."

Alex's face darkened. Anne saw the flash of emotion and his need to conceal it. "Thank you," he managed. "Ryan is doing fine. He lives with me now."

Merle's expression filled with compassion.

Alex pushed on. "I received an insufficient funds notice on the account she managed — Heaven's Child."

The man's brow furrowed. "Heaven's Child. Why would you get anything in regard to that?" he said. "It's been years since your sister passed."

"I thought the same thing." Alex paused. "You see, I thought the account was closed right after my sister died, so you can imagine my surprise to learn that it's still open."

"Closed? Why would it have been closed?"

"Since Marla wasn't around to manage it...Someone from Bring Them Home called me to tell me it was closed."

"No, we assigned Karina to take over management of the fund after she passed, but it's been open all this time."

"That's the woman we first met here?" Anne asked. "Does anyone else have access to the account?"

"Well, I guess there have been a few people..." He stammered for a moment. "I mean, we all have a degree of access to it..."

Anne glanced at Alex then looked at Merle—what did they know about this man? Nothing, really. For all they knew, he was the very one stealing the money.

Still, Alex held out the insufficient funds notification for him to read then told him of someone calling shortly after Marla's death regarding the funds. Merle breathed out heavily through his nose as he set the sheet aside.

"What do you make of it?" Anne asked.

He shrugged. "I don't want to assume anything," he said sincerely. "It's troubling though, that phone call. Why would someone do that?" He looked between Anne and Alex.

"They didn't want me to wonder the same thing my sister wondered," Alex said as he pulled out the note Marla had written to Edie along with the statement with the code on the back. "We found this too. Statements with her notations—she thought someone was stealing..."

The big man bent his head to read it. When he'd finished he blew out another heavy breath.

"I can't believe it," Merle said.

"You think she was wrong?" Anne asked.

"I don't know, but I can assure you I'll be looking into this. Is there more?"

Anne showed him the bank statements.

"What did Marla mean, 'Not an account'?" he said, pointing toward the line that detailed the deposit transaction with the name Daniel Lipps written in pen alongside it.

"We don't know," Anne confessed.

"Well, thank you for bringing this to my attention." Merle rose to shake hands, effectively dismissing them. "You can be assured that I'll look into this as soon as possible."

CHAPTER THIRTEEN

"What do you think?" Anne asked Alex as they pulled out of the Bring Them Home parking lot. She glanced at the dashboard clock. It was only ten o'clock.

"He struck me as a sincere person," Alex said. "But when we mentioned the theft…I don't know."

"He seemed eager to get us out of there, didn't he?" Anne finished for him.

Alex drummed the steering wheel as he drove. Anne could tell he was distracted, lost in thoughts.

"What's up?" she asked.

He didn't answer at first, then he turned his gaze to her for a moment before looking at the road. "This is all so…difficult," he said. "It dredges up so much. So much of that hard time." He sighed. "I wonder if I'm doing a good job."

"You mean in researching this?"

"Yes…No," he confessed, "in raising Ryan. Am I raising him the way Marla and Rick would've wanted? I honestly don't know."

"You're doing your best."

"Yeah, but that's a long way from being raised by your own parents. Dealing with their deaths has been hard. Sometimes the grief that comes over him…" This was something Alex rarely spoke of. Anne waited, not wanting to rush him. "I second-guess every decision I make when it comes to Ryan. I think I need to discipline, then I wonder if my discipline is too harsh. Back and forth. I push him then think I'm just being mean. That tug is constant."

"It's the same for me. You have to give yourself grace. Ask God for wisdom and then forgive yourself when you don't parent perfectly. God can redeem even the poorest parenting."

Alex chuckled. "That is a comfort. Knowing He can fix my blunders."

"Not only can He fix them, He can *use* them to bring about better things in Ryan. Those situations can teach Ryan how to forgive. And what skill is more powerful than that one?" She waited for him to meet her eyes. "Ryan knows you love him, that you're doing your best. He doesn't ask for more."

* * *

When Anne got home she picked up the phone to call her mother. Her folks had lived in Florida for five years now, since her father's retirement as a financial officer at the steel manufacturing company. They came to visit a few times a year, but it was never enough.

"Anne!" her mother's voice rang across the line. "I just got in from tennis. You should see my serve. I'm getting good."

"When did you take up tennis?"

"Last month," she said. "There was a deal on lessons at the Y, so I signed up."

Anne chuckled. "Did Dad take lessons too?"

"Oh no. He'll stick with golf. So what's going on?"

Her mom had a way of getting to the point.

"Did you know that Aunt Edie founded an international adoption agency?"

"Your aunt was always out doing this or that—I'm sure there was something like that on her list of accomplishments."

"But you don't remember it specifically? Bring Them Home adoption agency? It would've been in 1994."

"It sounds familiar," she said.

"Did she tell you that she met Mother Teresa?"

"Really?" Her mother laughed. "Seriously, honey, Aunt Edie was like Forrest Gump—meeting famous people wasn't unusual for her."

"Do you know if she wanted to adopt a little boy from India—Thomas Gee?"

"Honey, 1994 was a long time ago. I can't recall what I had for breakfast yesterday!" She laughed. "I need to go; your dad's calling me."

Anne said good-bye, then they hung up. Anne sighed as she looked at the phone. She'd been tempted to tell her mother about the medical test and her fears about the nature of the lump in her throat, but she didn't want to worry her mother. And she knew something like that would put the older woman on a plane the next day. No. Until she knew something for certain, she'd wait to tell her parents. There was no use making them worry when there was nothing they could do to help her other than hold her hand. Besides, she told herself, she had many friends in Blue Hill who were ready to hold her hand if need be.

* * *

The name on the statement that had been labeled "Not an account" had been Daniel Lipps. Anne was curious to know about this man, so when she got back to the library she did a quick search. There were several men by that name who came up, none in that area of Pennsylvania. Though, she realized, a donor could live anywhere.

She tapped her fingers on the desktop. When she looked up she realized Betty Bultman was staring at her.

"You're lost in thoughts," the mayor's wife said to her. Betty was a regular volunteer at the library, a matronly woman who'd lost her daughter in a car accident years ago. She'd become a friend over the past months.

"I'm sorry," Anne said. "I've been distracted."

Betty slipped the empty book cart into its spot behind the desk, then took a seat alongside Anne. An elderly gentleman came by, asking if they had any books on organic gardening. Anne led him to the spot among the nonfiction shelves, then returned to Betty, who was watching her intently.

"Is it your health you're worried about?" she said.

Anne's hand moved to the spot. "No," she finally said, "I'm not worried." Though in her heart she knew it was a lie.

* * *

When Anne went to the Pyles' to get Liddie and Ben after work, the Haydens were there. Pam sat on a chair in the backyard, a big glass of lemonade in her hand. Her eyes were closed and her face was tilted to the sun.

"Did my kids wear you out?" Anne asked.

Pam opened her eyes and laughed. "No. My own kids wore me out!" She motioned to the chair next to her. "So what have you been up to?"

"I went to see Mona Robinson yesterday. You were right, she knew all about Edie's trip. Thank you. It settled a lot of things for me."

"I should be thanking you," Pam said.

"Why?"

"We're going to adopt Klara." She smiled. "We decided this morning. We submitted her file to the Shriners so we don't know yet if that will go through, but we're going to update our home study and apply to adopt her as soon as we return to India."

"That's wonderful," Anne said.

"It's what I felt in my heart was right. We just couldn't see our way clear to get there." She gave Anne's knee a pat.

"I don't think Edie tried to adopt Thomas Gee," Anne said, telling her of Virginia's dementia. "I don't know why that mattered so much to me, but I can't help feeling a sense of loss about it."

Pam studied her for a long moment. "You can't save everyone."

"Maybe I *was* trying to save him," Anne confessed.

"I take my turn at saving the world too." Pam laughed. "Till I remember that God already did that."

CHAPTER FOURTEEN

I think I'm ready for the play," Liddie announced over supper.

"You still have a few days to practice." Anne buttered a slice of bread and handed it to Ben. Hershey lay under the table in the midst of their feet. Every once in a while she could hear the thwop of his tail as it hit the floor.

That familiar weariness was falling on her again, like a blanket across her shoulders, moving down, dragging her energy with it. She could feel her eyelids drooping.

"*Mo-oom!*" Liddie shouted.

Anne lifted her gaze. "Honey, don't shout."

"You're not listening to me and you're doing that nodding thing again."

"I'm sorry, sweetie."

"Come on," Ben said to his sister. "Let's clear the table and do the dishes so Mom can take a nap."

"You don't have to do that," Anne protested.

"It's okay, Mom," the nine-year-old boy said. He met her gaze. "Really."

When had he become such a little man? So perceptive, caring? Her thoughts turned to Eric. He'd been like that too. So perceptive. Sometimes she'd wondered if he could read her mind.

Sadness filled her. Missing him. Would she ever get past that? She doubted it.

She shook off the disconcerting thoughts.

"Okay, honey," she finally said to her son. "I'll take a nap."

The ringing of the phone woke her forty-five minutes later. Anne rubbed her eyes and reached for the cell that lay on her nightstand. Early evening sunlight was golden, low in her western window. Anne pushed "talk" and gave a sleepy, "Hello."

"Hi." The female voice was quiet, tentative. But Anne recognized it. "This is Karina from Heaven's Child." She paused.

Anne sat up straight. "Yes." She glanced at the clock. It was six.

"I copied your number from the guestbook so I could call you from home. I hope that's okay. I overheard you talking to Merle today…" She took a deep breath, as if she were trying to steel herself.

Anne waited.

"There's something going on. There's been something going on for a long time…" She sighed. "Someone has been stealing from Heaven's Child for a long time. I get phone calls from people, donors who I've never gotten checks from. I have no record of them. I didn't know what to do. I wondered if someone from the agency was doing it. I didn't have any proof so when you came in today it got me thinking."

Anne's heart was racing.

"It's got to be someone from Bring Them Home. Who else could it be?" Karina was saying.

"Okay…," Anne said. "Can you give me the names of the staff there?"

"There are only the five of us—me, Merle Meyer, Jinx, Ginny Stein, Ron Fields."

"Can you send me their contact information? I'll talk to them, see what I can learn."

"You can't tell them I called—that I told you." She sounded panicked.

"I won't. I promise."

There was a long pause, then, "All right."

Anne gave the woman her e-mail address, then another thought pressed in. "I have some statements," Anne said. "Marla wrote names, information next to different withdrawals. I assumed because those withdrawals were for various families getting scholarships." Karina was quiet, so Anne went on, "Could I send you a list of donors so you can look up some of those files? Information about who the recipients were? Something that might help us understand if perhaps one of those people is involved."

"I hadn't thought about that," Karina admitted. "Why don't you scan and e-mail me the bank statements at my home e-mail after I send the contact information for donors in my file." She seemed to want to say more.

Finally Anne said, "What's wrong?"

"I've been at the agency a long time, Mrs. Gibson. We do a lot of good in the lives of children…I'd hate for this to ruin the work that we do."

"I understand," Anne agreed. "I promise I won't do anything to jeopardize that. I'll be discreet, okay?"

"Thank you."

"And, Karina…thank you for this. For trusting me."

* * *

As soon as she got off the phone, Anne retrieved the statements Alex had left at her place. She wanted to study them more in depth before she e-mailed them to Karina. She took them to the living room and laid them out on the coffee table. She found a highlighter so she could note anything that might lead to a clue. Her first order of business was to make a list of donors for Karina to look up.

There were regular deposits, she noted. The same amounts came in on the same day each month. Associated with these were eight names. Anne assumed that since these names were listed with the deposits they were the donors, the people being swindled of their hard-earned money:

> Patrick Montgomery
> Ken Fischer
> James Louis
> John Smith
> Kip McLaughlin
> Gary Gove
> Lane Moxy
> Vic Michaelson

She glanced at the withdrawals. These were less predictable, though some were the same each month. But as she'd noted before, on the most recent statements there were ATM withdrawals in one hundred dollar increments from a Deshler location.

She thought about calling her friend Officer Michael Banks to see if the police could offer some support, but Karina's voice of fear returned. Publicity that the charity was a source of thievery would shut them down for sure. And until she knew who the thief was she wasn't willing to do that.

She typed up the list of names that Marla had written next to the withdrawals. Were these the ones stealing the money or someone else? She wondered about this as she sent both lists to Karina's e-mail address.

CHAPTER FIFTEEN

W hy didn't Merle have any idea that someone was stealing from Heaven's Child?" Anne asked when she called Alex to tell him what Karina had said.

"What do you mean?"

"I mean, this activity is right under his nose. But he seemed clueless about it when we talked to him."

"Maybe it's an act—maybe he's the one taking the money," Alex offered. "Or...if indeed all the social workers and CFO have access, then cash withdrawals are normal. There's no red flag there."

"I asked Karina to see if she could get me some information on the donors. Perhaps there's something there."

"We already know that the thief uses the ATM for withdrawals," Alex said. "Makes it a lot harder to catch the thief. Not like a signed check..."

"I was studying the statements again. All the withdrawals are from the same ATM, the one at the Holiday gas station in Deshler."

"Maybe we could ask them to see the video of that ATM from the time of the last withdrawal."

"If we were police with a search warrant, sure," Anne said. "I can't imagine any business handing over video like that." She paused. "But we could at least talk to them."

After she hung up from her call to Alex, Anne looked up the number for the Holiday gas station in Deshler. She called to ask for a manager when a teenage voice came on the line. A few moments later a deep voice said, "This is Bob."

Anne introduced herself and said, "I'm looking into a theft. Someone is using the ATM at your location to steal funds from a charity." She waited a beat to see if he would say anything. Not a word. Then she went on, "I'm wondering if we can take a look at the film footage from the time of the thefts to see if we can find the thief."

"Is this the police?" he said.

Anne cleared her throat. "Um, no." She knew she sounded sheepish.

"Seriously. You expect me to hand that kind of thing over to any Joe on the street? Are you at least from the bank?"

There was no point. Anne had guessed as much. But she felt obligated to give it a shot. She thanked the man for his time, though he seemed bent on delivering a lecture nonetheless.

Finally, she just hung up.

* * *

When the phone rang around nine o'clock the next morning, Anne knew it was the doctor. She dreaded picking it up, yet she knew she must. She pushed *talk* and said, "Hello."

"Is Anne Gibson there?"

"Speaking." *Enough formalities*, she thought, wanting desperately to hear the results, her heart pounding in her chest.

"This is Dr. Jones. I wanted to give you a call about your blood calcium levels. Your sugars were all fine, but the blood calcium was a 12.3."

"What's a normal level?"

"Usually between a nine and a ten."

"So what does that mean?"

"I want to run a few more tests...including a biopsy."

"High blood calcium could mean cancer?"

"Sometimes but not always," Dr. Jones said. "But, yes, sometimes high blood calcium can be a sign of cancer."

Though she'd been worried before, now a sense of peace filled her. She would be okay. So many people had said the same to her that she was finally beginning to believe it. When had that change happened? Had it been all at once or little by little? She wished courage would always be with her. But such emotions came and went, she knew. How could she learn to trust in God's goodness when she didn't always feel it? She needed to learn that it was still there even when she didn't feel it. That was what faith was.

* * *

When Wendy brought the kids home after Summer Fun, Anne was distracted, her mind returning again and again to the doctor's call. "Did you have a good morning?" she asked her daughter as she gave Liddie a kiss on the top of her head.

"Yep," the five-year-old bubbled. "You should hear my solo. I rock!"

Anne looked to Ben. "Does she?"

He nodded. "She's pretty good," he said. "Though I wouldn't let it go to your head, Liddie. It's just Summer Fun, not TV."

"*Just* Summer Fun?" she was protesting.

Anne's mind drifted. She treasured moments with these two, even their bickering! How could she bear it if the results of the biopsy weren't favorable? She inhaled a ragged breath, determined to keep calm.

"*Mo-oom*," Liddie was saying when Anne tuned back in to the present. "You're doing it again."

"What?" Anne asked, registering that her daughter was speaking directly to her. "Oh, I'm sorry. I was just thinking about something."

"But what could be more important than me and Ben?"

"Nothing," Anne said. "Absolutely nothing."

* * *

Anne sat on the table of the examining room later that same day, the sound of paper crinkling every time she moved. Her fingers touched the lump. It didn't seem to have gotten any bigger. But it had just been a few days. She closed her eyes and prayed.

The thing she hated most about all this was having to go through it alone. Yet until she knew the results of this test for certain she didn't want to worry her folks or her brother. She most especially didn't want to worry Liddie and Ben. She glanced at the painting on the wall. Why did clinic exam rooms have the worst art?

She shook her head at herself. This wasn't about her opinion of artwork. She missed Eric. More deeply than she'd missed him in a long time. The dull ache she'd thought had healed began to throb again, that pit of missing him.

"I'm so afraid," she mouthed to the ceiling. To God.

I haven't left you. The words rang in her heart. She needed them so badly, needed to believe God was there.

Finally, the doctor came into the room. She gave Anne a sympathetic look as she put her latex gloves on. "This won't be so bad," she said as she prepped her supplies for the procedure.

"Okay," Anne said, "I can cope with 'not so bad.'"

She closed her eyes. But there was something about that thick needle penetrating her throat, invading the spot that held her deepest fears. When she opened them it was done. The doctor snapped off her gloves and turned back to her. "I'll put a rush on this so we'll know soon, okay?"

"Okay."

* * *

On the drive home, Anne wasn't able to shake her conversation with the doctor. *Cancer.* The word cloyed at her like the disease itself. Choking, suffocating. She was only thirty-four. A part of her wanted to pretend it hadn't happened, she hadn't heard that horrible word in connection with herself. Yet another part of her knew it was all too real. Anne closed her eyes, longing for peace. She hated the rollercoaster that her emotions were riding.

Count it all joy when you suffer trials of many kinds, the verse from James 1 poked its head up.

"I'm not counting much for joy right now, Lord," she confessed.

Wendy's rebuke echoed then, "*You think God isn't in control of this? That He's off the clock on this one? 'Cause He's not. He's still taking care of the universe, and of you.*"

They were words she needed to hear, needed to remind herself of every day. Perhaps every moment.

When she climbed out of her car at the library, Alex was there. Wendy had closed up for her and taken the kids to play at her place. Anne wondered if Alex had been waiting in the lot the whole time she'd been gone. There was a plastic tote on the front porch. She glanced at him wondering what that was all about.

"Some more of my sister's papers," he answered her unasked question when she climbed the stairs to him. "These were at my folks' place. Since they're in Kenya now, I took the liberty of looking." He gave her a sheepish look. "I was hoping you could look through it with me?"

"Of course." Anne was glad for the distraction. She motioned him to follow her as she unlocked the front door.

They moved into the darkened library and to the elevator doors, where Anne pushed the *up* button. He studied her as they stood in the elevator, him holding that awkward tote between them. Without saying a word, he seemed to see right through her to the core of her fear. Seemed to know where she'd just come from.

"Are you okay?" he asked.

Anne felt the sting of unshed tears. She didn't want to cry in front of Alex. Not here, now. She gulped them back.

"You don't have to be strong, you know. You have friends who care about you."

She met his gaze.

"I worry about you," he said.

She drew in a deep breath. "I'm just…I'm going to be okay."

"Of course you are." He paused. "What is it?"

Finally it came out. "More tests. Maybe cancer."

He didn't say anything. Just watched her, patient. Understanding her need to let it be.

When they reached the third-story apartment, Anne opened the door. Hershey met them, eager to be let out. Anne took the dog outside and in a few moments they were back.

"So what is all this?" Anne said, looking at the pile of papers Alex unearthed with the lifting of the bin's lid. She was glad to forget, to research. In that at least she could pretend everything was normal.

"Just papers that Marla had. She kept her bills in one box so I was able to deal with all that when she died, but this was other random stuff. A friend of my folks came to help clean up and just shoved these in here…and then I kind of forgot about it till now."

Anne offered him a Pepsi, then took the seat adjacent to him on the couch as they both began to sort through the papers.

There were forgotten magazines, flyers, catalogs, statements from an insurance company, their 401(k), mostly items long past their expiration dates. There were several photos of Ryan, some with both parents smiling on vacation. The sign in front of them read "Old Faithful," and the ancient geyser sent up a fountain of steam behind them as they held a smaller version of the Ryan Anne knew in their arms.

There were school pictures too, from kindergarten. He'd been six at the time of his parents' deaths. That younger boy smiled at the camera, completely innocent, unaware of the tragedy about to strike.

Anne gazed at it as a pang hit her.

No surprises like that for Liddie and Ben, Lord. Please. They had their share when they lost Eric. She'd prayed it so many times since the doctor's call.

She set the photos aside on the pile of things to save and dug some more. Coupons someone must've clipped. A list of To Do items, a notebook with children's doodles. She placed these on the toss pile, then reached for the next packet. It was thick, a white nine-by-twelve mailer with a file folder inside. Anne tugged the contents out and began to look through. There were several documents, their titles centered and in bold: Motivation to Adopt, Preparation for Adoption, Child Requested, Adoptive Applicants, Marital History…

Wait. Anne's brow furrowed. This looked like an adoption home study.

"Alex…" She lifted her face. "I don't think Aunt Edie was trying to adopt, but it sure looks like Marla and Rick were."

"What are you talking about?" Alex turned from his own pile of papers to look at the copies in Anne's hand, taking them from her. "Adopting? Why wouldn't I know about that?"

He began to read the rest of the stack that was a good inch thick. His hand went over his mouth.

"What is it?" Anne asked.

"It's a referral." He held the sheet out to Anne. "They'd been matched with a seven-month-old boy."

Anne looked at the date of the letter.

"That was the week they were killed."

Alex's face was a pale sheet, as if he'd just heard the news of his sister's death all over again.

"They were probably on their way to tell us this news that night," he said, as much to himself as to Anne. "They'd called Mom and Dad and asked the whole family to meet at their place, that they had something to tell us..." He leaned over his knees and planted his fingers in his hair. "Why didn't she tell me before, that they were doing this?" He looked up at Anne.

"Maybe she was afraid," Anne offered. "Why didn't they have biological children after Ryan?"

Alex sat upright and blew out a hot breath. "They tried, but she kept having miscarriages." He paused. "You're right. Maybe she was afraid this wouldn't work out either."

Anne placed a comforting hand on his back. "After all that hurt it's hard to trust the future."

Alex met her gaze. "It's *still* hard to trust the future," he said. "There's not a day goes by that I don't look at Ryan and grieve. Not a day when I don't think he was cheated. You know that?"

"I know all about it."

"Of course you do." He sighed. "Of course you do. It's just not fair, Anne. It's not fair. And this baby, whoever he is — he lost out too on a really great family, a really great big brother..." His voice trailed off. He lifted his face. "Did they use Bring Them Home as their agency?"

Anne looked through the pages. "Yes, they did."

"And did they apply for a scholarship through Heaven's Child?"

Anne nodded. "I can't tell if they got a scholarship or not."

"I don't get this, Anne. I don't get any of it." Alex shook his head. "I knew my sister. We were close...or I thought we were."

"Just because she kept a secret doesn't mean you weren't close."

"It doesn't? It sure feels like it does."

Anne had known Alex's sister growing up. Not as well as she'd known Alex, but Marla had always been there, in the background, a girl with a huge smile and an easy manner. She had been the one in the neighborhood who took care of all the babies. Anne could remember her carting a wagonload of toddlers to the park in the afternoons. And it wasn't because parents were paying her for the task. She wasn't babysitting. She simply loved children, even when she was little more than a child herself. Alex's dad used to call her the "Pied Piper" because she usually had a baby on one hip and a couple other tots trailing after her.

So the discovery that she and her husband had been in the process of adopting fell in line completely with the woman Anne had known her to be.

The heartbreak she must've faced with all those miscarriages...Anne couldn't imagine it.

"Are you okay?" she asked Alex.

He nodded, though he didn't say anything. "To know that Ryan didn't need to be alone all this time. That there was another child out there meant to be his brother, that's a hard one, Anne."

"You would have taken him in too?"

"Of course. If Marla and Rick had adopted him. I would've taken him in a heartbeat."

Anne watched him. He paused, clearly thinking this new development through. "Maybe I still could."

"What are you saying?"

"What if I found him, Anne?"

"You mean now? Alex, it's been four years since your sister and brother-in-law died. I'm sure that little boy has another family he loves and who love him too."

His shoulders fell. "You're right. Of course you are. I didn't mean that—I couldn't tear a child from his family. But maybe we could meet him. It wouldn't need to be more than that. We could just know who he is, know his name and what his life is like now."

"I don't know, Alex. I don't know if that's wise. I'm afraid it will just open up old wounds, cause confusion…especially for Ryan."

But Alex wasn't ready to give it up yet. She worried for him, that this new discovery would lead to a greater hurt.

CHAPTER SIXTEEN

Once they'd finished going through the tote and tossed what they could, which was ninety-five percent of the papers, Alex headed home. Ryan was playing with a neighbor so he needed to get back.

Once he was gone, Anne thought about their discovery.

Rick and Marla had tried to adopt. It was ironic, since Anne had wondered if Edie had tried to adopt Thomas Gee.

Yet there was no proof that had ever happened, other than the word of a woman whose memory was less than trustworthy. There was no home study to document it. Not like Marla's.

Such a long, tedious process, and yet Marla hadn't breathed a word of it. Perhaps Anne's assumption that she didn't want to risk the hurt wasn't that far off base. She'd known couples who'd adopted only to lose the child when the birth mother changed her mind and took her baby back.

Marla must've been overjoyed to receive the referral, to learn that a child would indeed be coming into their home, a child all their own. And then she died. The contrast of joy to ultimate grief in a single day was almost too much to comprehend.

Anne was almost glad Alex's family hadn't known. At the time it would have seemed like a double loss.

She thought of Alex that night, the sight of his face when he'd read the referral letter. How his brow had furrowed in on itself. The pain in his eyes. For him the loss was the same.

All evening Anne couldn't get the discovery that Rick and Marla had tried to adopt out of her mind. She tucked the kids in bed still thinking about it. Finally, when she realized she wouldn't be able to sleep, she called Alex. He'd been thinking too. She could picture him pacing his one-level house.

"So Marla was working for Heaven's Child and trying to adopt at the same time..." Alex said when Anne told him she couldn't sleep for thinking about Rick and Marla.

"How does that knowledge connect with the theft from Heaven's Child?" Anne asked.

"Does it have to?"

"No. But it makes sense that it might."

"We'll have to think about that."

* * *

Karina, from Heaven's Child, called Anne later that evening. "I didn't want to call from work," she explained, "I'm too nervous that someone will catch me. But I did get them for you — the files of the people that Marla had mentioned on those statements. I put them in my briefcase as if I was going to work on them at home. Could we maybe meet somewhere? If you want to photocopy the files then I can return them tomorrow."

Anne gave her the address for the library. "I'll unlock the doors when you get here," she added. "Just call me at this number and I'll come down."

Karina was there a little more than half an hour later. She must've come straight from Deshler. The expression in her gaze said she was frightened.

"Thank you for doing this," Anne said, trying to ease her.

"Yeah," she said tersely. She handed Anne a printed list of workers at the adoption agency beginning with Merle Meyer.

Ginny Stein, the wild-haired hippie girl they'd met in the parking lot, was next.

Followed by Jinx Hendricks, the man in the wool hat and dark sunglasses.

Ron Fields, the agency's chief financial officer was last on the list. They hadn't bumped into Ron that day. Anne recalled Merle's mention of the high school friend who'd helped him establish Bring Them Home in 1994.

Anne met the gaze of the nervous young woman. "Has anyone quit since Marla's passing—anyone else who should be on our suspect list?"

"But how would a former employee have access to the account?" Karina said.

"I don't know," Anne admitted. "Still…"

"Um…Cheryl Bergen and Lincoln Krueger."

"Tell me about Cheryl Bergen," Anne said.

"Cheryl was a secretary. She's a sweetheart," Karina said. "She's quirky and a little weird. Who isn't weird though, right? I'll give her props, though. She's taken care of her sick mom for years now."

"What's wrong with her mom?"

"She had a stroke several years back. It could've easily killed her. It knocked out all her speech, her ability to eat on her own, walk…She's been bed-bound ever since."

"And Lincoln Krueger?"

"He was a social worker. Kind of a tough nut."

"Do you have contact information for either one?" Anne said.

"I can e-mail that to you when I get back," Karina said.

Karina kept wiping her hands on her skirt as if wiping off sweat. And she glanced around the nearly empty library as if certain hidden cameras were stationed throughout.

"Do you think someone followed you?" Anne asked, following the young woman's gaze.

"No. I…just…I've never done anything like this before."

Anne studied her to make sure she wasn't about to have a panic attack. Finally, her shoulders relaxed, her chest seemed to heave a little bit less.

"Karina, who takes that deposit to the bank?"

"I do."

"Anyone else ever take it?"

She shook her head.

"Okay," Anne said, "I was just wondering."

"I tried to look up the names on those lists you gave me," Karina said. "But none of those people on that first list of donors is in any of our files."

"None?" Anne said.

"We keep good records since we have to send out statements so donors can file their 8283 forms, and not one of these people got those forms from us, at least not that I can see."

"What about the second list?"

"I wasn't able to find anything out about this one." She pointed to the name Daniel Lipps with the words "not an account" next to it. "The other files I have here."

She pulled out a stack of manila file folders. But as Anne began to glance through them she could see that they were incomplete. It was as if someone had started a file but then hadn't finished them. There were applications, folders with their names on them, a few notes jotted here and there...

"None of these have home studies," Anne said to Karina who stood with her arms hugging herself as she watched Anne read.

The young woman's brow furrowed. "I know. I can't explain that—they should all have home studies. That's one of the first things we require when we issue grants."

Anne shuffled through the files one more time to be sure. "Well, thank you for all this."

"I don't know what help it is."

"You can never tell." Anne smiled at her.

"I hope we can figure this out."

"Don't worry," Anne said. "Everything will be fine."

She said the words, but in reality could she make such a promise?

* * *

Anne carried the photocopied files up to her apartment after she'd said farewell to Karina. None of the donors on the list were in her files, nor were any of the recipients. How could that be? Anne wondered how much money each had given over the years. So pulling out the statements again, she took a seat and got out a calculator, adding up total contributions from each source. One donor had given over $8,000 during the course of four years, another had given $19,000, a third had donated $32,000. Anne added up the total donations and withdrawals—$237,000 had disappeared from the account over all the years it had been in existence.

$237,000. Anne let out a low whistle. This wasn't a little pickpocketing. This was embezzling on a large scale.

Such large theft would surely have been noticed long before now if those donors never received receipts. Or had they?

* * *

The library was busy all morning the next day. Patrons seemed to have one question after another for Anne. It wasn't until eleven o'clock that she finally had a chance to sit down and think. She turned to her laptop computer, searching for the phone numbers of the donors on her list. She did manage to locate four of them.

She dialed the first name. No one picked up. She wondered if perhaps it was because they didn't recognize her phone number on their cell phone displays. Still she left a message in hopes someone would call her back.

Finally, an hour later, her phone rang, but by then traffic had picked up in the library again so she knew she'd have to keep it short. "This is Anne," she said.

"Anne," a man's voice said, "I'm Vic Michaelson. You left a message about Heaven's Child?"

"Thank you for calling me back," she said. "I am wondering a few things about Heaven's Child and I'm hoping you can help me."

"It's just a charity I give to. I'm not sure that I know all that much," the man said, "but I can answer some questions…"

"I hope you'll forgive me. I'm the Blue Hill town librarian and we're really busy right now. Do you think it would be possible to meet with you later today? Do you think you could come by the library?"

"That's not possible," the man said sounding a bit tentative, "but you could stop at the house. I don't really get around all that much anymore…got shot up in the Vietnam War, kind of messed with my legs."

"I'm sorry," Anne said. "Yes, I'd be happy to come to your place."

* * *

Vic Michaelson's home was falling apart. The front porch looked like it hung on by Scotch tape. It slanted heavily to the south and was piled full of stuff: old record albums, clothes that smelled dank and musty, buckets stacked in a pillar of plastic, various animal traps. Anne moved toward the white wooden door and knocked.

"Come on in," sounded from the depths.

Inside was no tidier. The first room was a kitchen, dark, with heavy curtains drawn against the sunny day. A small Formica table filled the center of the room with a game of Solitaire and a cold cup of coffee set out before an empty chair.

"I'm in here," Vic said.

Anne followed the voice.

He looked much older than a man in his sixties, as she'd surmised someone who'd fought in the Vietnam War would be, more like eighty. His hair was a rim around his bald head and what he did have stuck up in the back as if he'd just gotten out of bed. A gray mottled cat slept on his lap in the wheelchair he filled.

"I appreciate your letting me come out," Anne said.

He motioned her to a chair that was filled with old newspapers. She set them aside and took a seat.

"I don't get many visitors," Vic said. He had a kind smile, one that spoke of gratefulness for anyone stopping by, even a stranger looking for answers. "So what's this all about?"

"You donate to Heaven's Child, is that right?"

"I do," he said. "I've donated there for years. They do a good thing, helping young families adopt. That's something I believe in." He pointed to a photo on the mantel.

Anne rose to take it in. A family, by the looks of it his. There were six children of varying ethnicities. His wife was petite, pretty. She held a dark-skinned baby with chubby cheeks.

"They're beautiful," Anne said.

"That they are," he said. "Best thing my wife and I ever did. She passed a few years back."

"I'm sorry." Anne moved back to her seat. "Do your children live nearby?"

"A couple do. The rest come and see me pretty regular. More often now that Rose has passed. That's how it goes," he said, though she could see the tenderness in his eyes. Remembering a love long shared. "When we heard about Heaven's Child, we had to give."

"This is obviously something you care about."

"Something we should *all* care about," he added.

"So you've donated to Heaven's Child how long?"

"Five years. There was a woman — Marla Slater — who came to our church and talked on it, how it was a fund to help those who wanted to adopt but couldn't afford it." He shifted in the wheelchair and the cat lifted its head then settled back down. "It's expensive to adopt, especially internationally. And a lot of those kids have no hope of being adopted in their home countries. Did you know that in Korea few people adopt? All those children waiting for homes and people would rather go childless than take one of them in."

"Does Heaven's Child send you tax receipts every year?"

Vic screwed up his face as if he couldn't understand the question. "Well, sure they do," he said.

"Would it be possible for me to see it?"

He seemed hesitant, then "Etta!" he called in a loud voice. A tiny Asian woman poked her head out from the door off of the living room.

"You don't have to shout, Dad," she said. "Oh." She seemed surprised by Anne's presence. "I didn't know we had company."

Anne introduced herself, told the young woman the reason for her visit.

"Could you get my tax return from last year?" Vic said.

Etta's brow furrowed. "Your tax return?"

"I'm not going to keep it or anything," Anne assured. "I was hoping I could see a receipt from Heaven's Child, just to see what it looks like." Anne could tell the woman thought the request odd, but she went to get it anyway.

"My youngest. She comes a few times a week," Vic said while she was out of the room. "Makes me some meals, checks to make sure I'm breathing…"

"You're pretty lucky," Anne said.

"I am," he agreed.

Etta returned with the form in hand a few minutes later. It looked like a typical charitable donations receipt. "Is the amount correct?" Anne asked Vic.

"Yep," he said. "Why wouldn't it be?"

"Oh, no reason." Anne handed the document back to Etta and rose from her chair. "Well, thank you for your time, Vic. It was nice to meet you." She reached to shake his hand, which was warm. She offered her thanks to Etta, then said her good-byes.

As she made her way back to the car, she thought that everything looked as it should—correct documentation, amounts, the transfers that showed up on Heaven's Child's statements—so why would there be no record of Vic Michaelson in the database that Karina had looked up?

According to Anne's calculations Vic had given $23,000 to Heaven's Child over the years. She thought of his meager lifestyle, the struggles he faced every day, yet he gave so generously. So selflessly. That his money was being stolen, used for who knew what…it was just wrong! He'd given in good faith that his donation would be used to help families adopt.

So what exactly was his money being used for?

CHAPTER SEVENTEEN

Right after her interview with Vic, Anne and Alex headed to Deshler. She didn't want to raise suspicions by showing up at the Bring Them Home office so she called Ginny Stein at the number Karina had given as her home number and asked if they could meet at the Standing Stone Coffee Company in Huntingdon, a bright little café painted in oranges and lemon-yellow. Ginny agreed.

The social worker was waiting at the curved counter when they arrived. Anne took a stool next to her in the hopping little restaurant, with Alex on the other side of Anne.

"Thank you for coming," Anne said.

The thirtysomething social worker wore a purple and pink paisley scarf on her head, tied under her chin like Jackie O. Her white poet's top gathered at her tiny waist over an ankle-length patchwork skirt also in shades of pink and purple.

She smiled at Anne and said, "You have me intrigued. What is all this about?"

"I…," Anne began, but the waitress on the other side of the counter came over and laid a menu in front of her.

"Coffee?" she asked Anne and Alex. Ginny already had a cup.

"Yes, please," Anne said. Alex said he was fine with water.

"What flavor?" The waitress pointed to a sign that listed the many varieties they carried.

Anne settled on decaf *Congo*, which claimed to have "characteristics of an early spring garden and freshly-picked banana." The waitress turned to get her a cup, then moved down the line.

"This is a great little place," Anne said.

"I come here a lot. Their coffee is all fair trade, quality. And they go out of their way to educate the public too," Ginny said.

"Do you live near here?"

"Yeah. It's a bit of a drive to work in Deshler, but this is where I grew up. All my family is here, my sisters, all my nieces and nephews."

"Do you have a family of your own?"

Ginny shook her head. "No, haven't found the right guy yet."

"And you haven't adopted?"

"Not yet, but I will. Once I get my own place—I still live with my folks." She had beautiful hazel eyes that tipped down at the outer edges over high cheekbones, reminding Anne of Bette Midler's perpetual smile. "So...why did you ask me here?" She took a sip of her coffee.

Anne wasn't sure how to begin, and the fact that any of the social workers could be the thief wasn't lost on her either, so she paused for a moment before answering.

"Do you remember Alex?" Anne motioned toward him.

Ginny nodded. "Yeah. How could I forget those blue eyes?" She gave him a wink.

Anne noted the blush that climbed his face.

"My sister was Marla Slater," he said, clearing his throat slightly.

Instant sympathy filled the social worker's face. "I loved Marla—she was a kindred spirit. So, so sad when she died."

"It was," Alex agreed.

The waitress returned to take their orders, then scurried off toward the kitchen.

Anne turned slightly, to face Ginny more squarely. "We found out a few things about Marla and what she'd been doing before her passing that we want to get to the bottom of," Anne said once the waitress was out of earshot. "About Heaven's Child, as well as questions about whether she and Rick were trying to adopt."

"I know that they were trying to adopt," Ginny said.

"You did?" Alex said.

"It wasn't something she told people, I don't think. I knew because I was the social worker on the case. She was very private. She'd had so many miscarriages…" Ginny shook her head. "I can't even imagine that. After having a healthy son without any complications to not be able to carry a baby to term…She had a hard time believing she'd actually have more kids."

"So they got a referral?" Anne asked.

"I faxed it to her the day they died." Ginny blew out a breath, remembering. "It was the most tragic day ever. Both of them, gone."

"Did you know that her family had no idea they were trying to adopt?" Alex asked.

That piece of news seemed to surprise Ginny. "No. I thought they knew. I mean…they're family. I would've told you at the funeral if I'd known that she hadn't said anything." Ginny shook her head. "Sad."

"How did you come to work for Bring Them Home?" Anne asked.

"I met Merle Meyer when I was in college. He came to one of my classes and talked about nonprofits, and what they do at Bring Them Home."

"What year was that?"

"2005. I talked to him after class. I was majoring in social work and asked if I could help out there in my spare time. He was happy to have a volunteer. Then when I graduated he offered me a job."

"Rewarding work?"

"None more rewarding than seeing children join their adoptive families." Ginny shrugged. "There's just nothing like it." She smiled, then took a sip of her coffee.

"So Heaven's Child was created after you'd been there a few years."

She nodded. "Yep. 2008, I think. Edie Summers came in. She'd been thinking about creating the fund for a long time, I guess. She knew that Marla had a heart for the cause...so she was a natural choice to manage it."

"Was Marla housed in your offices that whole time?"

"Oh no. Marla worked mostly from home. She came in for meetings and if she was working on something special, but she wasn't around all that much."

"So can you tell us how all that worked? Fund-raising, all that..."

"Merle and Marla both spoke at a lot of fund-raisers. They'd set up booths at music festivals in the area. I remember Marla spoke at many churches to raise awareness of the need. She was an evangelist about it, you know. She was always quoting James 1:27 about orphans and widows." Her hazel eyes glowed with her passion. "It's why we do what we do."

"So you were involved with Heaven's Child too?"

"We all were. I mean *are*. Merle encourages the social workers to spread the word about the need for donations, as well as bringing families forward as candidates to receive scholarships. Since we're the ones working with the families we know their needs the best, so it just made sense to let us determine who the scholarship money would go to. We each have a set amount per year to give out, based on donations of course."

"So any of the social workers can just write a check from the account?"

"It's a little more involved than that. The grants are approved by Merle and Ron Fields, but then, yeah, we propose the candidates, get approval, then Karina writes up the checks that we present to the families. It's rewarding, seeing the shock on their faces, realizing they won't have to go into deep debt to bring their children home. It's so expensive to adopt. If only people could dig a little deeper — I mean if they aren't willing to bring a child into their home at least they can help others do it. You know, I get so mad sometimes at how much it costs that I start to understand why Robin Hood stole from the rich and gave to the poor." She chuckled.

The waitress came by with their food. She refilled their cups and moved on again. Ginny took a big bite of her Panini sandwich.

"Can you tell me about the other social workers? Jinx and Ron, right?"

"Ron isn't a social worker — he's a financial guy. Jinx is from upstate New York. Kind of a hard history, but he's pulled himself out of it. He's a good guy. Might be a little rough around the edges, but his heart is solid. He was at Bring Them Home long before I was."

"Does he have a strong sense of integrity?"

Ginny's brows came together. Clearly, she was curious about the question. "I...think so. I mean, I don't know if he has a police record or anything, but I've never seen anything that made me think..." She paused. "I take that back. There was once...he came to work looking pretty haggard. I asked him what had happened and he told me he'd spent the night in jail. I didn't know exactly why, but it sounded odd to me."

Anne took a bite of her sandwich.

"As for Ron," Ginny went on, "I don't know all that much about his private life, if that's what you're wanting to know about. He works hard at the agency. Is always there before anyone else, putting in long hours, staying late..."

"Does he have family?"

"I know he's married," she said. "I think he has a couple of kids, but I couldn't tell you if they're boys or girls or how many...I know it's weird. He's been there forever. Like since the place first started, but I know next to nothing about him. He's just very private, very task-oriented. Doesn't talk about his home life much at all."

After they said their farewells, Anne and Alex sat for a long moment in thought. "What do you think?" Alex finally said.

"She seems...nice." She met his gaze. "Didn't strike me as a thief," she said honestly in a low voice.

"What does a thief look like?" He raked a hand through his hair, then lifted his coffee for a sip. "She lives with her folks... doesn't seem like someone raking in $237,000, does it?"

"Unless she thinks of herself as Robin Hood," Anne said.

"That doesn't jibe though. Not if she's taking money from adoptive families."

"I agree," Anne said.

Before making the drive back to Blue Hill, they decided to drive past the address Karina had given for Ginny's home. Alex leaned forward in the passenger seat to study the expansive home with two-story marble columns.

"Nice house," he said to Anne.

"Yeah. Very nice."

He sat back.

Robin Hood, Anne thought. Like the famed thief, Ginny too was an idealist. She was quick to judge wealthy Americans for not supporting adoption, yet she lived in a house that most Americans could ill afford.

With a wooded three-acre lot, a stream that ran across the back of the property, it spoke of money . . . How did the free spirited girl reconcile the two?

Or had her conversation with Anne and Alex been purely an act?

* * *

It was a little after six o'clock when Anne and Alex arrived in front of Cheryl Bergen's modest little home in Blue Hill.

It was a plain house, white with no trim color. Not a flower or a bush in the front yard. A lone Eastern White Pine rose ninety feet into the air, dominating it like an angry parent with a disobedient child.

Anne moved up the ramp to the front door and knocked on the screen door. The inner door was open, and Anne could see a hospital bed in the room. The woman in the bed looked at Anne, but she didn't say anything. Anne said hello. A moment later Cheryl appeared. She was plain, like the house, with dishwater blonde hair and brown eyes. Cheryl was a heavyset woman, considerably shorter than Anne. She had round cheeks and smile lines emanating from her eyes.

"Sorry," she said, wiping her hands on her apron, "I didn't hear you knock. I was in the back making some raspberry jam."

"I'm Anne Gibson," Anne said. She held out a hand to shake, and Cheryl took it tentatively. Cheryl seemed curious.

"Do I know you?"

"You worked at Bring Them Home?" Alex asked.

"I did."

"My great-aunt Edie Summers was the founder of Bring Them Home. I'm wondering if you can help me figure a few things out about the history there."

The woman didn't exactly light up. Her brow furrowed and her eyes narrowed. "Okay...you know, I don't work there anymore. I quit a few years ago."

"Exactly how long ago did you quit?" Anne asked.

"Three and a half years ago..."

"We've been doing a bit of research," Anne put in. We were hoping you could answer some questions?"

Everything Anne said was true, though the nature of her questions might lead to other directions. She exchanged a glance with Alex who offered a faint smile.

Cheryl opened the screen door wide to let them in. "Please," she said, "come in. This is my mom, Inez." She gestured toward the woman in the hospital bed that dominated the front room. "That's a Hispanic name," she went on, "but there isn't a single Hispanic person on our family tree. My grandma liked to pretend she was exotic."

Anne couldn't tell if Cheryl was serious or if she was trying to be funny. She seemed to be sincere, yet there was a tension about her too. As if she were compensating for something. Though given the circumstances—two strangers at her door and an ill, vulnerable mother to care for—Anne could understand.

She led Anne and Alex toward a pair of stuffed reclining chairs and a small couch on the far side of the hospital bed in the living room. Two enormous cats rubbed at her feet, one on each side.

The small house was tidy, if a bit Spartan. Anne guessed the livable square footage at less than eight hundred square feet. A TV was mounted on one wall with a petite book case underneath it jammed with well worn paperbacks. There was a galley kitchen toward the back of the house, about the size of some people's walk-in closets. Anne could see a Formica table and two chairs tucked into one corner of the room. The back door of the house was visible from her spot in the living room. There was a bedroom just behind where they sat, and a bathroom in the space that must've originally housed the dining room toward the front of the house.

One of the cats jumped into Cheryl's lap the moment she sat down, while the other made himself comfortable at the foot of her mother's bed. A large oxygen tank hummed in the corner, its tubes connected to Inez's nose like a tether.

Inez closed her eyes. Her skin looked paper thin, with bluish veins showing through.

"She sleeps a lot," Cheryl explained, her eyes taking on a sad note. A moment later she seemed to shake it off and turned to Anne and Alex. "Would you like something to drink?" she offered. "I have Coke, Pepsi, orange pop...I'm parched so it's no bother."

"I'll take a Coke," Anne said.

Alex said the same.

Cheryl disappeared into the next room. The cat that had been on their host's lap moved to Anne, sniffing Anne's legs and stretching himself as if he wanted to jump up. Anne shifted away, hoping the cat would get the hint. He moved to Alex, who patted his thigh, and the kitty hopped into place.

"My neighbor brought over a whole bunch of raspberries," Cheryl said from the kitchen, "so I've been making jam all afternoon."

The house did smell of summertime, Anne realized, tangy and sweet. An open window on the other side of Inez brought in the warm breeze.

Cheryl returned with two large, sweating glasses of Coke that she handed to Alex and Anne, then she went back to the kitchen for her own beverage.

"Gotta love a Coke on a day like today," Anne said.

"Ain't that the truth?" Cheryl said when she returned. She offered a smile and moved to the seat opposite Alex and took a sip.

"Have you lived here long?" Anne asked, taking in the house with her gaze.

"I bought the house a few years ago. It's not much, but it suits our needs. I had to have it renovated for Mom's needs but" — she shrugged — "it works."

"Does someone take care of your mother when you're at work?" Alex asked.

Cheryl shook her head. "I work from home. But the county helps us. PCAs come when I'm gone. That kind of thing."

"That's good," Anne said.

Cheryl took another sip.

"So," Anne said, "I was wondering if you could tell us about your time at Bring Them Home."

"Your aunt was Edie Summers?"

"Did you know her?"

"Briefly," Cheryl said. "She struck me as a very caring person."

"What exactly did you do at Bring Them Home?"

"I was the office assistant. Really just a glorified secretary." Cheryl set her glass on the end table between the recliners and looked at Anne. "It's a job, you know? It was during college so I was glad to have it. I always liked kids, so helping kids get adopted kind of fit. I wanted to be a teacher, but then Mom had her stroke." Her gaze drifted to the sleeping woman. "I had to quit school to take care of her. Dad died a few years before that. Since I don't have any siblings, her care was left to me." She shrugged, then took another sip of her soda.

"How long have you been taking care of your mom?" Anne asked.

"She had her stroke four and a half years ago. I was twenty-one." Inez's chest barely rose. She was utterly still. Only the beating of her heart monitor revealed that she lived.

"That's hard," Anne said. "You do all this alone?"

Cheryl nodded.

"Did you like working at Bring Them Home?" Alex asked.

"Sure. I mean it was okay. The people were nice and I liked seeing kids get adopted. That was good. But..." She shrugged. "I was needed here."

"How long were you there?"

"I started freshmen year of college. So I guess three years? I worked for a little while after Mom's stroke...then it was just too much when she got out of the hospital. I guess I measure everything by when Mom's stroke happened..."

"That's kind of how those things work," Anne said. She understood all too well. Her measuring stick was Eric's death.

Cheryl went on, "It just got too hard to try to manage Mom and work. Once she got out of the hospital I had to choose."

"Did you know Merle Meyer and Ron Fields well?" Alex asked after a few moments.

Cheryl lifted her soda again and took a sip before answering. "I knew Ron better than Merle, just because I worked for Ron. I was really his assistant. They were nice enough, not overly generous but..."

Anne waited, sensing there was more coming.

"Ron could be a taskmaster. Like, he'd give me a big project to do with a crazy deadline and then he'd go golfing all afternoon with some donor. And if I didn't hit my deadlines he got angry."

"What kind of angry?" Alex leaned forward, his brow furrowing.

"He didn't yell or anything. You just knew he was displeased. He had a *tone* and he'd look at you." Cheryl shivered. "And he…" Her words trailed off.

"He what?" Anne prompted.

"Considering what Bring Them Home was all about—he had a pretty hefty income, if you know what I mean."

"You think he was taking money?"

She shook her head. "I didn't say that—just that…it's a nonprofit, yet he was living pretty high on the hog." She drew in a long breath. "By the time I quit I'd had enough." She looked at her mother, who stirred on her bed, then settled. "Taking care of Mom is hard. For him to expect me to put in extra hours like that when he was…It just wasn't possible." She set her glass down and met Anne's eyes, then Alex's. "Merle was always a good guy. He understood how hard it was for me. He'd ask how Mom was."

"Did you have anything to do with Heaven's Child when you were there?" Anne asked.

"Yeah…a bit." She shifted. "Not much though. I took the deposits, that kind of thing. It was really managed by Marla from her home." She looked at Alex. "And the social workers. They're the ones who figured out where the grants would go." She took another sip of her Coke. "Why do you want to know about that?"

"Marla Slater was my sister," Alex said.

"Oh. I'm sorry." Cheryl's face fell. She took a moment to compose herself, then said, "I felt awful when she died. That her husband died with her…She had a son, right?"

"Ryan," Alex supplied.

"What happened to him when his parents died?"

Anne could see that Alex was touched by her kindness. "He came to live with me," he said. His voice cracked and he struggled to maintain his composure. Finally he added, "He's a good kid."

"I'm sure he is." Cheryl nodded. "I bet that was really hard — to lose his parents at such a young age."

"It was."

Anne set her glass on the coffee table then stood up. "Well, we've taken up enough of your time." She glanced at her watch. "We should go. Thank you for the Coke."

Cheryl waved the comment away. "I'm glad you stopped by. Mom and I don't get visitors very often."

When they climbed into Anne's car Alex was unusually quiet. "She's a nice girl," he finally said.

Anne couldn't help but agree. The twenty-five-year-old had suffered more than her share.

CHAPTER EIGHTEEN

T hey drove straight to Lincoln Krueger's after leaving Cheryl. The two of them didn't say much on the drive, both lost in thoughts. Anne kept seeing Cheryl's longing glances at her mother, the meager home. Something about it seemed off, though she couldn't place what. She was simply a girl who was down on her luck. She wondered if Cheryl's assessment of Ron Fields was her lead — a man living off of donations? Perhaps. Though she didn't want to come to conclusions until she'd met the man for herself. Her thoughts flitted to Ginny's comments about Jinx Hendricks — a man who'd spent time in jail. There was clearly more than one lead here.

When she pulled her car to a stop in front of Lincoln Krueger's home, she and Alex both bent to study the place. Alex gave a low whistle.

The former social worker at Bring Them Home lived in a house that could've been featured in an Architectural Digest magazine. In classic Frank Lloyd Wright style, the house overlooked a waterfall that flowed beneath a section of the home that jutted over a steep ravine. Windows wrapped the entire level. There was no yard per se, rather the home seemed to be part of the woodsy landscape.

Anne and Alex climbed out of her car and made their way to the front door, ringing the bell.

Lincoln Krueger was perhaps the oldest-looking person Anne had ever seen. His face was weathered and leathery, with deep wrinkles. His jowls drooped like a hound dog's even though he was a thin, tall man. He peered down at Anne and Alex with dark beady eyes when they met him at the door. A petite woman in pink came up behind him, peering at them from several feet behind in the slate-tiled foyer.

"Good evening," Anne said, going through introductions, explaining their reason for being there much as she'd explained it to Cheryl when they'd appeared on her stoop.

Lincoln said, "Bring Them Home?" He looked confused. "Bring who home?"

"It's an adoption agency that you used to work at?"

"Oh…" He seemed to remember then. "I don't have time to talk to you about something that happened years ago."

"Would there be a better time that we could come by?" Anne said.

He pursed his lips and bent down to look her straight in the eyes. "No. There wouldn't be a better time."

He began to shut the door in their faces. Anne was tempted to shove her foot in the space, but he looked like someone who would have no qualms about bruising a strange woman's foot.

Alex stepped forward. "We just want to talk. That's all." That stopped Lincoln from shutting the door all the way. "And we can leave whenever you want us to."

"I'm…" He huffed.

"What does it hurt to give us a few minutes?" Alex added. There was a hint of pleading in his tone.

"Lincoln," the woman behind him said in a soothing voice, "it's all right." That seemed to be his undoing.

Lincoln sighed and flung the door open. "I suppose a few minutes," he said. "That's all, though. I don't have all night for some two-bit private eyes to interrogate me."

"We aren't private eyes," Anne assured. "Just…"

"Just get on with it." He turned his back on them and walked quickly toward the back of the house, moving with surprising speed for someone his age.

They followed Lincoln to a bright sunroom off the back of the house. From there Anne could see the town of Blue Hill. The water tower glinted in the late-day sunshine.

Lincoln huffed something to his wife then left, saying he'd be right back.

The woman in pink introduced herself as Lucy Krueger. "Forgive Lincoln," Lucy said. "He doesn't always know how he comes across."

She hovered over them like a hummingbird, constantly in motion, wringing her tiny hands, asking if they needed anything. Her light gray eyes met Anne's.

She offered them drinks which Anne and Alex declined. *Better not to stretch Lincoln's generosity too far*, Anne thought. Lincoln returned within a few minutes. He'd changed his clothes. The summer-weight polo and knee-length shorts were replaced by a heavy wool sweater and warm winter pants.

Anne wondered if Alex noticed that Lincoln had changed into warmer clothes, especially on such a warm summer day.

"Thank you for letting us talk to you, Mr. Krueger," Anne said.

Lincoln crossed his arms over his chest and sat back. He seemed a jurist awaiting his time to pronounce judgment on whatever case Anne and Alex had to present. Alex cleared his throat.

"You used to work for Bring Them Home adoption agency, didn't you?" Anne said.

"Yeah."

If all of his answers were going to be like that, this interview will be pointless, Anne thought.

"How did you like working there?" Perhaps an open-ended question would yield more answers.

"Fine."

Okay.

"Why did you leave?" Alex asked.

He shrugged.

"He retired," his wife offered as she reentered the room, a tray with cookies and lemonade in hand. She handed a glass to each of them. Hadn't they declined beverages? Anne took the glass anyway.

"Was he happy there?" Anne asked Lucy.

"He was." She smiled. "We never had children of our own so for him to have the opportunity to be such a blessing... that made up for a lot. It was something he really believed in."

Anne glanced at Lincoln when his wife finished. He sat motionless. A rock of unreadability. Anne was trying to reconcile what Lucy said of her husband—a generous man—to the surly man before her. She glanced at the wool sweater. His gaze moved with Anne's and he began to pick at the fibers as if he saw insects crawling across the surface. His brow was furrowed, intent.

"When did he get sick?" Anne asked Mrs. Krueger in a low voice.

The corners of Lucy's mouth lifted in a faint smile, gratitude for Anne's understanding. "About three and a half years ago. They tell me it's Alzheimer's, but that is so hard to diagnose. They can't really say for sure till it's too late to do anything."

"I'm sorry," Anne said.

"You couldn't have known." Lucy shook her head.

"Do you know a lot about what he did there?" Alex asked, leaning forward.

"Some," Lucy said. "He liked to tell me about the cases, though that really isn't allowed nowadays."

"Did he work with Heaven's Child at all?" Anne asked, adding, "It's the fund that offers grants to adoptive families."

Lucy sat back, trying to recall. She looked at her husband. "Do you remember Heaven's Child, Linc?" she asked.

"Heaven's Child," he repeated. "Nope. Is it a singing group?"

She turned back to Anne and Alex.

"When did he leave Bring Them Home?" Alex asked.

"Three years ago. When he got too bad."

* * *

"It has to be Cheryl," Alex said as they drove home.

"Why do you think it's Cheryl?" Anne said, shaking her head. "I don't think it's either of them. Lincoln—with his Alzheimer's— how likely is it that he can recall a PIN to take money out of an ATM?"

"True… Unless Lucy gets the cash out. You saw how nice their home is. How can a retired social worker afford that?"

"That sweet little woman?"

Alex lifted an eyebrow. "Sweet little women have done worse."

"Well," Anne went on, "that the stealing continues now that he and Cheryl aren't there rules them both out, doesn't it? I can't see how either of them would have access to the fund."

"It is a dilemma," Alex agreed.

* * *

The familiar tiredness seemed ready to take over. Anne could feel it tugging at her eyelids shortly after she got home. What would it feel like not to have these episodes? Not to be tired, constantly resisting the urge to sleep? She moved to the coffeepot in her kitchen and put on a fresh pot even though it was evening. She needed to stay awake until at least nine o'clock or she'd throw off her whole sleeping schedule.

When the delectable scent of coffee filled the room she poured herself a big cup and took it to the living room. She knew she should go downstairs and catch up on some work. She had some ordering to do for the library and a stack of books to enter into the system with barcodes and their Dewey Decimal codes to add to their bindings. Today had been so hectic she hadn't had a chance to keep up with checking in returned books or placing DVDs back in their alphabetized spaces in the long narrow drawers under the back counter.

After she drank her coffee and felt more awake, she headed downstairs to finish up those tasks. She knew they'd nag at her until she'd completed them.

An hour later, she looked around with satisfaction that she wouldn't be overwhelmed when she opened up come morning.

She glanced at the clock. The kids were at friends' houses that evening. Neither would be back for another hour.

Pulling out her laptop, Anne typed "Cheryl Bergen" into her search engine. She'd looked up all the others from the list Karina had given her except Lincoln and Lucy Krueger.

The young woman didn't have a Facebook page, which struck Anne as odd for someone her age, considering how popular the site was. Anne tried LinkedIn, the online site for business connections. There was nothing there. Cheryl seemed to have no criminal record. The only site that mentioned her at all was a dating site that had a very outdated photo of her and very little else. Nothing was filled out in the "About Me" section.

Anne sat back, staring at the picture of a much thinner, smiling Cheryl. She looked to be about twenty in the photo. She had given up her future to care for her ill mother. It was utterly selfless in a time when many people would have put the incapacitated woman into a nursing home.

Did they have nursing homes in other countries like India? Anne wondered. Or was that simply an American phenomenon? She thought of Thomas Gee and his daughter. What would become of his daughter if something happened to him?

The thought unsettled her. So many others like Thomas Gee lived around the world. Alone with no help. No way to help himself. The need was simply too great to fathom. She didn't have to travel to India to understand that.

Anne glanced at the page on her screen. Was she getting anywhere with all this? She typed in the name of Cheryl's mother—Inez Bergen.

There was an obituary for her husband—Glenn Bergen. Anne looked at the date. It would've been a year or so before Inez had her stroke. "That poor woman," Anne said to herself in the silence of the library. It was a lot to go through in the span of a year—her husband's death, her stroke.

How had Cheryl made it through that time? How did anyone survive such times? Anne sat back. She'd so wanted to help Thomas Gee and the orphans at Haydens' orphanage, yet maybe there was someone right here who she could help. Cheryl did seem lonely. Anne wondered if she had any friends, a church to support her. Then again, how could she get away for such things? Her situation was cruel, that was sure. Far too cruel.

* * *

On Thursday morning, Anne drove alone to the neighboring town of Lewistown to meet Jinx Hendricks at the Stone Arch Bridge Park. Alex had had to work, and since the Miller twins were working at the library and the kids were at Summer Fun she opted to go alone.

She thought back to her conversation with Ginny. She'd asked the social worker not to talk to the others about seeing her and Alex, and even though Ginny seemed obviously curious about the reasons for their questions, Ginny promised to keep quiet. Anne didn't want the staff at Bring Them Home to know she was interviewing them all, looking to see who might be a thief. She knew such conversations could taint later interviews and perhaps clue the thief in to what she and Alex were doing.

Anne parked her car and climbed out. The late June sun warmed her shoulders. Jinx was sitting on one of the park benches that looked out across Jack's Creek, an ancient looking bridge waiting idly in the distance.

Jinx Hendricks was the epitome of the word *character*. He wore a long leather jacket despite the day's warmth. Dark sunglasses shielded his eyes from sight. Anne made her way to the sinister-looking man, and he rose to shake her hand.

"Thanks for coming," Anne said. "Is it…Jinx?"

"That's right," he said. "It's an old story." He looked to be in his mid-fifties, with gray hair at the temples and a scar under his left eye. He sat back on the bench, Anne next to him.

"I'm sure you're wondering why I asked you to meet me here," Anne said.

Jinx laughed low in his throat. "You could say that." He pulled a cigarette out of his coat pocket, followed by a lighter. "You don't mind, do you?"

Anne shook her head.

"Alex Ochs — Marla Slater's brother — and I are looking into a few things regarding the time right before Marla died," Anne began.

"Okay…" He lit a match, then when the cigarette glowed orange he took a long puff. "Like personal things or things that have to do with work? Rick and Marla were friends of mine," he added.

"They were?"

"I know — it seems unlikely, doesn't it?" He laughed again.

Rick and Marla had been fairly conservative and straight-laced compared to Jinx, so the idea that they spent any significant time together didn't seem to fit. He gave a grin that revealed a gold tooth in the front of his smile.

"They didn't judge, you know? They were just real folks. Marla was a good egg—working with that foundation."

"Heaven's Child," Anne filled in. "That's part of why I asked you here. To find out more about Heaven's Child—how it works, who has access to the funds..."

"Access to the funds?" He twisted his dark brows and looked her in the eye. "Why would you want to know about that?"

"I'd rather not say. Just curious."

"Just curious," he repeated. He wasn't buying it.

Finally, Anne added, "Alex received a statement recently from that account—that and some statements that Marla kept. There were some things on them that didn't look right. We're wondering if someone's been embezzling." She hoped that would be enough to coax cooperation.

Jinx whistled, then nodded. "That's quite an accusation."

"I don't have proof," Anne confessed. "That's why I wanted to ask you what you know about the fund."

He looked across the water for a long moment. "It's a pretty straightforward charity. We take donations. The money goes to families that want to adopt but don't have the bucks. I think it supports a few other initiatives too—some schools in India, helping families in other ways. Anything that can help kids get adopted, stay off the streets." He shrugged.

"Can I ask you a personal question?" Anne leaned forward over her knees. There was a family of ducks on the water. The mother duck led the way with a trail of ducklings behind her. She didn't look back, simply swam ahead knowing her children would follow.

"Ask away," Jinx said.

"Why did you become a social worker?"

"What you mean is I don't fit the stereotype." His laugh was caustic, yet he didn't seem particularly offended. Anne wondered if he'd been asked the same question before. "Hey, just because I know how to dress doesn't mean I don't care about the injustices of the world. Kids need protecting. They need to grow up feeling loved, cared about. Not everyone has that privilege growing up." His words were weighted with personal history, Anne sensed. "You know..." Jinx blew out a long breath. "It gets hard after a while, working in this business. You start out all idealistic, think you're going to save the world. Then you find out the world's a lot harder to save than you thought. Not everyone is on your side."

Anne turned from watching the ducks that were climbing on to the opposite shore. "What do you mean?"

"Not everyone has good motives," Jinx said. He shook his head. "Money, man. It's the root of all evil. It's a cancer in our society." He sat forward and drew in a long breath on his cigarette, flicking the ashes toward the ground at his feet.

"Are you talking about something specific?"

"I'm just saying that I've seen things that aren't so good in this industry. That makes me sad."

"What kind of things?"

He sat up straight and looked her in the eyes. Anne glanced around, suddenly aware of his menacing stance. A couple was feeding the ducks breadcrumbs at the water's edge. The mother duck gobbled up the pieces.

Anne feelings of alarm eased a bit.

"Whatever you're walking on," he went on, "I'd tread carefully. Real careful. Sometimes it's just better to let things be."

"What do you mean?"

"I mean, you start shaking things up and the only ones who get hurt are the kids. You understand?" He paused. "Whatever you do—don't hurt the kids."

It was clear Anne wasn't going to get more out of him. *Perhaps he just has a flair for the dramatic,* she thought. Or perhaps he knew something.

CHAPTER NINETEEN

After her meeting with Jinx, Anne felt shaken. She'd called Alex and asked him to see what he could find on the social worker, especially in regard to Ginny's accusation that he'd served jail time. She'd tried looking it up when she'd returned from her talk with Ginny but had come up empty-handed.

"Are you okay?" Alex asked.

"I'm fine," she assured him. "I don't know if he was just trying to scare me or if there was more there, but see what you can dig up when you get a chance, okay?"

"I'm on it," he promised. "And, Anne, don't be a hero, okay?"

"I'm no hero."

"I know you," he insisted. "You might not see yourself as a hero. But you do that hero thing all the time and I'm telling you—knock it off."

Anne chuckled. She knew he was trying to protect her. Even if it was from herself.

She hung up, then drove the rest of the way to Deshler. She found Ron Fields at his home, a sprawling mansion with lush, rolling lawns, flower beds tucked here and there, colorful islands in a sea of green. His wife met Anne at the front door. She smoothed back her already perfect hair.

"Mrs. Fields," Anne reached to shake hands with her. "I'm Anne Gibson."

"Call me Meredith. Ron told me you were coming by." From the sound of her accent she was from the Midwest, probably Minnesota or the Dakotas. "He's in his office, working." She pointed down the hall to the right where double French doors opened to a dark, masculine room. "You can go right on in."

Anne thanked her, then went down the short hall, knocking on the wooden doorframe. Ron lifted his face and waved her in. He was a trim man with thick eyebrows and thin lips. The Chief Financial Officer, Ron had the greatest access to records and account information, Anne knew. She thought of Ginny's comment that she knew very little about him. Exactly how private was he?

Ron stood, reaching to shake hands with her. "Anne Gibson. That's a familiar name."

"It is?" Anne was puzzled for a moment.

"I knew your great-aunt." He motioned toward a wooden chair and Anne took a seat. His serious face transformed into a grin.

"She was proud of her librarian great-niece."

"That's sweet," Anne said.

"I probably saw her for the last time at Rick and Marla Slater's funeral four years ago." He sat back to study Anne. "You don't look all that much like her."

Anne laughed. "I guess I never really thought about it."

"She was something else, that woman. So," he said, clearly ready to get on with it, "what can I do for you?"

"I was hoping to pick your brain about the history of Bring Them Home."

He crossed his arms over his chest. "The history of Bring Them Home?" he repeated. "What do you mean?"

"Merle mentioned that you were involved from the start of the agency," Anne added. "Can you tell me about that?"

"Certainly." His lips formed a thin line. "As I recall, Edie had gone on a missions trip to India. When she came back, she got in touch with me and Merle. Mona Robinson had told her about us. She thought that my financial know-how and Merle's salesman personality might make a good adoption agency." He laughed. "I think we've done okay. We've placed an awful lot of kids over the years."

"And what was my aunt's role in all of that?"

"She did a lot of fund-raisers and greasing palms to bring it together." He shook his head. "She was good at getting people to open up their pocketbooks." He sat back in his chair. "It was a gift she had, much like Merle. You should've seen those two work a room. Me—I'm not so good at that. I'd rather stay tucked away with my calculator!"

Anne glanced around the luxuriously decorated office. A large globe sat in solitary orbit in one corner, flanked by burgundy leather chairs. A green banker's lamp rested atop the massive walnut desk that held a couple framed photos, a cup of pencils, and an oversized computer screen.

"Merle told me that you stopped in and talked to him a few days ago," Ron said. "He mentioned that you have some concerns."

"Yes. About Heaven's Child. What's your role with that entity?"

His face darkened a bit, his brow furrowing. "Your aunt Edie was involved in creating that as well. Did you know that?"

"Yes. How did Marla come on board?"

"Marla was a good administrator. Edie knew that Heaven's Child would need someone with a deep commitment to the cause to take it on, so once it was established she asked Marla to take it over."

"How many scholarships does Heaven's Child give out every year?"

"Thirty to forty, I'd say. We gave out about three hundred thousand dollars in adoption grants last year, even more the year before that."

Anne let out a low whistle. "That's a lot of help."

"We wish we could give more. We need to find ways to get the word out so people can give. I think there are a lot of people who want to give. When people hear about the need, getting them to give isn't hard."

From the way he spoke on the subject Anne could sense that he was passionate about adoption. So why did Ginny Stein characterize him as closed and private? Anne pondered the thought for a moment.

"Can you tell me about some of the people at Bring Them Home? Like Ginny, what does she do?" Anne knew that one question often led to the next. She hoped this question would open other doors.

"She's a social worker—helps families with home studies, walks them through the adoption process."

"And she lives with her folks?"

"I don't ask personal questions at work, especially of women." Ron shrugged. "It's just wiser...for me."

"And Jinx?"

"Pretty much the same."

"You have never had any...issues with him?"

Ron furrowed his brow. "No. Not really." He laughed. "He is a bit of a kook, don't get me wrong. But he believes in what we do. Believes strongly in it."

"Do you work a pretty long work week?"

"Depends on what you call long. I was raised on a farm in southern Wisconsin. My dad worked from sunup to sundown seven days a week. Kids nowadays don't get that. At Bring Them Home I probably put in fifty hours in any given week. I don't know how not to do that."

Anne understood. Hadn't she done the exact same thing the night before? Some weeks she felt as if there was never a time that she wasn't working in one capacity or another—library work or house work—doing laundry, cooking, cleaning.

"Not like Ginny and Jinx," he went on. "Those two show up when they're good and ready. We're lucky if they're in the office before nine."

"You think they aren't hard workers?"

He shrugged. "Merle is in charge of them. I'm just saying what I see. Whether they get their work done...I can't say."

"And what's your relationship with Merle?"

Ron's lips quirked into a smile. "Best friends since high school. He's the possibility and I'm reality." He laughed. "We're a good team. Not that we always see eye to eye, mind you. Sometimes we go at it."

"How so?"

He shrugged. "Let's just say he's good at spending money. Not real good at sticking to a budget. So I get to nag him like his mother."

He glanced at his watch and Anne sensed that he was ready to be done.

"I don't want to take up any more of your time." Anne stood. "Thank you."

"I don't know if I helped you at all." Ron stood too.

"You have." Anne smiled, then said farewell and let herself out.

* * *

While he thought they could work harder, Ron believed in his team. That much was obvious. Which meant that the thief could be any one of them. Other than Jinx, they all seemed to live rather posh lives. Cheryl Bergen's accusation that Ron lived awfully well off for someone at a nonprofit rang true. While that was compelling it wasn't exactly proof of wrongdoing.

By the time Anne got home from Deshler, she was running late. She went about her regular routine, assisting patrons whenever they came to the checkout desk. She was glad she'd caught up on chores the night before because the steady stream of patrons kept her busy.

By three o'clock she was ready for a nap. More than ready. The afternoon haze was coming on fast—she could feel it in her eyelids. Her cell phone buzzed as she climbed the stairs to her apartment. It was Alex.

"Hey, how did the interview with Ron go?" he asked.

"Interesting," Anne said.

"Could I come over later?"

"Later would be good—I need a nap right now."

"Have you heard back from the doctor?"

"No. Still waiting on labs."

"Why does it take so long?"

She knew the question was rhetorical.

"How long a nap will you need? I can pick up the kids at Wendy's, keep them here till you want them." She could hear the teasing in his voice.

"Give me a half hour?"

"Let's make it a full hour. I'll take them to the park. They'll be good and hungry for supper."

"You're an angel."

* * *

True to his word, Alex was there with kids in tow an hour later. He even brought food. Anne could smell fried chicken when he came up the back steps.

"What's this?" she said.

"You've been busy. I knew you wouldn't have time to cook supper."

"So you made chicken?"

He waggled an eyebrow. "You think I can't?"

"I didn't say that."

"I'll have you know I can fry up amazing chicken. I just happened to get this at the deli at the grocery store."

Anne punched him in the arm and he pretended to be wounded.

"Grown-ups!" Ryan said. "Come on, Ben. Let's go to your room." The boys retreated down the hall.

Liddie stood in front of them, with Hershey sitting at her side obediently.

"Can I have some chicken?" she asked sweetly. "I'm hungry."

"Sure, honey."

Anne moved to the cupboard that held plates and pulled down a stack. Alex got out the chicken with sides of coleslaw, mashed potatoes and gravy, and dinner rolls with butter packets, setting them out on the kitchen counter. Anne served Liddie a plate and the little girl sat down to eat her meal.

Alex fixed himself a plate of fried chicken and sides and joined Liddie.

When Anne brought her meal to the table, Alex was talking to Liddie about what she'd been learning at Summer Fun.

"The people in India eat with their hands," she said as she lifted her fried chicken to her mouth and took a bite. "Sometimes they use their bread like a spoon too."

"You're learning a lot," Alex said.

"Yeah, the Haydens are good teachers. I'm going to miss Natalie when they leave." She turned to her mother. "Do you think we could go to India to see them?"

"India's a long way away, honey," Anne said. "It costs a lot of money to travel so far."

"So how can all the Hayden children come to America?"

"I'm sure they save up. It's part of why they only come every few years."

The little girl took another bite. Anne did too. The aroma filled the small apartment, a homey scent.

"Well, I'm going to save up then," Liddie said. "Maybe we can all go when I'm a teenager!"

"You do that, honey."

"Can Ryan and I go too?" Alex asked. There was a twinkle in his eye when he spoke to Liddie. Anne could see that he enjoyed her spunky attitude.

"Of course you can go!" Liddie said. "And we can take the Pyles and..." She looked at her mother. "Who else?"

"Whoever you want, honey."

Liddie screwed up her face in thought, then began to list off her friends from school.

"I hope it's a pretty big airplane," Alex said.

"We might have to take a couple," the five-year-old suggested. "Just to be safe."

After they'd finished their meal and Liddie bounded off to see what the boys were up to, Anne and Alex cleaned up, then convened at the table.

Anne told Alex about her meetings with each of the Bring Them Home employees. "What were your impressions of Ginny Stein?" she asked when conversation returned to the case as a whole.

"She struck me as an idealist. A bit unconventional. I could see her carrying protest signs in the 1960s."

Anne smiled at the image. "She lives with her parents. So if she is the thief, she isn't spending the money on extravagant living."

"True," Alex said, "but people can have other vices."

"And I don't want to rule anyone out till we know more about them."

Anne typed Ginny's name into the search engine on her laptop. The young social worker had gone to Berkeley where she'd gotten her degree. They already knew that she went to work for Bring Them Home right out of college. Her LinkedIn network was quite extensive, including endorsements from several leading children's rights groups, though there was no résumé. Her hobbies included tennis, rock climbing, playing the ukulele, and skydiving.

"So she's a risk taker," Anne said, adding that detail to her list. "I'd think there's a bit of thrill involved in stealing."

"And skydiving isn't a cheap hobby," Alex added.

The next site pulled up Ginny's Facebook page, all basic information. There were several photos of her with young men, one with his arm around her in a possessive gesture. The caption read, "My beau" and was tagged with his name—Kirk Johnson. Anne clicked on the link that took her to Kirk's Facebook page. While Ginny's page looked fairly benign, Kirk's page was filled with posts depicting gambling establishments. One caption read, "Next week we'll win the big one, buddy!"

Anne went to his "About" page to see if she could determine how long the two had been a pair. There was nothing there that gave any clue.

"A boyfriend who gambles...," Alex said.

Anne added the detail to a bulleted list in her notebook. "Remember, she also knew about Marla and Rick adopting."

"I did a bit of digging about that myself today too," Alex said.

"You mean finding the boy in the referral?"

He nodded.

"And?"

"Not much...but I've been thinking about it. Maybe all of this is for a reason. Discovering the referral. Maybe this can be a healing thing."

"What exactly are you saying, Alex?"

"I know you think it's not a good idea, but I want to find him," Alex insisted. "I want to know who he is now."

Anne studied him for a moment. She understood. It was hard to let loved ones go. Especially when there might be a piece of them out there somewhere, some tangible evidence of their lives and the things they loved. This boy represented that to Alex. He was the epitome of what Marla had longed for, the child she'd loved without even knowing him. For Alex to know him would be to have a part of his sister back. Anne couldn't begrudge him that.

She supposed figuring out who had stolen the Heaven's Child money was much the same—Marla's unfinished business. They owed it to her to find the thief. Yet Anne couldn't help feeling that it would end badly, that it would open old wounds and bring Alex—and Ryan—back to that dark place. She wanted desperately to protect them from that kind of hurt.

"You can argue all you want," Alex said before she had a chance to say anything, "but I want to at least try."

Anne could see in the stiff way he sat that there was no point in trying to argue. He was digging in. He wouldn't listen to even the most persuasive reasoning.

"All right," she said.

"That's it?" he said, obviously surprised. "All right?"

"What do you want me to say? You'll do what you think is best. Now..." She turned back to her bulleted list. "What did you discover about Jinx Hendricks?" She wrote the name as she asked.

Alex was silent for a long moment. He knew what she was doing. Still, he let it go.

"There was a Facebook page for a man with the same name, but it wasn't him. I couldn't find him there at all. No LinkedIn page. There wasn't even a White Pages listing. So I went back to the Bring Them Home Web site. His real name is Jerry Hendricks. There was a bio for him."

He laid a sheet of paper with the printed information on the table in front of Anne.

Jerry "Jinx" Hendricks is a long-time advocate for children. He joined Bring Them Home when it was first established and has worked in both the private nonprofit sector and across the public child welfare continuum for more than eighteen years. Hendricks previously worked for the Pennsylvania Department of Human Services where he helped develop and implement adoption policy that continues to benefit children across the state.

He held a position in Pennsylvania Department of Children and Family Services coordinating its Post-Adoption and Guardianship Services, and was the Foster Care Manager for several years. Hendricks also has experience training, facilitating support groups, working in early childhood prevention/early intervention with at-risk families, and in Child Protection Services.

"Hard to believe that's the same man I met with today," Anne said.

Alex held up a photo.

"I guess there's no arguing with that. But he's so…different now. So jaded." She studied the photo for another minute. "What do you think happened to him?"

"Hard to say. Though someone who's worked with all those government agencies…Imagine all the things he's seen during the course of his career. Kids living in less than ideal conditions, sent back home to be abused again, politicians making behind-the-scene deals that affect real people's lives...I'd think someone like that is bound to be jaded."

"You make a good point," Anne conceded. "Did you discover anything else? Did you find out anything about that jail time Ginny mentioned?"

"Nothing about jail time, but I did find this." Alex raised an eyebrow and laid another sheet in front of her, this time a newspaper clipping.

Anne read out loud from a news piece:

"'Jerry Hendricks of Willow Grove, Pennsylvania, who was awarded the honor of Eagle Scout himself as a high school senior, is bestowing the same honor on his son Preston.'" She looked up at Alex. "Okay...that's surprising."

"A family man," Alex said.

She bent to read the rest of the article, mostly about Jinx's son who would be participating in the event that coming week. Anne glanced at the date—six years prior. "Well, that confirms what we learned from the bio—he was, at least at one time, an overachiever."

"And there's this." He laid a third sheet of paper in front of her.

"My, you have been busy," she said, impressed with his detective work in her absence.

"I learn from the best." He gave her a wink. "Read it."

The headline read, *Eagle Scout Killed in Head On Collision.*

"Oh no," Anne said. She placed a hand over her mouth as she read about the tragedy. Jinx's son, cut down in the prime of life, just twenty at the time of the accident. Five years ago. "That could make someone rather jaded too."

"It sure could."

They paused for a moment, feeling for the man who'd lost someone so precious.

After a few moments, Anne said, "So this is everything you found on Jinx?"

Alex nodded. "Tell me about your interview with Ron Fields."

"He seemed like a nice man. He spoke fondly of Aunt Edie and was passionate about adoption. Hardworking. Of course you knew that—Ginny said as much. But for someone who works for a nonprofit, Cheryl was right, Ron lives in a pretty pricey house. Most expensive neighborhood in Deshler, I'm sure."

"Does his wife work?"

"I don't know, but Merle had already told him about our visit."

"So who knows if he's hiding something."

Anne nodded and turned to her computer to type in the chief financial officer's name. She clicked on the link for his LinkedIn page.

According to his résumé, Ron had graduated from the University of Wisconsin Madison in 1985 with a master's degree in finance, and his bio on the Bring Them Home site said he married Meredith Wright in 1986. Anne wrote her name down. They had four daughters, all adopted. He'd worked for a Fortune 500 company until 1994 when he cofounded Bring Them Home with Merle Meyer and Edie Summers. One endorsement read, "Ron is an advocate for children. He gives selflessly and endlessly to see that children everywhere are cared for."

"Doesn't exactly sound like an embezzler, does he?" Alex said.

"Not really," Anne said. "But then what does an embezzler look like?"

"There's not much else here," Alex said, scanning the rest of the page at Anne's side.

She was feeling tired again. "Do you want a Coke?" she asked.

"Sure."

She got up to go get one for each of them. When she returned, he was looking up Ron's wife, Meredith.

"What'd you find?" she asked as she set his Coke next to him and took the chair adjacent.

"Meredith does have a job," he began. "She's an investment banker with Wells Fargo."

Anne let out a low whistle. "That would account for the expensive home."

"But look here," Alex said, raising an eyebrow. "Meredith also has a pretty colorful background."

A haggard looking mug shot of the perfect-looking woman stared back from the screen. "What was she arrested for?"

"Theft." He turned the screen toward Anne so she could read.

Shippensburg native, Meredith Wright was indicted on two counts of felony theft for burglarizing a home in a western suburb of Pennsylvania with her boyfriend Mark Nichols. A date for trial has not been set.

Anne was incredulous. "I wonder if her boss at Wells Fargo knows about this." She looked at the date—the early 1980s. It had been years before she married Ron. Anne added the information to her list. "This isn't exactly narrowing things down, is it?" she said. "Is there anything stating the outcome of the trial?"

"Not that I can see," Alex said.

"Well, people can change."

"What do we know about the president—Merle Meyer?"

"We know that he does a lot of fund-raisers for Heaven's Child. Of course he has access to the account—that's part of our problem. The way he structured the thing, they all have access. Anyone could be the thief."

Anne typed in his name and clicked on his LinkedIn account. His photo looked several years old, and he wore a mustache and goatee in the shot. According to his profile, he'd worked at two other adoption agencies before creating Bring Them Home with Aunt Edie.

Anne read out loud, "'Merle is an accomplished fund-raiser, bringing in over a million dollars in funds for his previous agencies. He has a heart for children, helping to place over 250 children in adoptive families over the course of his career.'"

Anne pressed the *back* button and clicked on the next link from the search. This site cited past criminal activity, any arrests, convictions, felonies. Merle's name was listed.

"This site claims that in 1987 Merle was arrested for possession of marijuana," Anne said. "Then in 1988 he was arrested for theft. Merle stole a car from his own grandmother."

"He stole from family?"

"It's probably more common than we realize," Anne said.

"Gotta appreciate a grandmother with that level of tough love, though," he said. "To call the police on her grandson."

"You're assuming she knew that he was the thief when she discovered it missing." She read the article. "It was just an arrest, no conviction afterward."

"How old would he have been in 1988?"

"Early twenties, maybe?" Anne guessed. "All of this is old news. We need something more recent." Anne returned to the search page and clicked on the next link, the foreclosure section of the Deshler newspaper. It was a standard foreclosure notice, with Merle and his wife listed as Mortgagors. A property valued at $407,000 and purchased ten years prior.

"That would give someone motive to steal," Alex said.

"Yes it would." Anne shook her head.

"Did you visit Merle's house? Does he still live at this address?"

"No, I didn't," Anne said, reaching for the sheet of paper with the contact information for all the Bring Them Home employees that Karina had brought her. She bent her head to study it. "It's the same address," she said.

How had Merle avoided that fate that had seemed written in stone, or at least in the newspaper?

Finally, Anne said, "Well, so far we have five possibilities and none of them eliminated."

Chapter Twenty

Anne headed to the newspaper archives first thing the next morning. Grace Hawkins was busy talking on the phone when Anne got there, so she motioned to her friend that she wanted to do a bit of research, then headed back when Grace gave her a thumbs-up. The newspaper archives smelled of groundwood paper and ink. As a librarian it was a scent Anne loved — the perfume of knowledge.

Anne settled in front of the microfiche machine, its oversized blue screen glowing. She glanced at the notes she'd written regarding the arrests of Merle Meyer and Meredith Wright and pulled up the files for the newspapers from the months that followed. There was bound to be something of interest there. She hoped.

She scanned through several sheets before finding what she was looking for. *Nichols Guilty of Felony Theft* the title read.

Former Blue Hill resident Mark Nichols was found guilty of two counts felony theft for stealing a set of golf clubs and a golf cart from the Shippensburg Country Club last month. When asked about the incident the twenty-five-year-old said, "I was just looking for some fun."

His girlfriend, twenty-one-year-old Meredith Wright, pled guilty to a reduced charge and is serving six months probation. The prosecuting attorney on the case stated that Ms. Wright was "extremely helpful in the case" and was not in any way a threat to the community.

It sounded like a couple of irresponsible kids not knowing when they'd crossed the line. Yet at twenty-one and twenty-five, they clearly should've known better. Anne sat back. The article was dated in the late 1980s. She sighed. It wasn't exactly evidence of embezzlement from a fund that wasn't established until 2008.

Anne looked for Merle Meyer next. She didn't find anything about the 1987 marijuana possession or the 1988 theft of his grandmother's car, but she did find an article about a missions trip he took in 1991. The title read, *Meyer is a Man on a Mission.*

Merle Meyer is headed around the world as of Monday. The twenty-seven-year-old is taking the journey of a lifetime as he heads from Mexico City, Mexico, to Mindoro, Philippines, to Accra, Ghana. While abroad he will be helping local missionaries with all manner of projects, from reroofing a church to teaching Sunday school to children in the small villages outside of Accra to helping with medical missions in the Philippines. "I'm confident Merle will be a huge asset to the people he meets," Pastor Jenks from the Deshler Community Church of Christ said.

Clearly something had happened to change Merle from the course he'd been on as a youth. Glancing at her smartphone, she looked up the church that was listed in the article. Pastor Jenks still served that congregation.

Glancing at her watch, she decided to make the short drive over to have a chat with him.

* * *

Anne parked in the lot of the Deshler Community Church of Christ. The pavement was in dire need of replacing. The asphalt was heaved in many places or completely missing—deep pot-holes looked like a connect-the-dots puzzle across the gray expanse. Tufts of grass poked up here and there. Anne climbed out of her car and made her way into the cool brick interior.

The church secretary lifted her gray head when Anne entered. "Good morning," she said. "Are you looking for Pastor Jenks?"

"Yes, I am," Anne said.

She pointed Anne to the sanctuary where the older man knelt in prayer at the railing. Anne moved into the second pew from the front, waiting for him to finish, not wanting to disturb the hushed moment.

After a few minutes he rose and turned toward her. "I thought I heard someone come in," the white-haired man said as a broad smile filled his face. His eyes were gray, and he reached to shake hands with Anne.

"I'm sorry to intrude," Anne said, rising. She introduced herself.

"I welcome intrusions when it comes to God's people." He motioned her to sit back down, then sat in the front pew, turning to talk to her and resting his arm across the back.

"What can I do for you?" he asked.

"I've been doing some research for a friend, and I came across your name in a newspaper article," she said.

"Which article are we talking about?"

"It was about Merle Meyer, many years ago. He was taking a missions trip around the world."

Pastor Jenks nodded as the memory returned.

"How well do you know him?"

"Merle Meyer?" His brows knit together. "Like my own son. Actually, he and my son graduated together."

"Does he still attend here?"

"Sure does. He and his family have come here for several generations. Are you looking for Merle?"

"No. This is about something else."

The pastor sat back, waiting for Anne to go on.

"He was arrested in the late eighties. Do you know about that time?"

"I do indeed. Hard time for that young man. He was struggling deeply, still trying to figure it all out. Gave his family some very rough days."

"But he came through it?" Anne guessed.

"Yes, he did. Took a bit. He went on a youth retreat, and that time turned his life around. He started coming back to church, got involved in helping others…"

"And that was when he went on his missions trip around the world?"

Pastor Jenks smiled. "It is. It's gratifying as a pastor to see people really commit themselves to serving Christ. It took a lot to get Merle there." He chuckled. "He and his family are a testament to how people can make an impact on the world." He shook his head. "It's a good, good thing."

* * *

Anne called Karina on her private number first thing when she got back to the library but got no answer. The Miller twins were at the front desk, Remi checking in books while Bella helped patrons with their checkouts.

Anne was still thinking about Merle Meyer. One question remained—how Merle had avoided foreclosure when it had already reached the newspapers. Usually, by that time a person had missed months and months of payments and had failed to negotiate any sort of agreement with the bank.

When traffic in the library eased Anne called Karina again. This time she picked up. "Is the address you gave me for Merle Meyer correct? I'm just wondering if he's moved within the past four years." She read the address from the foreclosure notice to Karina.

"That's the same address," Karina said.

"Do you know anything about his foreclosure?"

"No." She paused. "Foreclosure? He never mentioned it."

"Not even a word?"

"Nothing."

Anne thanked her and hung up.

Merle Meyer's address was approximately halfway between Blue Hill and Deshler. Anne told the Miller girls she'd be gone for less than half an hour at lunch. She just wanted to get a glimpse of his home.

She wove through the rolling hills, past farm fields and stands of hardwood trees, until she saw it — a three-story mansion surrounded by pastures and white horse fencing. A pristine horse barn added to the pastoral setting. Several horses grazed in the distance.

Anne glanced at the paper where she'd written the address to be sure it was correct. How had they been able to keep that out of foreclosure?

* * *

Anne had written down the names of the references Merle listed on his LinkedIn account. She picked up the phone and called the first one when she had a break that afternoon. Considering that the withdrawals were in one hundred dollar increments she knew it wasn't all that likely that the thefts would have kept Merle's home out of foreclosure, yet she needed to know what had happened, how he'd avoided that fate. And the thief had taken over two hundred thousand dollars, a significant enough sum to help anyone who was hurting financially.

"Rand and Rand Law Firm," the deep voice said.

"Good afternoon. My name is Anne Gibson. I'm the librarian in Blue Hill. To whom am I speaking?"

"This is John Rand."

"Merle Meyer has you listed as a reference on LinkedIn. I was hoping I could ask you a few questions."

"Merle Meyer? Sure." She could hear the man shuffling in his chair.

"How do you know Merle?"

"He's a client of mine. His agency is, actually."

"How long has he utilized your services?"

"Goodness, ten years? I'd have to look it up."

"Since he has you as a reference I'm wondering what can you tell me about him?" Anne knew their legal relationship meant that the man could share only limited information. She hoped a more open question would leverage something of importance.

"Merle's a straight shooter. The kind of guy who'd go to bat for the underdog. He's done it time and again for me and he does it constantly for the people who come to his agency."

"For you personally?" Anne probed.

"Sure has. Visited me in the hospital when I was there. I had severe burns after a propane explosion. Merle stepped in and helped my family in very practical ways. Took my boys to their ball games. His wife brought over I don't know how many meals. Kept us going. You can't even fathom that kind of friendship till you see it in person. That's what he does for orphans, you know. Just a really good guy batting on their team."

"Has Merle ever had any financial difficulties?"

He paused and Anne wasn't sure if he was going to answer. Finally, "He and his wife were in some trouble a few years back. But after all he'd done for me and mine, well, it only seemed right to help them out."

"You mean the house foreclosure."

"Yeah."

"So you brought his mortgage up to date."

"I did. That's what friends do."

Well, that answered one question. Though the possibility that Merle could have taken the money remained. Yet if Merle was as self-sacrificing as his friend claimed, the likelihood that he was the thief was growing slimmer and slimmer.

* * *

Jinx Hendricks lived in a micro house on the edge of Blue Hill, in the backyard of a man named Lon Hogan. Lon met Anne at the front door when she stopped in later that afternoon. His hair reached to his waist and was pulled straight back from his face in a ponytail. A five o'clock shadow tinged his dark complexion, offsetting pale blue eyes.

"Jinx isn't here right now," Lon said when Anne told him who she was. He held a guitar in one hand as he pushed the screen door open.

"Can I ask you a few questions about him?" Anne asked.

Lon raised a curious eyebrow. He stepped back and let Anne into the flat-roofed house. Despite a large front picture window, the interior of the house was dark, with dark-paneled walls and plants hanging from macramé plant holders that clung to the ceiling. He set the guitar on a stand in the corner, then led her to an orange-and-tan floral couch that looked like something straight out of *The Brady Bunch* TV show.

"How did you and Jinx become acquainted?" Anne asked.

"He's my brother-in-law." Lon laughed. "I married his twin sister Jenny."

"I didn't know Jinx had a twin."

Lon nodded. He shifted on the couch and crossed his left leg over the knee of his right.

She glanced through a back window at the tiny house that belonged to Jinx. It was the size of a nice garden shed, up on wheels with a tiny covered porch off the front of it. A long extension cord wound from it toward the house.

"When did he come to live there?" Anne asked.

"Not long after his divorce. Can I ask what this is about?"

"I'm sorry," Anne said. "I didn't mean to sound so mysterious. I'm doing a little digging to learn about a foundation that my aunt created—Heaven's Child. It's run through the adoption agency where your brother-in-law works."

"And so...what? You think Jinx is a thief?" he guessed. "I wouldn't put it past him."

"What makes you say that?"

He pointed out the back window. "I'll admit, ever since his divorce Jinx hasn't been the same. He used to be this Boy Scout—

top of his class, overachiever. You name it. Then his son got killed and his marriage fell apart, and well, he fell apart with it. I mean, look at how he lives. He's a freeloader. Took on that weird name…Jerry Hendricks never would've done any of those things."

"You don't care for your brother-in-law?"

"Sure I do. I mean, he's my wife's brother. I *have* to care about him. But when he was younger he was a different person. It was a lot easier to like him."

"You mean the Eagle Scout."

"Exactly. He's fallen a long way from that kid."

"So if he is a thief, where do you think he'd spend the money?" She took a risk.

Lon shrugged. "Knowing Jinx, he'd give it away. Just because he could."

* * *

Alex came in to the library around the same time Anne returned from Lon's. He held a sheet of paper in his hands and said, "Information on Ginny Stein."

Remi and Bella Miller were still manning the front desk, so Anne motioned him to her office in the back.

"How did you get this?" Anne said, glancing at the names — a professor Ginny'd had in college, two roommates, several couples who'd utilized her as their social worker for adoption.

"I found her résumé on Monster.com," Alex explained with a wink. "I *am* an employer, after all, so I have access to that side of the Web site."

"And I'm just sure she was looking for a construction job." Anne lifted an eyebrow.

"You never know. These are people who know Ginny." He handed Anne his cell phone. "Should I call, or do you want to?"

She called the first number, the professor, and got voice mail. Anne hung up. "There's no sense in leaving a message," she explained.

She dialed the next number, a roommate. "I thought she lived with her parents," Anne said to Alex.

"I think this was in college."

The line rang. A few minutes later a breathy sounding voice answered. "This is Bonnie." Anne could hear crying in the background.

"Did I catch you at a bad time?" Anne asked.

She heard what must've been the closing of a door, then quiet. "I can hear you now," Bonnie said. "It's naptime, so…"

Either she was a mother or she took care of others' children. Anne introduced herself and told Bonnie the reason for her call. "We're looking for information about Ginny Stein. You were roommates?"

"Is Ginny missing or something?" the woman asked.

"Oh no," Anne said, "we're doing some research." She glanced at Alex. "She has a boyfriend—Kirk Johnson?"

"Is he in jail again? That guy's trouble," Bonnie confided. "I don't know why she hangs out with him. He has a rap sheet a mile long."

Anne jotted the information down so Alex could keep up with the conversation. He pulled up a chair alongside her desk as she talked.

"How long have they gone out?"

"Oh, several years. She keeps hoping he'll propose, but he never will."

"Has Ginny ever been arrested?"

Bonnie hesitated for a moment before answering, obviously weighing whether she should confide such information. Then a few moments later she said, "She was arrested once for identity theft."

"She was?"

"It was a few years ago. That's why she lives with her folks, because she can't get credit."

"Was she convicted?"

"No, she managed to get off. Good lawyer or something. Daddy has sway."

They talked for a few more minutes. Finally, Anne thanked the woman for her time and hung up. She handed the phone back to Alex then groaned as she raked her hands though her hair.

"What's wrong?" Alex said.

"Don't you see? We aren't narrowing anything down here! Everyone is a suspect."

Chapter Twenty-One

Half an hour after Alex left, Anne's phone rang. Only a few patrons milled about, two on computers in the media room on the second floor, and a mother and her three preschoolers reading in the Children's Room, but there was no one on the first floor where Anne was.

She took the call in her office. "Hello. This is Anne."

"Anne, it's Dr. Jones."

Everything in the room stopped moving. Anne blinked, and it was as if she'd hit the slow-motion button on life. The doctor's voice sounded far away. She could hear her, and yet there was an echo in Anne's ears, like a shout across a wide canyon. Doctors didn't call with good news. If tests were negative they'd send letters, have their nurse call. They only called when the news was bad. Anne felt her heart beating. One beat. Two.

"I have your test results back," the doctor said.

Anne waited. Her vision narrowed.

"The biopsy was negative."

The words didn't register.

Wait. Negative. Had the doctor really said that? That meant no cancer. Suddenly everything snapped back into regular time.

"So I'm okay?"

"Yes," the doctor said, then she went on, "except the PTH test showed that you have hyperparathyroidism."

"Hyper what?"

"Parathyroidism. There are four glands next to your thyroid," she said. "They regulate the calcium in your blood. Your blood calcium and parathyroid hormone levels are high, so you've been leaching calcium from your bones."

"So…I could get osteoporosis?" Anne guessed.

"Exactly," the doctor said. "I need you to get a bone density test to see how much damage the disease has caused, whether you're at risk for broken bones. Then we're going to want to get you scheduled for surgery."

"Surgery?"

"We need to take the offending gland out. It's a pretty straightforward operation. You should be able to go home the same day."

"Are there risks?"

"There are always risks."

Anne was trying to wrap her mind around what had just occurred. She scribbled down "hyperparathyroidism" as well as a few of the details the doctor said, then Dr. Jones transferred her to scheduling to set up a date for the bone density test and the surgery.

As soon as she hung up, she typed the long word into her search engine, clicking on the Mayo Clinic link that talked about the disease. She began to read:

Hyperparathyroidism is an excess of parathyroid hormone in the bloodstream due to overactivity of one or more of the body's four parathyroid glands. These glands are about the size of a grain of rice and are located in your neck.

The parathyroid glands produce parathyroid hormone, which helps maintain an appropriate balance of calcium in the bloodstream and in tissues that depend on calcium for proper functioning.

Anne reached for her phone again without thinking and began to punch in Alex's number.

What am I doing? She stopped. *I can't run to Alex every time I feel needy.* She placed her cell phone face down on the desk and covered her face with her hands.

Lord, it's You I need, she prayed. *Thank You that it's not cancer.* The thought came and with it relief. A weight lifted from her chest. *It's not cancer!* She should be elated. And she was.

Yet knowing she still needed surgery, that there was still something wrong with her, was disconcerting. What if something happened while she was on the operating table? What if the bone density test showed that she'd suffered significant bone loss? New fears flooded in. She closed her eyes, willing her mind to settle. If Eric had been there, he'd have placed a calming hand on her back.

I miss Eric, Lord. I miss him now, when he would've been here supporting me, loving me. I miss him telling me the truth, reminding me that it's going to be okay.

She hadn't realized she was crying till she pulled her hands from her face and saw the curious four-year-old girl's eyes staring at her. "Are you sad, Ms. Gibson?" the child said from Anne's office doorway.

Anne wiped the tears away and smiled at the little girl. "I'm fine, sweetie. I'm just fine."

* * *

Alex stopped by the library again later that afternoon, just as Anne was hitting her afternoon slump. He wore a dark-colored baseball cap and a plain black T-shirt. He ambled to the checkout desk in his familiar gait, pausing to chat with one of the Miller girls.

"What do you have there?" Anne asked, pointing to the cup of coffee he held in his left hand.

"For you," he said, holding it up. "I knew Wendy wasn't coming to your rescue today, so..." He set the cup on the checkout desk in front of her.

"You're a life saver." Anne circled her hands around the warm paper cup.

Then Anne noticed the sheet of paper he held in his other hand. "More information?" Anne lifted an eyebrow.

She wanted to tell him about the doctor's call, yet she held back. She didn't want to cry again here in the middle of the library with patrons milling about.

"Since we're hitting dead ends trying to figure out who's stealing from Heaven's Child, I did a bit of research about that boy," he said.

"The one your sister and Rick wanted to adopt? Did the agency tell you where he was placed?"

Alex shook his head. "No. Ginny said that they can't give that information out till he's of legal age, but I did manage to find this."

He laid a Deshler newspaper clipping from the prior month on the desk. The headline read, "Accident on I-99 Leaves Woman and Child Fighting for Their Lives."

"This is the same boy?" Anne lifted her face.

"Yes. It's the same child described in the referral."

Anne scanned the lines till she found the mention of the child in the referral. About the same age that child would have been too. She could see the lines in Alex's face—it pained him to know the boy who could have been his nephew may have died.

"I'm sorry," she said.

"It doesn't say he died, just that he's in critical condition." He poked his finger at the paper.

"So did you search for an obituary?" she asked.

"I did. There wasn't one."

"So he survived."

"Yes. But don't you see?" Alex said, his face was glowing with excitement. "He's not only alive, but as of one month ago he still hadn't been adopted. He's in foster care, and we know the name of his foster mother."

Anne didn't want to answer him. She knew how he'd react. Yet she could see the end result of this trail, and she worried that he and Ryan would be disappointed. There had to be a reason the child had never been adopted. What if he had some fatal disease or a disability that Alex couldn't manage? Whatever the reason, it could devastate Alex.

"What is it?" he finally pushed.

"Why are you chasing this down?" she asked.

"I have to," Alex said. "For Ryan. He could've had a brother. He didn't need to be alone all this time."

"He hasn't been alone. He's had you."

"You know what I mean. Besides, we could be a family, like a real family."

"What are you saying? That you want to adopt this boy?"

"I don't know...I might."

"You know how hard it is to raise children alone." Her words echoed those she'd said to her own children just a week prior. Yet it was true.

"Of course I know how hard it is," Alex said. "I also know how rewarding it is. Think of it, Anne. Ryan could have a little brother. Would you deny him that?"

* * *

In the end Anne had let it go. She hated arguing. She wanted to be a friend, even if that meant sticking by Alex when he made decisions she didn't agree with. So when he asked her to come with him to meet this foster mom, perhaps meet this child, she couldn't turn him down. Even though in her heart she knew it could devastate him. It was precisely *because* it could devastate him that Anne needed to go along.

Finding the address of the woman in the newspaper article wasn't difficult. A search on the Internet, a few clicks, and they had it. So after work that Friday they headed straight there.

The house was in the country, a two-story Colonial surrounded by tall pine trees and a massive garden to the east. Free-range chickens pecked at the ground as Anne and Alex pulled into the gravel driveway that formed a U in front of the house. A lazy-looking hound dog lifted its head from the wraparound porch that circled the first floor.

"Are you nervous?" Anne asked Alex, noting the way his hands wrung together as they climbed down from his pickup.

"A little," he admitted.

There were children everywhere, it seemed. Sounds of their laughter rang in the summer air when Anne and Alex made their way to the front door. A large wooden playset with slides and swings created a hub of activity in the front yard. A girl about eight years old approached them first. Her jet black hair was in pigtails that stuck off the side of her head like Pippi Longstocking's.

"Who are you?" she asked revealing a missing front tooth.

"I'm Anne and this is Alex. We're looking for your mom."

"My mom doesn't live here," the girl said.

"Well, maybe your foster mom?"

Alex gave the woman's name.

The girl bolted for the front porch, shouting, "Anna Mae!"

Several long minutes later, a woman who looked to be in her mid-thirties came out of the house. She moved slowly, like someone twice her age, and Anne could see that she wore a brace on her left leg. She motioned for them to join her on the porch that stood several tall steps off the ground.

"I'm sorry," she said, when Anne and Alex finally reached her. "I have a hard time with those steps still."

Anne and Alex introduced themselves.

Anna Mae had long blonde hair that reached to her waist, and her eyes were so blue they looked liquid. She motioned toward the padded furniture that lined the front of the house, and they each took a seat.

"I'm so sorry about your accident," Anne said. "Do you know how long recovery will be?"

"It's already been a month, but they're telling me another eight weeks. I'll just be glad to get rid of this brace. How did you know I was in an accident?"

"We read about it in the paper," Alex said.

Anna Mae looked down at her leg. "It's slow going," she admitted. "The doc says I'm lucky to be alive, so I'm counting my blessings. But there's no telling how long it will be before I can walk without pain. I hope eight weeks is enough." She studied them both, then added, "But you didn't come here to find out how I'm doing just from reading some newspaper article. Did you?"

"No," Alex admitted. "There was a boy in the accident too. We're hoping to find him... to meet him."

"You want to meet a five-year-old boy? How do you know Noah?"

"We don't know him." Alex let out a nervous laugh. Then finally the whole story came out—the Slaters' desire to adopt, the home study they'd kept a secret, the referral, their deaths as they made their way to tell the family the good news that they were about to welcome another son.

"I still don't get it," Anna Mae said. "What does meeting Noah accomplish now? What's the point of it?"

"To be honest," Alex said, "I'm not sure. I just want to meet him. He was meant to be my nephew." He looked her in the eyes. "That means something to me. I don't know." He glanced at Anne. "Maybe I could adopt him." Anne was surprised that he'd confided as much.

Anna Mae's smile was not unkind. She shook her head. "If only I could give that to you," she said. "Noah was taken to another family after the accident. Social Services said I couldn't handle him with the injuries I sustained. He was too rambunctious for me to keep up with. The other kids"—she gestured to the mayhem of play in her yard—"they listen to me pretty well, help me out. But Noah was a handful. A sweet boy but still a handful…"

"Did he suffer injuries in the accident?" Alex asked.

"He was fine as far as the accident went. Had a mild concussion—but he'd recovered fully before he left us."

"Do you have any idea which foster family he's with?"

Anna Mae shook her head. "They don't tell us those things. I wish I knew. All I know is that he was placed with a family in Bellefonte."

"Why wasn't he adopted after Rick and Marla died?" Anne asked, curious as to why the child hadn't made his way to another adoptive family.

"He had some health issues. Needed heart surgery."

"As a baby?" Alex asked.

She nodded. "He had the surgery, but he'll always have to watch out for problems with his heart. It looks scary on paper. Prospective families see that and they get afraid, so they take the next referral they get." She sighed. "Everyone wants the perfect, healthy child, so it bumped him off the waiting lists and into foster care. The irony is that if those same parents had given birth to that boy they wouldn't have thought twice about keeping him." She looked out across the yard. "I know everyone has their own struggles."

Chapter Twenty-Two

I'll call the county and ask them where he is," Alex said as they made their way back to Anne's house in his pickup truck.

"He's a minor—do you seriously think they'll just hand out that information to any stranger who shows up?"

Alex sighed, staring out the car window as he drove the winding roads back to Blue Hill. Late afternoon sunshine whispered through deciduous trees, sending echoes of light onto the road surface.

"What else am I supposed to do, Anne?"

There was a long silence. She didn't want to answer him. She couldn't give him the answers he wanted. "Let it go, Alex. Marla and Rick are gone."

"Don't you think I know that? Come on, Anne. Don't be condescending."

"I wasn't trying to be…"

"Sure, you weren't. Every time I've brought this up you've discouraged it. Like I'm not an adult who can make up my own mind. I'm not a child, Anne. I know what I'm doing, just because you don't like it…"

They pulled up in front of the library and Anne waited for him to say more.

"I didn't mean…," Anne began again.

"Just save it," Alex said, lifting a hand like a police officer stopping traffic. "I'm done with this conversation."

Anne got out of the car, slammed the door, and moved up the walk.

She felt like a heel, and yet indignation rose up too. She'd tried twice to apologize to Alex and both times he'd shut her down.

Well, fine, Anne thought. *I have better things to do than save you from yourself.*

* * *

Anne's heart was heavy that night. She and Alex hadn't made up. She hated that, but he was being obstinate. No good could come from his search. He didn't have the resources to take in a child with health issues, especially as a single parent. It would only break his heart. Didn't he understand that? She was just trying to protect him.

When did it become your job to protect Alex from himself? That thought pointed a gnarled finger. *You didn't even tell him that the doctor said you don't have cancer.*

Anne sighed. She finished chopping onions for the tacos she was making. The two Hayden kids that Ben and Liddie had befriended — Natalie and Isaac — were over for supper. Anne leaned out the third-story window and called down to the foursome to come up. The clamber of feet filled the back staircase and within minutes the house was an echoing chamber of children's voices. Hershey was in the middle of all of them, a happy Lab with an enormous grin.

Anne set the fixings on the kitchen counter so the kids could go through a line to fill their shells rather than the endless passing of dishes that tacos always seemed to present.

When they were all settled with their heaping plates around the table, Anne offered a prayer of thanks.

"Mrs. Gibson," Isaac said as he took his first bite of taco. Sauce dribbled down his chin.

"Yes, Isaac." Anne handed him a napkin.

"I know the man in your picture." He dabbed at his face, then took a drink of his soda.

"Man? What picture are we talking about?" She looked at Ben.

"I showed him the pictures you found of Aunt Edie in India," Ben said.

"You mean the orphanage director—you know him and his wife?"

"I know him too but no, I was talking about Mr. Gee. He comes around sometimes. He talks to me."

"And you recognize him from when he was a little boy?" Anne found that hard to believe.

"Yeah, because he has the same scar on his chin that he had when he was little."

Anne had seen the scar in the picture. She remembered wondering where he'd gotten it.

"Is he a nice man?" Anne was curious to know the boy's take on the man his mother had described as sad and lonely.

"Yeah, he's very nice. He tells me stories."

"What kind of stories?"

"Stories about a little Indian boy with an American mother." That piqued her interest.

"Are these fictional stories?" She watched the boy as he gave it thought.

Isaac shook his head. "No…I don't think so."

"So who are they about?"

"Him when he was a boy."

* * *

Mona had given Anne her aunt Edie's travel journal, but Anne had felt she'd known the whole story behind Edie's trip to India after her talk with the retired missionary, so she hadn't taken the time to read it other than a cursory glance. Suddenly, with Isaac Hayden's revelation that Thomas Gee had an American mother, her interest was renewed.

Once dishes were washed and put away, Anne pulled the leather journal from the nightstand where she'd put it. The leather cover crackled in protest and Anne wondered how long it had been since anyone had read the words her great-aunt penned here.

The inside cover read,

Edie Summers
India, 1993

Anne began to read the first entry:

I am on a plane, traveling about as far from Blue Hill, Pennsylvania, as is humanly possible while still remaining on this planet. India, they tell me, is about as foreign a place as I can imagine. I've talked to many people about the culture there. They all say that I simply can't prepare emotionally for what I will experience. The depths of poverty will be unimaginable, and there is nothing I can do to fortify my senses against what that will do to me. And perhaps I don't want to fortify myself. Perhaps the true devastation of that sight will inspire me. I hope so.

I only know that God is with me. He loves the poor more than I can comprehend. So it is only with His power that I can go. Prompted by His love to reach a lost world. I only ask that He will open my eyes to see how a middle-aged single woman can make any kind of difference in a sea of hurt.

Anne turned to the next entry, dated the next day.

Well, I've finally arrived in Mumbai, India, and I want to cry. I'm sure the jet lag weighs in to what I'm feeling and the heat is unrelenting. Perspiration drips off my face and neck from morning till night. There is no relief from it.

The shanty towns around Mumbai – I've never seen anything like them. One home is connected to the next in a maze of tin and lumber, all poorly constructed. Their interiors are dark, a tunnel from one to the next. It is so oppressive.

How can people live like that, especially in this heat? It makes me ashamed to live as I do, all alone in my majestic Victorian house. I know that God has a purpose for me there as He does for these people here. Yet I can barely stand to see it.

The wonder, however, is that in the midst of this gray swirl of dust that is India, there are bright spots. The women wear bold-colored saris, their beautiful smiles white against brown skin – it is as if all that dark, dusty mass is the canvas for them. They are the artwork of India.

And yet isn't that truly how God sees all of us? His artwork here in the midst of a decaying world? I asked Him to open my eyes and oh, how He has! For all that grieves me here, there is joy. And that is baffling to me. Joy in poverty. The same kind of joy that God gives to us in our hopelessness. It's something to take hold of.

Then the next excerpt, two days later:

I visited Lance and Laura Stieb's orphanage today. Those children have stolen my heart! Especially one little boy – Thomas Gee. He has the most infectious grin, and he runs to do whatever I ask. If I say I need a tissue he's up and looking for one. So generous, even with so little to offer. At his young age he understands what many adults in the western world fail to comprehend. Life is not about acquiring but about giving, just as Christ, who was God, gave up everything for us.

Who can comprehend that but a child?

I wish I could adopt the boy. Oh, that India didn't have such stringent laws on international adoption for single people. I've told him that while I can't take him home he can still be my faraway son. I will write to him and love him from afar. He says this is good enough. I don't think it is but I will pray that God will provide for him. How it breaks my heart to leave him here!

Anne read the entry again. Aunt Edie had loved Thomas Gee, had wanted to make him her son. And in a way he was her son, though not legally. She had loved him, and what was being a mother if not that?

Every entry revealed a part of her great-aunt that Anne had only glimpsed in her youth, a woman of deep love, who cared for the world even if their lives were nothing like her own:

I am challenged by this place, she wrote in Kolkata. *Tomorrow I meet with Mother Teresa. What will I say to her? What kind of help can I offer to a woman who has done so much? Part of me wishes I could stay here, live in India and help these people. And yet I am afraid too. Afraid* that I have too little to give, that I wouldn't have the stamina, the determination to run that course.

Aunt Edie thought of moving to India? That thought startled Anne. How different life would have been for Anne if her great-aunt had made that choice.

She read on:

I met Mother Teresa today. What a humble, dear woman. I walked with her as she tended the sick and dying at her mission – Missionaries of Charity. The sight will forever be etched in my memory – both her unflinching kindness and the devastation those poor people face every day.

That she would take time out of her chaotic schedule for me, a spoiled woman from the West. Yet she acted as if she had all the time in the world, that I was as important as those she tended. How humbling that was. There was no rush, no hurry to ask me what I was about and move me on. She listened to my desire to help. She honored me. Yet who am I? I asked her this and she said, "The Son of God thought you were worth an awful lot. He can do anything. You are simply His vessel."

I'd forgotten that. I'd been so busy trying to figure everything out that I forgot He already has a plan. I don't have to save the world. He already did that. I don't have to struggle to make things happen. I can simply rest and let Him use me. Oh, there's power in that! Freedom. So I will pray and ask God what these small hands can do.

And that will be enough.

Anne read for a while, each entry detailing that day's events, as well as the heart of her great-aunt. The final entry said the following:

I'm back in Mumbai, ready to fly out tomorrow for the States. I'll give this journal to Mona Robinson, who has become a dear friend to me these past weeks. I couldn't have made it through my time here without her. Not only is she a knowledgeable travel companion, she understands my desire to help. Not just for two weeks but for a long time to come.

After much conversation with her, I've decided to start an international adoption agency in the Blue Hill area. If people understand the great need I have seen here I know they will respond as I have. They will give and make these children theirs.

She suggested I contact Merle Meyer and Ron Fields, friends of hers who are knowledgeable about adoption law, to get started. I pray my meetings with them go well, that they will be as moved as I have been to make a change for the children of India and the world.

Lord, Edie had written at the end of the entry, *I cannot begin to fathom Your love for this world. My heart is broken by what I've seen here, yet I know that Your heart is more broken. That You came as Jesus said, "to bring Good News to the poor" — such Good News indeed! Your love for children is Good News.*

Anne closed the cover and sat back. Such a generous heart Aunt Edie had. It inspired Anne to be more like her. *So how can I do that, Lord?*

Her thoughts returned to Thomas Gee and to the photos of children Liddie and Ben had brought back from their time with the Haydens. To little Klara, whom the Haydens longed to adopt. She sensed the answer was in Mother Teresa's words—to simply wait and let God use her as His vessel.

* * *

For some reason Anne had been thinking about Cheryl all day. She wondered if that was the answer to her prayer, to help ease the burden that girl carried alone in caring for her mother. The scripture she'd read that morning reiterated what was on her heart:

As much as you did this to the least of these you did it to me.

Anne realized she didn't need to worry so much about Thomas Gee, a man on the other side of the globe whom she could do little to help, when there were people here in her own neighborhood that she could reach out to. She would pray for Thomas of course, ask God for a way to help him and others like him. But for Cheryl, Anne could be a friend. Her thoughts turned to the meager home, the hospital bed with monitors beeping...Hospital bed?

Didn't Cheryl say that she worked at home? What exactly could a college dropout do from home that would pay for something as expensive as a hospital bed? Anne reached for her laptop and looked up the cost of the item. A new hospital bed listed at around thirteen thousand dollars. Though of course she could've gotten it used and she had mentioned that the county helped out...But would the county pay to remodel her home so Cheryl could keep Inez with her? That Anne wasn't so sure of. Still, it was probably much cheaper than the cost of putting the disabled woman in a nursing home.

Anne glanced at the bedside clock. It was only seven thirty yet she was tired. What would it be like not to be so tired all the time? That would be something to look forward to.

Her thoughts returned again and again to Cheryl, until she finally decided she needed to see her. She called Bella Miller and was happy she was free to come over and sit with the kids for an hour, so she could stop by Cheryl's house. When she arrived, the TV was on loud. Voices emanated through the screen door when Anne knocked on its wooden frame. Inez was there, lying motionless in the bed, her eyes rheumy, her skin pallid. She blinked slowly.

"Cheryl?" Anne called into the house, knocking again. She could hear movement in the back.

Finally, the young woman came out. She seemed surprised to see Anne. "I didn't hear you," she said. Then she laughed. "That's twice now, isn't it? Maybe I should get a doorbell."

There was a moment of awkward silence before Anne said, "Could I come in?"

"Forgive me." The girl's face flamed. She pulled the screen door open and motioned for Anne to have a seat. "I forget my manners sometimes," she said.

The interior of the house was warm, matching the warm weather outside. Anne wondered if they had an air conditioner. She'd think someone in Inez's condition would need that.

"So what brings you back my way?" Cheryl asked.

"I was just thinking about you. I hope you don't mind my intruding like this."

"No, not at all." Cheryl moved to stand on the other side of Anne, between her and the door to the kitchen. "I can get you something to drink, if you'd like."

"Sure," Anne said.

Cheryl scooted back into the kitchen. Anne could hear her getting ice and opening a can of soda.

Anne moved to the doorway. "You've been on my mind lately," Anne said again. "How you manage your mother's needs by yourself…"

"You're too sweet," Cheryl said.

Anne noticed that the small Formica table was covered in papers, a laptop computer open in their midst. A small printer hummed on a cart-on-wheels in the corner. "I'm sorry. I caught you in the middle of something," Anne said.

"Oh, it's fine." Cheryl waved the apology away. She handed Anne the Coke, then led the way back to the small living room. "I was just doing a little work."

"How do you support yourself? Now that you don't work for Bring Them Home?"

"Freelance work," she said. "Data entry, that kind of thing."

"For one company or several?"

"Several." Cheryl took a sip of her Coke, then added, "It's easier than working in an office. Taking care of Mom...I'm here if she needs me." She shrugged.

"That's perfect." Anne sat back. "Can I ask you something?" She waited a beat before going on. "How do you handle all this? I mean, emotionally? Do you have friends, people who support you?"

She could see that Cheryl hadn't expected the question, that it unnerved her. Her eyes clouded and her lip quavered. "I do okay." She shrugged.

"Would you mind if I came by from time to time? Maybe we could do something." Anne laughed. "That sounds lame. What kind of things do you *like* to do?"

"Why would you do something like that?"

"Because I...care."

Cheryl stared at Anne for a long moment. "I don't know what to say. Thank you."

Anne and Cheryl set up a regular date. Thursday mornings before the library opened Anne would go over for coffee, take something for breakfast, and the two of them would chat. It was a simple start. Cheryl could be at home for her mother, yet still have a friend.

The young woman seemed so grateful, yet Anne felt she was the one being blessed.

CHAPTER TWENTY-THREE

Anne woke very early Saturday morning. She lay awake, her mind roiling through all she'd discovered in the past few days: talking to Anna Mae about the boy from the referral, her argument with Alex, the Haydens' decision to adopt little Klara, reading Aunt Edie's journal. The outcome of her biopsy and blood work. And of course getting to know Cheryl Bergen better.

Finally, she got up and padded to the kitchen, pausing at Liddie's open door. The little girl was sleeping on her stomach, just as she had when she was a baby, her mouth gaping, making little murmuring sounds.

Anne couldn't think of anything more beautiful. She sighed and shut the door, careful not to wake her. Here she was, stressed about this or that, chasing down leads when the thing that mattered more to her than anything else on the planet was those two children. What was wrong with her? She thought of Alex, still aching for his sister and brother-in-law as she ached for Eric. Did grief ever really end? No, she realized. It just took new forms.

She sat in one of the chairs that looked out on to the back lawn. From here, on the third story, it offered a lovely view of Blue Hill as the faint early-morning sun sent brilliant shades of pink and lavender across a purple-blue sky. Wisps of clouds, brushstrokes in gray.

She tugged the afghan from across the chair's back and tucked it around herself, then noticed the Bible lying on the small table alongside the chair. Anne reached for it and let the pages flip open where they would.

There was something about the Word of God that never failed to comfort her. Like the afghan across her back, it warmed her, filled her with reminders that God had taken care of others across the ages, so many others, and in miraculous ways when He needed to. He would do no less for her and her children. He'd promised as much when He'd said, "I will never leave you or forsake you."

She glanced at the page that fell open and read the verse from John 14:27: "Peace I leave with you; my peace I give you; I do not give to you as the world gives. Do not let your heart be troubled and do not be afraid." Anne smiled and let her fingers trail the words on the paper.

"Thank You," she whispered into the morning, repeating the words to herself. "Do not let your heart be troubled."

The only answer was found there. He understood the anxiety that came with life on planet earth, the devastation of grief. He cried with those who cried. He'd cried with her when Eric had died and she'd felt so alone. He'd cried with Alex and Ryan for all they'd lost. No one was more compassionate than Him. No one was more capable of consoling than Him.

Maybe discovering the existence of Ryan's almost-brother *was* for a reason as Alex had said. Maybe Alex's idea of meeting him could bring a measure of healing, knowing the child who could have been his nephew.

* * *

Alex finally showed up at her door again before she opened the library on Saturday morning. His head hung low and his blue eyes looked down when he stopped by her place.

Anne felt guilty that he was the one to come to her. She should be more humble, more willing to be the first to bend. Hadn't she been the same way with Eric? So stubborn. She didn't like that about herself.

She cared about Alex, from the time she was five years old; he'd been one of her dearest friends.

"I was hoping we could talk," he said.

"Of course." She motioned to the chair next to her in her sunny living room.

He was silent for a few long moments. Anne watched him, waiting, not wanting to rush him. He drew in a deep breath. "I've been struggling," he finally admitted. "All this stuff with Marla, Heaven's Child, adopting a boy...It brings everything back to that day." His eyes shimmered. Anne could almost see the memories in his gaze.

"I know," she said.

He raked a hand through his hair.

"I'm like a washing machine with too many clothes on one side. My balance has been thrown off." He met her gaze. "I want so badly to figure out who has been stealing that money all this time—four years! That's a long time for someone to keep stealing. It's one thing to grab some cash once, but to keep doing it month after month? I'm almost afraid to find out who is doing this. And yet the pain it dredges up...If it was someone Marla trusted..." He shook his head. "And yet it's not as if anything we do will change anything. None of it will bring my sister back."

"Justice isn't a bad thing," Anne said.

He pursed his lips, considering that. "I'm not so sure, Anne. Justice doesn't cure. It doesn't give anyone hope. Only forgiveness does that. And the longer I sit and think about it, the more anxious I get."

"Do you want to stop looking for the thief?"

"No." He paused, blew out a breath, then leaned across his knees, toward Anne. "I need to keep looking, to finish what Marla started. It's this boy—the one who Rick and Marla wanted to adopt. I think I should take him, make him my son."

Anne didn't say anything.

"I know you don't agree," Alex went on, "that you think it'll be too much for me to raise two boys."

"You're right. I didn't think meeting him was a good idea. But I've been thinking. Maybe becoming a family, knowing him, could be a good thing."

"You think I can handle it?"

"It won't be easy. A five-year-old is a lot of work, but I think you can handle anything you set your mind to."

"Even as a single dad?"

"You've been a single dad to Ryan these past few years, and you've done a great job."

"You think so?"

"I know so."

Alex blew out a heavy breath. "You tried to apologize and I didn't let you," Alex said.

"I am sorry," Anne said. "If you want to look for this boy, I'll help you. I'll support it. Regardless of your reasons."

"And you'll help me find the thief?"

"Of course."

Alex released a swoosh of air, pent up frustration. Anne felt the relief of forgiveness then too. There was nothing as freeing.

"I have some news," she added.

He looked her in the eyes, expectant.

"I don't have cancer."

He gave her a hug.

Quickly, she moved away and allowed the moment to pass. She was afraid of the pull that drew her to him. She'd already lost Eric. She couldn't bear to lose Alex too.

"So what's causing the exhaustion?" he asked.

"I have hyperparathyroidism—it's a malfunction of one of my parathyroid glands. They regulate calcium levels in the body."

"So…it can be repaired?"

Anne nodded. "A little surgery. The doc says I'll be out of the hospital the same day."

"Oh, Anne, that's great."

She glanced at him. Relief filled his gaze.

"You know," she said. "I'm thirsty. Want a Coke?"

"At eight o'clock in the morning? Why not!"

He laughed, and Anne scurried off to the kitchen to get him a cold beverage.

He followed her into the small room and took a chair at the table in the corner. He pulled out the list of possible thieves they'd made earlier, his hand resting in his hair like a plow in a field, making furrows in tufts.

They'd added new, relevant facts: that Merle's friend had given them money to repay the outstanding debt on his mortgage, that Jinx had fallen from his former model-citizen state to essentially being a homeless freeloader, that Ron Fields's wife had a less than stellar past, and that Ginny Stein had been arrested for identity theft and had a boyfriend with a long rap sheet. Not that past indiscretions meant they'd committed this particular crime, but simply that a trend of failure and justification often led to greater and greater excuses, greater and greater crimes.

They stared at the sheet for several long minutes.

"I don't know," Alex finally said. "Where do we go from here?"

Anne sat back. "We're overlooking something. That's all. There's something right in front of us that we aren't seeing."

Alex blew out a breath. "If Marla knew the money was being stolen, why didn't she tell someone? Why didn't she come to me so I could help her find the thief, put a stop to it before they took over two hundred thousand dollars?"

"She tried. She wrote to Edie..."

"But did Edie even read it?"

Anne shook her head. "It was sealed...I doubt that Edie saw it. Surely, she'd have looked into it if she had."

Anne went to retrieve the letter she'd found before, hoping it held some clue.

The second half of the letter seemed particularly meaningful:

When I go through my records everything seems to be in order. Yet I've gotten calls from several donors whom I have no record of. They show me cancelled checks made out to Heaven's Child, even receipts they've gotten for those same funds, and I haven't been able to reconcile the two.

I'm not asking you to solve this for me. I know you have a lot on your plate, and I don't want to burden you. But you know the staff at Bring Them Home better than I do. I'm hoping you can advise me, offer your wisdom. Because I deeply need it.

"Wasn't that what Karina said?" Alex turned to Anne. "That she got phone calls from people who weren't in her database."

"I don't understand how that could be," Anne admitted, "when some of those same people are getting tax receipts."

"Somebody's going to a lot of work."

"Do you have that statement that Marla wrote on?" Anne asked. "The one with the codes?"

Alex pulled it out of his satchel and handed it to Anne. She studied it for several long minutes.

C.B.—?; J.H.—30; G.S.—35; R.F.—?; L.K.—5; M.M.—?

"Don't you see?" Anne finally said. "These are the initials of the staff from Bring Them Home." She pointed to each as she spoke, "Cheryl Bergen, Jinx Hendricks, Ginny Stein, Ron Fields, Lincoln Krueger, Merle Meyer…"

"So what at the numbers and question marks about?" Alex asked.

"Maybe the amount of money she thought they'd taken, or how many grants they'd filled?" She looked at Alex. "I'll ask Karina." Anne dialed while Alex watched. "Karina," Anne said as soon as the woman answered. "I'm looking at a bank statement from December 2009. Can you look up how many grants Jinx, Ginny, and Lincoln wrote that year?"

"Um…sure?" Karina said. "I'll call you first thing Monday morning."

When she hung up Alex looked her in the eyes. "So you think that Marla suspected those three?"

"Perhaps," Anne said.

* * *

The kids' play was coming up on Sunday instead of the regular morning service, with a special dress rehearsal Saturday morning. After Alex left, Anne got them out of bed and into their costumes.

Liddie was portraying life in Korea. She wore a traditional *hanbok*, an ornate robe with overlong sleeves, and she walked on *namaksin*, traditional Korean wooden shoes. Her hair was pulled up rather sloppily beneath the Korean *jobawi*, an embroidered silk hat with flaps over each ear.

"Don't you look cute?" Anne said.

Liddie gave her an indignant look. "I'm not meant to look cute," she said. "I'm meant to be *authentic*."

"Okay." Anne tried her best to keep a straight face. "How do you know that word?"

Liddie said, "I know a lot of words, Mom."

Ben came out of his room wearing the traditional clothing of Ghana, a brightly colored smock over a pair of dress slacks. Hershey padded after him.

Ben met his mother's look. "Don't laugh," he warned.

"Why would I laugh? You look wonderful."

Ben crossed his arms over his chest. "Right."

"Come on," she said. "This is going to be fun."

He stood alongside the table, picked up a strawberry, and tossed it in his mouth. "We sit down to eat breakfast," Anne said. "We don't stand like animals at a feeding trough."

"We need to get to church." Ben looked at the clock. "Practice is starting in half an hour."

"Church is five minutes away."

Anne patted the chair next to her. The boy took his seat, and they bowed their heads to pray.

* * *

Saturday afternoon was warm. Though there was air conditioning in their third-story apartment, Anne hated being cooped up on a sunny summer day. She called Pam Hayden and Wendy Pyle and asked them if they'd like to grill out at the lake with her.

Liddie jumped up and down when Anne asked her if she wanted to go swimming. "I love you!" she oozed, giving her mom a big hug.

"Help me gather what we need so we can meet the Haydens and the Pyles at the lake."

Both kids scurried off to pull together their beach attire, towels, as well as the necessary sand shovels and buckets for castle-making while Anne got supper supplies ready. Within half an hour they were in the car and on their way.

"Are you ready for your performance tomorrow morning?" Anne asked the kids in the rearview mirror as she left the city limits for the lake.

"I am!" Liddie bounced up and down in her seat. She wore her swimsuit already, a cute two-piece with a sailor motif. "Want me to sing my solo for you?"

She started singing. Ben rolled his eyes and looked out the window. When Liddie finished, Anne said, "That was good, honey. How about you, Ben?"

"I'm fine." She could tell by his tone that he wasn't in the mood to discuss the matter so she let it pass.

"Hey," Anne said, "I need to tell you two something." She'd been looking for the right moment to tell them of her upcoming surgery.

They must've known by her tone that what she was about to tell them was serious because both children straightened in their seats and gave her their full attention.

"What is it, Mom?" Ben said.

"You don't need to be worried," she began. "I went to the doctor last week and found out that I need a little surgery."

"Surgery...like when the doctors..." Liddie made a cutting motion across her neck.

Anne laughed. She shook her head at her five-year-old. "The doctor is just going to take a little gland out that's causing me problems. It's the size of a piece of rice."

"Will it hurt?" Liddie said.

"No, baby. The doctor will give me medicine so it doesn't hurt. I'll be home the same day, so you'll barely even notice that anything's different."

She looked at Ben. He was so serious. His brow furrowed.

"You going to be okay, Buddy?"

Ben nodded. "I will if you are."

"I will be."

Chapter Twenty-Four

By the time Chad Pyle pulled the bratwursts off the grill, the kids had all but forgotten their concern over Anne's upcoming surgery. Anne sat on folding chairs with Pam Hayden and Wendy Pyle while the men hovered over the glowing coals and the children splashed in the water.

"So it's easily fixed," Wendy said of Anne's operation. "Aren't you glad you went? You would've never known and spent your whole life sleepy. Or worse, you could've broken a hip."

"Either way it's a good thing I have you and Alex to bring me my afternoon coffee." She winked at her friend, then turned to Pam, who seemed unusually quiet. "Have you heard anything from the Shriners about Klara?"

"Yeah," she said, "they turned us down."

"Already?" Anne felt sorry for the couple—she'd gotten their hopes up only to have them dashed.

"I got a call this afternoon—the programs nearest Blue Hill are all full. We'd have to fly to Minneapolis if we wanted to get her into the system."

"Could you do that?" Wendy asked, leaning forward.

"We could, except we don't know anyone in Minneapolis. We'd have to pay for lodging, all those added expenses. And if any of her stays are long, that can add up fast."

"Maybe there's something like Ronald McDonald Houses where you could stay," Anne offered.

"Maybe," Pam said. "We have to figure it out."

"Does this mean you might not adopt her?"

She could tell the missionary didn't want to answer the question. Finally, Pam repeated, "We'll have to figure it out."

Anne felt gut-punched. She'd been so hopeful that Klara could become a Hayden. The thought that it might not happen was devastating.

* * *

"Why don't you join me and Mildred at the Keystone Cafe after church?" Anne said to Alex when she saw him the next morning. "I have an idea."

She and Alex took their seats. A hush fell over the congregation as the lights went down, the only remaining light in the sanctuary that of the colored windows along the sides.

Then the children began to sing. Their tune was quiet at first, a rhythmic African song. The kids began to file toward the front, their voices as one. To Anne it was lovely, the sound like angels. When they gathered across the front they looked like a rainbow, with their bright costumes and grinning smiles. They moved into the next song and began to sway. This tune held a lilting quality and Liddie's sweet voice lifted above the rest.

Liddie grinned at her mother as she sang, then turned, fully lost in the moment. Unabashed, unashamed. Even Ben seemed to relax as the program moved on. Each child had their lines to perform, a blurb about each country — what their primary religion was, how many citizens knew Christ, the traditions they celebrated.

When each had said their parts and the songs finished, Cory Hayden moved to the microphone. "Thank you for coming today," the missionary said. "We have been so privileged to serve your children these past two weeks. They share much in common with the children of India who we love so dearly." He turned to motion to the kids. "They're all heaven's children."

Anne glanced at Alex. She could see that he'd caught the connection. Heaven's Child. A new idea began to form instantly.

Perhaps the Shriners had fallen through for Klara, but that didn't mean that God had given up on the little girl finding her adoptive family. She was, after all, also heaven's child.

* * *

Alex and Anne reached the café on Main Street, parking in the front and climbing out. The kids had headed to the Summer Fun picnic after church, an event that would likely eat up much of the afternoon, so it was a perfect opportunity to get together to ponder the case, especially now that Mildred was back from her trip to Hawaii. Anne hoped their dear friend could offer new insight.

The Keystone Cafe was a hopping little place, tucked in one of the historic downtown buildings. The decor was pure charm with checked white-and-salmon floors and whitewashed brick walls. The food was sophisticated and delicious—offering both Italian fare, as well as grilled sandwiches that rivaled any Anne had ever had in New York.

Mildred Farley had gone on ahead after church. She was seated at a table in the back when Anne and Alex got there. She wore an aqua-colored pantsuit with a large daisy brooch. A jaunty blue hat offset her white hair.

"How are you?" Mildred said as she stood up when Anne and Alex drew near. Her skin was tanned, and she had a renewed vibrancy about her. She gave Anne a hug and a peck on the cheek, doing the same with Alex.

"Did you have a good time?" Anne asked, taking her seat.

"Oh, I did indeed," Mildred said, returning to her chair. "I didn't do much other than lay on the beach."

"You never struck me as a sun worshiper, Mildred," Alex teased.

Mildred laughed and waved the comment aside. "I can assure you at no time did I don a bathing suit. And I had an enormous beach umbrella to shade me. No, I'm more of the read-a-book variety of beachgoer." She took a sip of her ice water and added, "But it was lovely. Just lovely. We saw dolphins, went on an ocean excursion…"

The waitress arrived, Susan Kendrick, an acquaintance of Anne's. She laid the menus on the table and asked what Alex and Anne would like to drink, then left to retrieve their coffees.

"So"—Mildred leaned in and looked at Anne—"what have you found out about your aunt Edie's visit to India?"

"A lot actually. Do you know Mona Robinson?"

Mildred pushed her lips together in thought, then said, "Yes, I think I remember that name. She was a missionary with the Stiebs, no?"

"Yes she was. She became a good friend of Aunt Edie's too. I spoke with her about Edie's time there—she was very helpful." She paused as Susan returned to deliver Anne's and Alex's coffees.

"Are you ready to order?" Susan asked.

Anne ordered the Greek Geek, a salad with red onions, black olives and feta cheese, while Alex and Edie both opted for the special — the Keystone Meatball, a sandwich with Italian meatballs and fresh mushrooms smothered in a marinara sauce with mozzarella and parmesan on a hoagie bun.

When Susan left, Anne continued telling Mildred about her visit with Mona Robinson. "You already knew about her trip, the impetus for creating Bring Them Home adoption agency and then later Heaven's Child..." She exchanged a glance with Alex, who took a sip of his coffee. "That was where she met Thomas Gee and met with Mother Teresa."

"Right...," Mildred said, obviously eager to hear what else they'd learned.

"I found out why she didn't tell us about any of it," Anne said, "I brought this along." She opened the journal to a bookmarked page. "It's a travel journal she kept. Mona gave it to me."

She handed it to Mildred, who read out loud for Alex's benefit:

"I have been challenged by the example I've seen in Mother Teresa. So humble. Never talking about her own great deeds, and there are many. But more concerned about those she's helping, anyone she comes in contact with. It prompts me to consider the Scripture from Matthew 6:1–4 that talks about seeking the praise of others when it is His favor that truly matters. Lord, help me to break this need in myself. Help me to know that Your words 'Well done' are all I need."

Mildred lifted her eyes when she finished reading, "I guess I can't argue with that." She shook her head. "Still, she could've said something to me!"

Anne laughed with her and sensed that they were both missing Aunt Edie, her generous spirit, her tenacity.

Mildred handed the journal back and looked between Alex and Anne. "And Thomas Gee?" she asked.

"Someone she cared for. She wrote to him for a long time, but that was all."

Mildred nodded. Anne began to tell her about their discoveries regarding Marla and Heaven's Child. The note she'd written to Edie asking for help in discovering the thief, their assumption that the thief was a member of the Bring Them Home staff. Then that Marla and Rick had been trying to adopt, had gotten a referral the very week of their deaths. Anne didn't mention Alex's desire to meet that boy, perhaps adopt him. She left that to him, if he chose. It wasn't hers to share.

Mildred's brow furrowed. "I don't understand. How could someone steal from a charity? To take money from children in need..."

"It happens all the time," Alex said. "People find ways to justify it. They tell themselves that God can provide through other means. They tell themselves that their needs or desires are more important than those of the recipients from the charity—after all those people are often distant, not someone they know or care about. Or they use stealing as a way of getting back at someone for an injustice done to them." He shrugged.

"Do you think that's what this is? Someone getting payback?"

Anne was surprised that Mildred used such a term.

"I have no idea," Alex confessed. "I only know what Marla suspected and Karina too. We don't have proof that the money is being misappropriated. We only have Marla's suspicions and possible motives."

He sat back and Anne took over. "We've talked to all the staff at Bring Them Home, as well as former staff." She laid out what they'd learned in her absence.

"So who is your top suspect?" Mildred asked as Susan returned with their food. Anne could smell the meatball sandwiches. It made her mouth water. A few moments later she brought out Anne's Greek Geek salad.

"Right now *everyone* is a suspect," Anne confessed. "Except Merle Meyer."

"You think it's a conspiracy?" Mildred asked.

"It's possible." She exchanged a look with Alex. Yet to think that everyone at the agency could be involved in stealing from a fund that was meant to help families pay for adoption seemed unthinkable. Anne couldn't imagine how deeply such a scheme would have hurt Marla and Edie if they'd known about it.

Finally, she shook her head. "I don't think so. We need to narrow it down somehow. One thing that was interesting was that the files of the cases that Marla had listed on the statement, the ones receiving grant money—none of them had home studies."

"Why would that be?" Alex asked.

Anne paused to consider. "I think they were dummy files, meant to look like real cases."

"Fictional cases?" Mildred raised an eyebrow.

"Sure," Anne went on, the idea gaining traction. "So that if anyone wondered where that money was going they'd look in the files and see that there were indeed recipients."

"Until they checked further," Alex said. "And saw that there weren't checks made out to any of them, just ATM withdrawals."

Anne nodded.

"Who would have done that, do you think?" Mildred said.

"I think we can eliminate Lincoln Krueger," Anne began. "He's a retired social worker. He has Alzheimer's. I just can't see his wife doing it...The rest all have access and possible motives. Well, except for Cheryl Bergen. She doesn't have access now that she doesn't work at Bring Them Home."

"So that leaves Ron Fields," Alex said. "He lives in fancy houses. Ginny Stein, whose boyfriend has a police record."

"She has a record too," Anne reminded him. "And Jinx Hendricks..." Anne told Mildred a bit about him, his devastating losses of both his son and his marriage. That he lived in a micro house in the backyard of his sister and brother-in-law, jaded and suspicious of the world.

"What we need is solid evidence," Mildred said.

Anne pulled out the statement that bore Marla's writing that they'd stared at countless times.

"We haven't figured this out either." She pointed to the letters and numbers she'd first noticed on the backside of the statement. "But I think this is something. I called Karina to see how many grants Jinx, Ginny, and Lincoln filled that year."

"Do you think this could be the amount each stole?" Mildred asked.

"That only adds up to seventy—even if it was in thousands, it doesn't align with the $237,000 that's been taken." Anne paused, wrinkling her brow. "Except that the thief has stolen more since Marla died..."

Anne quickly added up the amount withdrawn only to the time that Marla died — $85,000.

"Just add up the transactions that were ATM transactions," Alex said. "Add up the check withdrawals separately."

Anne did the math again — $70,000 came out via checks. That lined up with what Marla had written on the statement, except that there was another $15,000 through cash withdrawals before Marla's death.

"So," Anne was thinking out loud now, "the checks are the amounts each person doled out in actual grants — $70,000 at the time of Marla's death."

"And the thief had stolen only $15,000 by that time."

"So the rest of the $237,000 stolen has been after Marla's death."

"That remainder could have been avoided if Marla had caught them."

"That kind of thinking helps no one," Anne said.

"I know," Alex said. "But I can't help think it."

"This does show one thing," Anne said. "Marla considered Ginny, Jinx, and Lincoln suspects."

Mildred lifted her sandwich and took a bite. Sauce dribbled down her chin and she wiped it with a napkin. "If only you could *demonstrate* the theft somehow," she said.

"You mean like send in a donation and watch the funds go through the system?" Anne said, an idea forming.

Mildred nodded.

"I think there might be a way to do that."

CHAPTER TWENTY-FIVE

A nne rolled the driver's side car window down and slipped the envelope into the blue mailbox in front of the post office.

"What will this do?" Alex asked from his spot in the passenger's seat.

"I'm not sure it'll do anything," Anne confessed. She pushed the lever into *drive* and moved back on to Main Street.

"So we'll just wait and see?"

"Do you think you can figure out what Marla's password was? For the Heaven's Child bank account?" Anne asked as they made their way back to the library where Alex had left his car.

"If it's the same. It'll likely be changed since her death." He chuckled. "You ask me this *after* we send a check for one hundred dollars to Heaven's Child?"

"What can I say? I have confidence in you."

"I'm not sure that confidence is founded."

"Can you do it or not?"

"I can try."

Anne parked in her usual spot alongside the library and the two of them climbed out.

Wendy looked up from her spot at the checkout desk when they came inside. "Oh, you're back," she said. "Someone was trying to get a hold of you, Alex."

"Of me? Here?"

"I think they tried your house and Ryan told them you were at the library."

"Any idea who it was?"

"Some social worker." Wendy read him the name she'd written down earlier and a phone number.

"That's strange," he said, pulling his cell phone from his back pocket and dialing the number. "This is Alex Ochs," he said. "I'm returning a call for…" He read off the name Wendy had written down.

Anne watched his face as he talked. Curiosity, then recognition. Then shock.

"Um, thank you," he finally said. "I didn't expect this." He motioned for Anne to get him paper and pen, then he bent to write a phone number and a name. "Yeah, I just want to meet him, I think. I'll give her a call." Then he hung up and looked at Anne. His eyes were wide, as if excited and scared at the same time by what he'd just learned.

"Well?" Anne asked.

"It was the social worker in charge of the little boy Marla and Rick wanted to adopt. Apparently, Anna Mae called her after our visit. She explained the situation with my sister and brother-in-law, that I wanted to meet him." He crossed his arms over his chest. "While there are privacy laws for people who adopt, there are no such laws for this kind of situation. She said she thought it might be beneficial."

"Beneficial? How?"

Alex shrugged. "She gave me the name and number of the foster family that has him now. He's nearby." He looked Anne in the eyes. "We can actually meet him, Anne."

"When?" she said.

"I don't know." He confessed. "I need to think about it."

"Why?"

"I...I don't know about it now, if it's the right thing to do. I need some time to think about it."

* * *

Alex had tried every password he could think of. He and Anne sat side by side in her office after the shock of the social worker's news began to wear off. The bank's login page had turned up an "incorrect password" message.

"They'll lock me out if I try too many times," he said, groaning as he sat back in the chair.

"This is not a bust," Anne protested. "It has to be something logical." She typed "heavenschild" into the password box and pressed "Go."

The computer seemed to be searching, then the account's statement popped up on the screen.

"*Lookee* there!" Anne said.

"I'll never hear the end of this," he murmured.

Anne slugged him in the shoulder as the page loaded. There had been no withdrawals since the prior statement, though there were several deposits. The account sat at a balance of four thousand dollars.

"How long will it take for your check to clear?" Alex asked.

"Just a few days. It's so much quicker than it used to be."

"We'll keep an eye on it."

But the check still hadn't gone through the Heaven's Child account by week's end. Anne clicked on to her personal account to see if the check showed up in that account. There, two transactions down, the check had cleared two days after Anne had sent it.

She called Alex right away to tell him.

"I don't get it," Alex said. "How could it have cleared your bank without clearing the Heaven's Child account first?"

"I have a pretty good idea," Anne said. "Can you come over?"

He agreed and was at Anne's apartment within a few minutes. Anne was dialing her cell phone when he came up the back stairs. He gave her a questioning look, but she held up a finger and said, "Is Karina there?"

Ginny Stein had answered the line. Within a few moments Karina came on. "This is Karina."

"Karina, it's Anne," she said. "Can you read me off the account number for Heaven's Child?"

"Um...sure?" the young woman said. Anne could hear her shuffling papers for a few moments before she began to read the six-digit number.

"That's what I thought," Anne said when she'd finished. "Did you get a check from me a couple days ago?"

Again a pause. "Yes, I see it here," Karina said. "Why? What have you found out?"

"I'll tell you in a little bit," Anne said before saying farewell.

"So?" Alex said. "I don't get it."

"There are two accounts for Heaven's Child," Anne said.

"Two? Why would there be two?"

"Think about it—if you're trying to hide your stealing from the people who manage an account it's a lot easier if there is a real one and the one you're actually stealing from."

"So someone set up a second account? When?" Alex said.

"The week Marla died," Anne said. "And I have a pretty good idea who."

* * *

Anne went out to her car. Alex followed, completely baffled. Anne enjoyed keeping him in the dark, at least for a few minutes. They climbed into her sedan, and Anne started the engine.

When Alex could stand it no longer, he said, "Where are we going?"

"Cheryl Bergen's."

"I thought you'd ruled her out."

"I wanted to. I like her," Anne said honestly, "but it all adds up." She backed out of her spot and moved toward the tiny house just off of Main Street. "She needed money to pay for a house, remodeling it for her mother, a hospital bed, and monitors…She had motive, access—now that we know it was a second account. She could've easily created the dummy files before she left, to keep Marla at bay."

"But she's…"

"Sweet? I know." Anne met his gaze. "Yet desperate times call for desperate measures."

Anne made the last turn toward the small house where Cheryl and her mother lived. She knocked on the front door, calling Cheryl's name.

It wasn't until she pulled open the screen door that she realized something was wrong. Inez's eyes were rolled back in her head and her body was convulsing.

"Cheryl!" Anne called louder.

A moment later she heard the back door open. The younger woman came in with a load of folded towels under her arm.

"What's wrong?" Cheryl was instantly on alert. She moved to her mother's bedside, her eyes growing wide at the sight of her mother's frail body jerking back and forth. "Call an ambulance!" she screeched.

Alex instantly reached for his cell phone, telling the dispatcher what was happening and where to come. Anne made sure there was nothing in the way that would injure the unconscious woman. She seemed to settle, but the stillness that followed was even more terrifying than the seizures.

Cheryl was wailing, clutching her mother's hand, frantic with fear. Anne gently pulled her away as the EMTs arrived, giving them access to the woman who appeared dead. The convulsions had torn the heart monitor from her chest, so the eerie sound of a flatline filled the tiny house.

One of the EMTs turned it off while another bent to listen to her heart.

"She's alive," the thin, thirtysomething man said to Cheryl.

She inhaled relief. Then said to Anne, "I need to go with her."

Anne looked at the EMT, who shook his head. "How about if I drive you?" Anne soothed. "We'll meet them there in a few minutes. They need to do their work on your mom. We need to let them."

Cheryl nodded obediently, though Anne knew she was frantic.

"Just hang out here for a minute," Anne instructed while they got Inez ready to load into the ambulance. On the count of three, the strong men hoisted her frail body onto the stretcher that folded into the back of the ambulance.

Cheryl and Anne followed them to the door, watching as she was loaded into the back. Lights flashed as the vehicle moved down the street and out of sight.

"I need to go," Cheryl was murmuring.

"Do you want Alex to take your car, so you can get back home later?" Anne asked.

"Oh." Cheryl met Anne's gaze. "Yeah, that makes sense." She handed her keys to Alex.

Anne led Cheryl to her car, driving the short distance to the Blue Hill hospital. Alex followed in Cheryl's green compact.

Anne sent up a prayer for the young woman and her mother.

"I should've been in the house," Cheryl said. "I had no idea what was happening. Thank God you were there." She glanced at Anne. "If you hadn't come…" She shook her head and tears rolled down her cheeks.

Anne placed a hand on the young woman's shoulder. "Do you have anyone else I can call? Any family?"

Cheryl shook her head. "No. I don't have anyone."

* * *

All that night and into the wee hours of the next morning, Anne and Alex sat with Cheryl. Anne had called Wendy to ask her to take Liddie, Ben, and Ryan. Her friend instantly agreed.

Anne didn't have the heart to tell the young woman what she suspected. Not now.

Just after midnight, when Cheryl went to the bathroom, Alex pulled an envelope out of his jeans pocket and handed it to Anne.

"What's this?" she asked.

"Proof," he said, though there was only agony in the word. "It was in her car." Inside was a statement with Heaven's Child's letterhead addressed to Vic Michaelson, the donor Anne had spoken with, the Vietnam vet who'd given twenty-three thousand dollars to the charity.

"Sometimes I hate being right," she confessed. "You were right about justice too. Forgiveness is far more healing."

"Unfortunately, that isn't our call," Alex said.

A weight tugged on Anne's shoulders. She placed the envelope into her purse. "Cheryl isn't going anywhere," Anne said. "At least not right now."

An hour later, a doctor met them in the waiting room. Anne glanced at the clock: 1:03. Her eyes ached from being up so late. Cheryl had been pacing the room, but when she saw the doctor, she made a beeline to hear any news.

"It was another stroke," he said, his expression grim. "She's holding her own now."

"Can I go see her?"

"We're going to keep her in ICU today, see if there's any improvement. You can go in for fifteen minutes. You'll need to wash up, wear a gown." He glanced at Anne and Alex as he spoke, including them in the instructions. "She's fragile, so I want you to keep it calm. Don't excite her at all."

Cheryl nodded solemnly. "Can Anne come with me?" she asked the doctor.

"I suppose," he said, obviously reading the younger woman's fragile state.

Alex told them to go on ahead. He'd stay in the waiting room. Anne and Cheryl did as the doctor had instructed, then made their way to the darkened room, lit only by a perimeter ceiling light and the monitors attached to Inez's body. Cheryl's hand moved to her mouth, covering the lower half of her face as she stared at the woman she loved.

"Hey, Mama," she said. She took Inez's hand in hers and stroked the back of it. "I'm glad you're still here."

Inez didn't respond, not even a flicker of her eyes.

Cheryl and Anne stood in silence until their time was up. A nurse came in to check on Inez, so Anne and Cheryl returned to the waiting room.

Cheryl sat heavily and Anne took the chair next to her. Cheryl had stopped crying sometime during the night. Now she seemed calm, or perhaps it was shock or exhaustion.

"Are you okay?" Anne asked.

Cheryl nodded. "You know, don't you?"

Anne waited, not wanting to assume.

"I saw Alex give you the envelope." Cheryl looked at Anne, though Anne didn't register betrayal in her expression. Cheryl added, "You know about Heaven's Child, I mean." The tears returned then, a silent stream down her cheeks. "I didn't know what else to do," she confessed. "The bills were mounting up. I didn't want her to go to a nursing home. I'd promised her… That money was right there, every month." She looked Anne in the eyes. "At first it was an ATM withdrawal. Just a few hundred. It was too easy. Then I could see that Marla was catching on. She kept asking where the money went so I made up some fake files, fake cases. But I knew that I'd be found out. When she died, I went to the bank and created a separate account." She shook her head.

"The people who'd been giving through automatic drafts—they became my monthly paycheck so I could take care of Mom, could pay for her hospital bed and her medicines. As long as I sent them receipts, they were none the wiser. Bring Them Home had their donors still giving to them in the new account. If I hadn't overdrawn the original account, you would've never found out."

Anne didn't respond. She waited, knowing Cheryl needed to say more.

"But I'm *glad* you found out. That's the weird thing. I've been living with this guilt for so long, knowing I was stealing. And not just stealing from anyone. I was stealing from children!" She shook her head. "It's so despicable. So utterly selfish."

Anne gave her hand a squeeze.

"But we'd lost everything. First Dad…then when Mom had the stroke…" She sighed. "I'm not going to justify it any more. I'll turn myself in. I've made a bad situation worse. I'm done with that." She looked Anne in the eyes. "Do you think God will forgive me?"

"He already has. That's what He does."

"What will they do with Mom if I go to jail?"

"I'll help with that," Anne promised. She glanced at Alex who had turned to listen to the conversation. "We can talk to the county. Find a good situation for her."

"You'd do that for me?"

Anne nodded. "I would."

CHAPTER TWENTY-SIX

Inez was moved out of ICU the same day Cheryl was arrested. Anne stayed with the young woman as long as she could, until the officer took her into the back of the police station. Merle Meyer met Anne and Alex at the precinct just as they were about to head for home.

"I can't believe it was Cheryl," he said.

"I can," Anne said. "She's no different than any desperate person, looking for help." She thought of Thomas Gee, once a boy, struggling to survive in a cruel world.

The mountain of a man seemed to understand. "She has a lot of people to repay," he said.

Anne nodded. She glanced at Alex. He looked as exhausted as she felt.

"Can I ask you something, Merle?" Anne asked. "Is Heaven's Child just grants for adoptions or can the grants be used for other things?"

"What do you have in mind?" he asked.

* * *

He was a beautiful child, the five-year-old boy who would have been Alex's nephew and Ryan's baby brother. His name was Noah. He had curly, dark hair and equally dark eyes. Deep dimples etched his chubby cheeks.

Ryan was on the floor with the boy, showing him how to work the remote control car. Noah laughed loudly as Ryan put the miniature sportscar into action. He flattened his body on the hardwood floor as it zoomed toward him. Then he reached for it and Ryan showed him how to make it go. "Let me try!" he squealed.

Alex seemed mesmerized by the sight. Anne had been watching him as he gazed at the two boys and what could have been. She wondered if he would pursue the idea to adopt Noah, to finish what his sister had started.

Noah's foster mother came back into the room with a tray of lemonades. She was in her early thirties, pretty. Her eyes shone when she glanced at little Noah.

She handed glasses to Anne and Alex, then set one on the coffee table for Ryan.

"He likes you," she said to Ryan as she took a padded rocker adjacent to the couch where Anne and Alex sat.

"How long have you had him?" Anne asked.

"Since he got out of the hospital after the accident. He's such a sweetheart, just an answer to prayer." She took a long drink of her lemonade. "We've wanted children for a long time but haven't been selected for adoption by any of the birth mothers since we finished our home study. So when the social worker called to tell us a little boy was available to foster, we were all over it."

She looked first at Anne, then Alex. The joy in her expression was hard to miss.

"So you want to adopt him?" Alex said.

She nodded. "Very much."

Anne could see that the revelation stung Alex, yet she could also see acceptance. The boy would be loved. For Alex, that would be enough.

Ryan glanced up. "Could I come play with him sometime?" he asked.

"Of course," the foster mother said. "You can be like a big brother to him."

Ryan seemed to like that idea. He bent down to show Noah another trick the car could do. Noah chuckled again, deep in his throat. A sound of joy.

Anne hoped it wasn't an empty sound in Alex's ears.

* * *

When they finally said good-bye, Anne wasn't sure what to say to Alex. She waited for him, knowing that when he was ready, he would share his heart.

"He'll be happy," he finally said. Anne knew he meant Noah. "That's all I needed."

"I know."

"We'll be happy too." He glanced at Ryan in the rearview mirror. "Won't we, Bud?"

"Sure will, Uncle Alex!"

* * *

"Come on in." Wendy Pyle met Anne and Merle Meyer at her front door. Alex came in behind them. Reverend Tom was already there.

Anne had called Wendy earlier, asking if the Haydens were still there. It had been a full week since she had seen the missionary family. They had been on the road since Summer Fun had let out, meeting with some of their supporters, speaking at church events to raise awareness of the need for help in India.

Wendy gave Anne a wink as she said, "Pam, Cory, someone's here to see you."

"We almost have everything all packed," Pam was saying as they came down the hallway. When she saw the foursome in the living room, she exchanged a curious glance with her husband.

"What's going on?" Cory said. He looked at the reverend.

"It seems your friend Anne has been doing a few things behind your back," the pastor said. He raised an eyebrow and turned toward Anne.

"Don't look at me," Anne said, motioning toward Merle Meyer. "Merle has something to tell you."

"Now you really have my curiosity going," Pam said.

She and her husband turned toward the big man. A chuckle rumbled his belly. He reached into his jacket pocket and pulled out an envelope. "Don't listen to a word Anne says." He winked. "She mentioned that the Shriners had turned your little Klara down, so she talked to me about Heaven's Child…"

"Heaven's Child?" the missionary said.

Merle handed the envelope to Pam, who tore it open. As she read her shoulders started to shake, a hand flew to her mouth. "I can't believe it." She held the letter out to her husband.

"Tell me what it says already!" Wendy said.

Everyone laughed.

"It says," Anne said, "that Heaven's Child will take out a health policy that will cover Klara's care—surgeries, medicines, physical therapy." She turned to speak to Cory as well. "And not only her surgeries but any travel costs associated with bringing her to the States as well."

Pam was already bawling. Cory wrapped an arm around his wife's back and held her tight. "This is so generous," he said.

"No," Alex said, "it's just the *right* thing."

"I have to tell you," Anne added, "I'd always thought of myself as a generous person until I met you." Her face grew serious. "Your love for children, the way you sacrifice your own needs and daily conveniences so you can give to others—it challenges me." She glanced at Reverend Tom, then Merle Meyer. "To give up everything to care for orphans... well that's a powerful thing."

She gave Pam's hand a squeeze. "Thank you for that."

Epilogue

Anne could hear people talking, yet she couldn't quite get her eyes to open. She didn't recognize any of the voices. She was aware of a dull pain emanating from her throat. The darkness returned.

When she woke again she was able to open her eyes. The voices she'd heard before were still there. Now she recognized them as the nurses who'd talked to her just before her surgery. She glanced around the room—curtains, stainless steel tables holding other patients, monitors, IV stands. She was in the recovery room.

"How are we doing, Mrs. Gibson?" The nurse moved to the head of her bed and bent to look in her eyes. "Are you in pain?"

Anne nodded and whispered, "Yes." It hurt to talk. She could feel the bandage on her throat. The nurse turned to adjust the medication dripping into Anne's wrist. A few minutes later the pain seemed to ebb. Anne closed her eyes again.

When she woke she was in a private room. Alex was there with the children.

"How are you doing, Mommy?" Liddie asked. The five-year-old was next to the bed, her eyes searching her mother's.

"I'm doing okay, baby."

"I'm not a baby, Mom."

Anne couldn't help but smile. She grimaced in pain.

"Is that normal?" Ben asked Alex.

"I'm sure it is," Alex assured.

Anne was grateful that Alex was there to comfort her children. She turned to look at him. "When did you get here?" she asked.

"Just fifteen minutes ago," Alex said. "The nurse called as soon as you got out of surgery."

"Did they say how it went?"

"Perfect." He smiled into her eyes. "Just like you."

The compliment warmed her from the inside. "I'm not perfect, Alex. If anyone should know that, it's you."

"True," he said.

Liddie was still studying her mother. "Did they take all your rice out, Mommy?" she asked.

"Rice?" Alex asked.

"It wasn't rice, silly," Ben said. "It was the *size* of a grain of rice."

Anne started to chuckle, but the motion caused instant pain in her throat. "Don't make me…" she said.

Yet even though it hurt, the joy of having Alex and her children near her made it all worth it.

* * *

Within a few days Anne was back to her old self. She couldn't sing yet, but she'd been told that the ability would return in time.

The Haydens had returned to India. Anne could tell that the children missed Natalie and Isaac. They'd written, but it was never the same as being together in person.

Anne was glad to be back at work in the library.

The people of Blue Hill had rallied around her when they heard of her surgery. So many dropped by with Get Well cards and meals that she had a full freezer. She'd forgotten that about small-town life when she'd been living in New York, the way neighbors came out in times like this.

She was pushing the book cart into the Nonfiction Room to shelve some books when Ben came flying into the library. Several heads lifted to look at the nine-year-old.

Anne moved to him and said, "What is it?"

"A letter from India!" His eyes were wide and excited. He pointed to the foreign looking stamps and marks on the thin paper.

"Who's it from?" she asked.

There was no return address. Anne took the letter to her office and pulled out her letter opener.

Ben had followed, watching with interest, clearly hoping it was from Isaac.

My dear Anne Gibson, she read out loud for Ben's benefit.

I am pleased to make your acquaintance and to hear of my dear friend Edie Summers through our mutual friend Pam Hayden. Your great-aunt was a joy to me, a mother when I had none. She gave me courage to think I could grow into a man of faith, that God could use me in this difficult place, India. I had forgotten about that, but your kindness to my friend and her daughter Klara has reminded me.

I thank you. It is because of you, they tell me, that they have made our dear Klara their own daughter. It fills my heart to know that child will not grow up alone, unloved. She will know the love of a dear mother and father, as I knew the love of your great-aunt, though distant. As I care for my own little girl. Your great-aunt was a mother who showed kindness when none was deserved. I still keep her letters as a treasured memory of my childhood.

She showed me what true motherhood is – to give as she did. And as you do. You give hope to the hopeless. That is gift indeed.

I have asked Cory Hayden if I can help at the orphanage. I am good with my hands, a hard worker. He knows this to be true. So he has given me a job of maintenance around the orphanage. I am thankful for the post. It is an opportunity to serve, to give back to those who gave so much to me.

Yours truly,
Thomas Gee

Anne hadn't realized she was crying till she felt the wetness on her cheeks.

"See, Mom," Ben said. "God can use us to help anyone. Even a man on the other side of the world."

* * *

Inez had gone to the local nursing home, where she was doing relatively well. Anne visited Cheryl in prison every week until she was released on probation. The judge had been lenient with her, and Anne could see that Cheryl didn't take the kindness lightly. She'd vowed to repay every cent and she was working toward that end.

"I can't thank you enough," she told Anne when she stopped by the library to let Anne know that she had found a job at a nearby garden center. "I finished my first day. I really like my new boss."

"I'm proud of you for getting the job," Anne said. She gave the young woman a hug.

"You didn't give up on me. Everyone else would have! But you..." She gave her head a slight shake. "You were a friend when I didn't have a friend."

Anne gave her hand a squeeze. "I was only doing what I'd want someone to do for me."

"Well, you're an extraordinary woman, Anne Gibson. Extraordinary indeed."

About the Author

Emily Thomas is the pen name for a team of writers who have come together to create the Guideposts series Secrets of the Blue Hill Library. *Finding Home* was written by Traci DePree. Traci is the author of twelve novels, including the best-selling Lake Emily series, six books in Mystery and the Minister's Wife, another Guideposts series, as well as two other books in Secrets of the Blue Hill Library. She has five children, three adult daughters and two younger ones whom she homeschools in a rural town in southern Minnesota. She and her husband, John, have been happily married for twenty-nine years. To learn more about Traci and her upcoming titles, join the conversation at facebook.com/traci.depree. She loves getting to know her readers.

A Conversation with the Author

Q. *Have you ever visited an orphanage? If so, what impressed you most?*

A. I have. I spent a summer at an orphanage in Milot, Haiti, when I was sixteen. And I have many friends and family who work with orphans around the world. The thing that impressed me most is how amazingly normal these children are, eager to love and be loved. The need for families is huge and the rewards…surpassing anything you can imagine.

Q. *If God were to call you to be a missionary on a foreign mission field, where would you enjoy serving?*

A. I have longed for God to call me to the foreign mission field! Wherever He led me would be awesome. I have a deep affinity for African, as well as Asian countries. I have long wrestled with God on this issue, until I finally realized that wherever I am is His mission field. God loves people everywhere so there is no end to the ways I can show that love in tangible tidbits. It's why I am intentional about volunteering.

Q. *What was the most challenging time for you personally during the adoption process?*

A. Waiting! We filled out paper after paper, then we waited. Then more papers! The stack was huge. In all it took a year and a half from start of home study to bringing our daughter home. But when my husband and I set out to adopt we made a promise to each other that unless God closed the door we would see the adoption through any hurdle. Of course God loves adoption so He made a way through. Jem was worth every moment of waiting.

Q. *As a multi-cultural family, what are the biggest challenges you see your Asian daughter facing? What special experiences has your family encountered as the result of your adoption?*

A. I can't say that we've had very many big challenges yet. Our biological children were a lot more work! (We have three grown daughters and another just a few years older than Jem.) But Jem is still young so who knows what's ahead! She does think of her birth parents often and grieves not knowing them. I talk with her openly about them, wondering what they are like, if they regret their decision. Then I remind her that I'm glad she's my daughter!

Q. *Who in your own life demonstrates the gifts and graces of Aunt Edie.*

A. My sister Amy is Edie and so much more. She has a heart to save every orphan. There are so many children that her life (and her family's) touches. I'm so proud of her and my brother-in-law for the work that they do encouraging orphans and finding them families through their work. I love to see children find forever homes too! It reminds me that in Christ we too are no longer orphans.

Recipes from the Library Guild

Blue Hill Community Church BBQ Beef Sandwiches

3–4 pounds chuck roast
1–2 bottles chili sauce
1 jar pickle relish

Place the roast in a slow cooker on low, six or seven hours, till the beef falls apart. Drain fat and shred any meat that is still clumped. Add one or two bottles of chili sauce and one jar of pickle relish.

Serve on hamburger buns. Serves eight.

FROM THE GUIDEPOSTS ARCHIVES

This article by Karen Kingsbury originally appeared in
Guideposts magazine.

I brushed the bangs from my forehead and clicked *send* on an
e-mail, answering a question from a fan about a character
in one of my novels.

A child from Haiti. The words popped into my head like an
e-mail popping into my inbox. It had been a really long day:
working on my new book in the morning, taking care of family
and household stuff in the afternoon, then back to my study to
answer fan mail in the evening. I tried to dismiss the thought. But
it wouldn't be dismissed.

At that time my husband, Don, and I already had three
children but wanted more. Don had a good job as a high school
basketball and football coach. I had published half a dozen novels.
By any yardstick we were a blessed family.

But when our youngest, Austin, now two, was only three
weeks old, he had undergone major surgery to correct an inherited heart defect. He survived, but the ordeal practically killed
me. My doctor said that it was fortunate that neither of our other
children had inherited the condition. And Don and I didn't want
to take a risk with our next child. We started talking about

adoption—tentatively at first, then just about every day. We met with an adoption facilitator to explore our options.

"There are plenty of kids in America who need good homes," she told us. "But if you really want to go where the need is greatest, consider Haiti. It's the poorest country in the Western Hemisphere."

The facilitator mentioned one orphanage in particular—Heart of God Ministries, just outside the Haitian capital of Port-au-Prince. Don and I had agreed to take things slow. The orphanage had a Web site. But we hadn't yet looked at it.

But then one day, with the kids in bed, Don up in our bedroom reading and me down in my study with my writing done for the day, I couldn't resist. I typed in the name of the orphanage and clicked.

Heart of God's homepage popped up. "See our list of adoptable kids," said a banner down at the bottom.

Kelsey, our oldest, was twelve. Tyler was seven. Don and I wanted to fill the gap between him and two-year-old Austin. I narrowed my search down and clicked again.

A boy's face appeared on the screen. A boy with big brown eyes and a gentle, tentative smile. I could almost hear God whispering in my ear, *Adopt that boy.*

"Emmanuel Jean's grandmother dropped him off a year ago," said the text. "She believed with all her heart that a loving American family would make him their son."

I ran up to our bedroom and pulled Don away from his book. He followed me into my study and leaned over the screen.

"Are you sure?" he asked. "There are hundreds…"

"I know, I know," I said. "It sounds impulsive. Crazy, even. But I just know God wants that boy to be our son."

Don pointed to another banner that offered a free video.

"I guess we'd better get it," he said.

A package showed up about a week later. We hadn't brought up the idea of adoption with our kids yet. We waited till they were all tucked into bed before slipping in the video.

E.J. appeared. Same big brown eyes. Same sweet smile. And the same unmistakable feeling in my soul: He was meant for us.

The next day Don and I printed out E.J.'s picture, placed it in an empty chair in the living room and called Kelsey, Tyler, and Austin in.

"How would you guys feel about having a new brother?" I asked the kids.

"He looks really friendly," said Kelsey.

"He's five?" Tyler chimed in. "That's right between me and Austin!"

Don and I felt so encouraged we took another look at our finances. Why not adopt two children at once and save ourselves the time and expense of doing it again later! We got back on the Web site and found another boy, a close friend of E.J.'s. Like him he had a warm, sweet smile that tugged at my heart. Sean.

We initiated the adoption process. The first package of forms that came in the mail was thicker than our phone book. With each new form we tackled, the reality of what we were getting into hit Don and me harder.

Lying in bed one night, I felt my confidence — that sureness I'd felt when I first saw E.J.'s face on my screen — faltering. A noisy parade of what-ifs marched through my head. Were we taking on too much? Could we do this? Was the decision to adopt two boys really right?

Our adoption facilitator had made clear that Rule Number One of bringing a new child into a home with other children is to love all of them equally. You have to know that your adopted child is your child, end of story. I had three children I'd raised from birth—children who were as much a part of me as the blood that flowed in my veins. Who was I kidding to think I could let two total strangers into my house and be able to treat them with that same closeness? I hugged my pillow. *God, can I really be the mother you want me to be? To five children?*

Two months after E.J.'s face appeared on my computer screen, I boarded a plane for Port-au-Prince. Don would stay with our kids back in the States.

The orphanage—a low brick building surrounded by a wall topped with razor wire—lay on the outskirts of town. Inside, forty-two kids lived in a 1,400-square-foot space. Pigs rooted in garbage just a few feet from the front door. I knocked.

A woman, the head of the orphanage, greeted me. "It's a special day when a parent comes to adopt a child," she told me. "All of the children are so excited that you've come."

She led me out to a walled-off patio with a single cement bench. The kids followed after us. She called two boys out of the crowd—both so skinny their shoulders barely kept the necks of their shirts up. I recognized them instantly. Sean and E.J. I leaned down to hug them, when all at once another little boy emerged from the crowd.

"Hi, Mommy," this one said. Then, in a gesture so familiar it was as though he had known me forever, he brushed the bangs from my forehead.

Who was this child?

The orphanage director explained. The three boys—Sean, E.J., and this third boy, Joshua—were like brothers. For all intents, they were brothers. "Joshua knows you are Sean and E.J.'s mother now," she said. "That makes you his mother too."

It made no difference to Joshua that I wasn't taking him home. In his mind I was his mother nonetheless. How could that be? Trust. A trust beyond all questioning, all judgment, all logic. A trust that could only come from one place.

E.J. and Sean were allowed to come with me to the guest quarters. Joshua waited with the other kids to say good-bye. Surely, the reality would set in, and I dreaded the thought of hurting his feelings. I waited for his tears to come.

"Good-bye, Sean, good-bye, E.J.," he said. Then he turned to me. "Good-bye, Mother!" he said without a hint of doubt.

Doubt. It's something we adults are pretty good at. Sometimes it seems like the longer we live, the better we get at it. But it was a skill six-year-old Joshua had yet to learn. A little Haitian boy with no education, few prospects and barely enough meat on his bones to keep his clothes on, he nonetheless had room in his heart for faith. Faith that I was his mother. He simply knew. The same way I knew that night when those words popped into my head about adopting a child from Haiti. Who was I to tell him he was wrong?

I called Don that night to report on the day's events. I worried it would sound more like a plot from one of my novels than a real-life scenario.

"Honey, I don't know how to say this exactly, but there aren't two boys here for us, there are three." I told him the whole story. "I just can't bear the thought of leaving Joshua behind."

"Well then don't," said Don. "Two, three…bring those boys home."

Only Sean and E.J. could go back to the States with me on that trip. We had to go through the same complicated legal procedures to adopt Joshua. Six months later he joined our family too.

I won't say there weren't any rough patches, because there were. America—with its grocery stores full of food, its hot and cold running water and its completely alien ways, was a huge challenge for all three of the boys. But they had a family to love them every step of the way. And that's what counted.

Six years later the challenges haven't gone away. But these days they're the kind that any normal American family faces. For one thing, we've got three kids in their teens now, and I don't need to tell any parent out there that that brings a whole new world of hurdles.

Sometimes my life does sound like the plot from one of my books. But that's not so bad, considering whose plot it is.

Read on for a sneak peek of another exciting book in
Secrets of the Blue Hill Library!

Agree to Disagree

Anne Gibson smiled as she handed a book to her loyal library patrons, Betty Warring and Nellie Brown. The elderly sisters loved to take turns reading to each other and were slowly getting through the library's biography section.

"This just came in," Anne said. "I saved it in case you two might be interested."

Betty frowned as she peered at the title over the top of her glasses. "But we're on the Ns. This is the Duke of Wellington."

"Oh, you and your alphabetical system," Nellie said. "We can go back to the Ns later. This looks interesting."

"You're so impulsive," Betty grumbled. "It's why you always got in trouble when we were kids."

"I doubt that if we check a book out of alphabetical order, we'll get in trouble." Nellie winked at Anne. "We'll take this one. Thank you for thinking of us, Anne."

"Not that we've been reading as much as we normally do," Betty said. "It seems all everyone talks about is the new Beau-Mart that's coming to town."

"And by 'everyone,' she means herself," Nellie said to Anne.

"I recall hearing you talk just as much as me about it," Betty said.

"Well, it is rather exciting," Nellie said. "We've never had a big-box store in Blue Hill before, and there are so many sides to the issue."

"There's only one side as far as I'm concerned," Betty said. "It'll ruin Blue Hill if Beau-Mart ends up building here."

"What do you think, Anne?" Nellie asked.

Put on the spot, Anne hesitated. "Well, as you said, there are so many sides to the issue. I've been listening to all of them."

"You lived in New York for many years, didn't you?" Nellie said. "You're probably used to lots of big stores."

"It's true, we had a Beau-Mart about ten minutes away from our house in Brooklyn." Anne finished checking the book out to the two ladies and handed it to Nellie. "I hope you enjoy this one."

"I'm sure it'll be a nice break from all this chitchat about Beau-Mart," Nellie said. "It does seem to be polarizing people in town, don't you think?"

"Bye, Anne," Betty said as the sisters left the library.

The front door had barely closed before a striking Hispanic woman in her fifties entered the library. She had a chic pixie haircut that framed her oval face perfectly, and her deep brown eyes were dramatically rimmed with a hint of eyeliner making her appear more like an Aztec princess than a modern woman. Anne had seen her a couple weeks ago when the Beau-Mart representative had first come to town, but they hadn't spoken. The woman had been picketing by herself outside the Blue Hill Inn, where the rep was staying, and passing out fliers to anyone who passed by.

"Hi." The woman had a deep voice, slightly gravely, but her smile to Anne was wide and friendly. "I'm Isabel Alvarez."

"I'm Anne Gibson. I'm the librarian here. How can I help you?"

"I was hoping I could leave these here at the checkout counter." Isabel dumped an enormous purse on the counter and proceeded to pull things out of it as she dug for something at the bottom. Lipstick, tissues, pens, paper clips, a tube of toothpaste, and a roll of cloth medical tape piled up beside her purse. Several other things spilled out and fell onto the desk behind the counter, where Anne scooped them up.

"Sorry about that," Isabel said. "My purse is always so full…"

"No problem." Anne handed her a pocket mirror and a strange object, the size of a tube of lipstick, that was a folded piece of metal with foam padding on the inside.

"Here they are." Isabel pulled out a stack of fliers, a bit rumpled on the edges, and slapped them down on the counter. "Could you please pass these out to your patrons?"

"I'm afraid I can't pass out fliers unless they've been approved by a member of the Library Guild." Anne glanced at the top flier and was dismayed to see *BEAU-MART* across the top.

Isabel paused in the act of putting her things back in her purse. "What do you mean? These are important."

"Since this is a public library, and the contents are the property of the community, anyone who wants to pass out literature has to be approved by someone from the Library Guild first."

"But do you realize the damage Beau-Mart is going to cause in your community?" Isabel leaned forward, her dark eyes intent. "It will spell doom for local pharmacies, grocery stores, sporting good stores, clothing stores…"

"Regardless of what I think," Anne said, striving for a low, calm voice, "I'm afraid it's library policy."

"But Beau-Mart is the Evil Empire," Isabel said. "They are out to enslave us all and destroy the planet in the process."

Anne thought Isabel a bit melodramatic, but the woman's voice had carried to the nearby History Room, because a few patrons had come out to the checkout desk to see what was going on.

"That's just your opinion," said a man with short white hair and a square face. "Beau-Mart could be good for this community." Anne recognized the man but couldn't recall his name at the moment.

"How could it be good if it puts Newlands' Grocery Store out of business?" demanded an angry voice. Anne recognized him as Clark Bronski. His wife, Evie, and their three-year-old son often came to the library, but Anne didn't see them. They were probably on the second floor.

"You're one to talk, Clark," said the white-haired man. "You probably tore down the fencing between your grazing land and Hugh Zumfelde's property on purpose last week."

Clark had gone white. "That was an accident. The cows took down the fencing. It wasn't my fault they were blocking the access road to Hugh's land."

Anne cleared her throat. "Gentlemen…"

"The timing was convenient, wasn't it?" said the white-haired man. "It prevented the Beau-Mart representative from looking over Hugh's land that day. I'm a friend of his, and he said that the representative rescheduled the appointment but also expressed concern about the sturdiness of the fencing, thanks to your cows."

"I had nothing to do with that."

"You just wanted to prevent his property from being chosen by Beau-Mart," the man said.

"And what's wrong with that?" Isabel jumped into the fray.

"Everyone, please!" Anne didn't like having to raise her voice, but she couldn't let this argument go on, especially not being egged on by Isabel.

There was a moment of silence. Clark looked self-conscious. "Sorry, Anne. I'll go get Evie and Connor." He walked up the stairs.

The white-haired man frowned at him, then turned and stalked out of the library.

After the two men left the checkout desk, everyone else who had been drawn by the heated voices disappeared back to the other rooms in the library.

Isabel looked around, her face obviously disgruntled at losing her audience, but then she gathered up the things she'd taken out of her purse and turned to leave.

"Isabel, don't forget your fliers." Anne held out the stack of paper.

The sour look on Isabel's face made Anne wonder if she had left it on purpose, but she took the stack of papers with a breezy, "Thanks." Then she walked out the door of the library.

Anne heaved a sigh, but the anxiety from witnessing the angry exchange between Clark and the other man still lingered in her chest. Anne was worried about how divided the town seemed to be over having Beau-Mart build a store here.

"Mommy, is it time yet?" Anne's five-year-old daughter, Liddie, hurried up to the checkout desk, already wearing her swimsuit. Her excited smile lightened Anne's spirits.

Nine-year-old Ben followed her, also in his swimming trunks but wearing a T-shirt. "Is Mrs. Pyle here yet?"

"Not yet." Anne glanced at the clock. "Soon. Be sure to thank her for including you two in her outing to the community center pool this afternoon."

"Hey, are you two going swimming?" One of the library helpers, Remi Miller, was coming down the stairs from the second floor. "That sounds fun."

"We still have the backyard waterslide we used when we were kids." Remi's twin sister, Bella, followed her down the stairs.

"*Ooh*, waterslide." Liddie clapped her hands. "Then I wouldn't have to wear my purple dragon."

Remi and Bella looked confused, so Anne said to them, "It's Liddie's floater ring. It's shaped like a purple dragon."

"Oh." Remi laughed. "Our cousin's daughter has one shaped like a pink unicorn."

"Pink unicorn?" Liddie's chocolate brown eyes were wide. "If I had that, then Ben could wear my purple dragon and they could be friends."

"I don't need your purple dragon," Ben said, groaning. "I can swim without it."

At that moment, the library's front door opened and Wendy bustled in. "Hey kids! Ready to go?"

"Go get your towels and change of clothes," Anne told Ben and Liddie. "And don't forget Liddie's purple dragon," she added as the two kids pounded up the stairs.

"I'm really glad I was coming here anyway today." Wendy put a clipboard on the counter in front of Anne. "Now you can sign this?"

"What is it?" Anne glanced at the paper on the clipboard, and her heart thudded as she saw the words STOP BEAU-MART in bold letters across the top.

"It's a petition to prevent Beau-Mart from building a store in Blue Hill." There was a stubborn set to Wendy's chin. "We can't have them ruining our town."

Anne bit her lip. "You really think it would ruin the town?"

"Of course." Wendy looked at her in surprise. "You don't think so?"

"It would definitely change things," Anne said slowly.

"It would ruin the village charm," Wendy said. "And think about all the local stores that would be forced out of business. We can't stand by and let that happen."

"I definitely wouldn't want that," Anne said, "but the Beau-Mart representative has been looking at properties to the south of town. Surely, it wouldn't affect the stores in downtown Blue Hill?"

"It'll ruin the economy for miles around," Wendy insisted.

"Will it?"

Wendy's face grew red. "What exactly are you saying, Anne?"

"When I was in New York, I used to work with a couple women at the library who were struggling to provide for their families," Anne said. "They repeatedly talked about how Beau-Mart's low prices saved them. They wouldn't have been able to buy enough food for their families if the prices hadn't been so low, not to mention everything the schools required them to buy for their kids."

"If people want to go to Beau-Mart, they can go somewhere else." There was a mulish cast to Wendy's bottom lip.

"The next closest would be twenty miles away, and that takes gas," Anne said. "The new Beau-Mart would be in the south of town, near the lower-income housing area. I think the people there would really benefit from having it, and I wouldn't mind shopping there."

That last comment made Wendy's blue eyes flame like gas jets. "I can't believe you'd side with Beau-Mart over this."

"I'm not taking sides, Wendy," Anne said. "I just think there are valid reasons for having a Beau-Mart in Blue Hill."

"So you're not going to sign my petition?" Wendy rattled the clipboard against the desk.

Anne stared at the clipboard. The agitated feeling in her chest from the men's argument earlier had increased tenfold. She didn't want to argue with her closest friend, but she simply didn't agree with Wendy on this issue, and she couldn't, in good conscience, sign a petition she didn't believe in. "I'm sorry, Wendy, I can't."

"I'm very disappointed in you, Anne." Wendy shoved the clipboard back into her bag and stalked out of the library.

Anne could only stare at the closing library door in shock. She'd never had such an awful disagreement with Wendy before. Then she heard a sound that made her heart break.

"Mommy?" It was Liddie's frightened voice.

Anne turned to see Ben and Liddie at the bottom of the stairs, holding their swimming carryalls, staring wide eyed at her. Liddie was clinging to her older brother, and Ben had an arm around his younger sister in a protective gesture.

Oh no. Had they heard her entire exchange with Wendy?

And even worse, Wendy had left the library without taking them with her to the pool. She probably hadn't done it to be cruel, she'd probably been so upset with Anne that it slipped her mind, but Anne felt horrible that her children would suffer because of her disagreement with her friend.

"It's all right. Come here, honey." Anne knelt down and opened her arms, and Liddie ran to her. Her little girl was trembling. Ben walked toward her more slowly, his face a little stern.

"I don't like angry voices." Liddie's tiny voice was muffled where she had her face against Anne's shoulder.

"Don't be afraid. Sometimes adults disagree with each other. It's nothing to do with you two."

"I don't like that she said those things to you." Ben frowned.

"Does that mean you and Mrs. Pyle aren't friends anymore?" Liddie asked.

"Of course we're still friends." Anne hoped so anyway. She had to find a way to heal the breach between them. "Why would you say that?"

"Because when kids have fights on the playground, sometimes they're not friends anymore," Liddie answered.

"Well, when you grow older, you'll learn how to forgive and forget."

Liddie sniffled. "Mrs. Pyle left without us."

Anne's heart seemed to break all over again. "I know, I'm sorry, honey. I think she was so upset that she just...forgot about you two." Would Wendy come back later with apologies for forgetting the kids, or was she still so upset that she'd stay away from them all? Anne didn't want that to happen.

Liddie's sniffles seemed to grow louder, or maybe that was just Anne's worry making it seem that way.

There was a tentative cough from behind her, and she turned to see Remi and Bella standing on the other side of the counter.

"We, um, might have an alternative," Remi said. "If your kids wouldn't mind not going to the pool...?"

"We can go home and get the backyard waterslide," Bella said. "It'll be great in your backyard, and we don't mind watching the kids for you this afternoon."

Anne wanted to kiss them. "You two are lifesavers. Well, kids?" She looked down at two sets of eyes that seemed to be lightening. "How about water sliding with Bella and Remi in the backyard instead?"

"No purple dragon?" Liddie seemed sad she couldn't wear her favorite floater.

"You can ride your purple dragon," Remi said with a grin.

"You can go superfast too," Bella added, and Ben perked up.

Anne sent Ben and Liddie to clear a place in the grass while Bella went home to get the waterslide. She admitted she still felt upset about the argument with Wendy, but she just wasn't sure what to do about it.

There was no one at the checkout desk, so Anne took a moment to pray. *Dear Heavenly Father, thank You for Bella and Remi being able to help out like this. Please help me with this issue with Wendy. I don't want our friendship to be torn apart just because of something as silly as Beau-Mart, but Wendy seems so adamant about it.*

Anne sighed. It wasn't just her and Wendy, but other people in Blue Hill too. *Lord, please don't let our town be further divided over this.*

But Anne had a bad feeling that things were only going to get worse.

***

Anne heard the library phone ringing, and she turned from the scene in the backyard with Ben, Liddie, Remi, and Bella shrieking and laughing over the waterslide. Their fun seemed to ease the anxiety in her chest over the Beau-Mart argument with Wendy.

"Hello. Blue Hill Library. This is Anne."

"Anne, this is Mildred. I know this is last minute, but are you free for an hour or two this afternoon?"

Mildred's voice sounded excited, which immediately got Anne's attention. "I think so. What do you need?"

"Well, I have an appointment with the Beau-Mart representative to look over my property, and I'd feel better if someone came along with me."

Anne was surprised. She hadn't even known Mildred owned property in Blue Hill that Beau-Mart might be interested in. "Sure, let me check to make sure I can leave the library." She put the phone down and went to the History Room, where Betty Bultman was shelving books. "Betty, would you mind holding down the fort for me this afternoon? Just for an hour or two."

"I don't mind at all." Betty gave Anne one of her warm smiles. "It's rather empty right now anyway."

"If things get hectic, you can ask Bella or Remi to help out," Anne said. "Once they dry off, that is. They're in the backyard."

"Yes, I heard them." Betty's eyes twinkled. "They're enjoying that waterslide just as much as your children, I daresay."

"More than I would have," Anne said cheerfully. "Thanks, Betty." She went back to the phone. "I'm free, Mildred. Did you want me to pick you up?"

"If you wouldn't mind? Your car has better cushioning than mine, and the property is among the foothills south of town."

Anne was glad she'd offered, because she wouldn't have wanted to ride in Mildred's Buick LeSabre on winding, bumpy roads, especially since the car wasn't as new as Anne's Impala. "When shall I pick you up?"

"In twenty minutes? I'm scheduled to meet the representative at the access road to my property at two o'clock, and it'll take us a little while to get there."

Soon Anne was following Mildred's directions down a country road, heading south of Blue Hill.

"Stay on this road for another five miles, almost until you reach the highway," Mildred said. "Then the access road will be on your right, but we'll park along the side of the road and wait for the Beau-Mart representative."

"I didn't even realize you owned property out here," Anne said.

"An uncle left it to me years ago. It's farmland that's been leased to Ray Wilson for longer than I've owned it."

"Wilson? Related to Beth Wilson?" Beth was a young mother who came to the library often with her five children. Her youngest, Reggie, was a four-year-old terror.

"That's Ray's daughter-in-law," Mildred said.

"But if you're hoping to sell the land to Beau-Mart, what about Ray?"

"Actually, he wants to retire. His son, Beth's husband, doesn't farm — he's an accountant — and he wants his dad to move in with them. So if I could sell the farmland to Beau-Mart, the timing would be good."

"Well, you have a good chance," Anne said. "You said the access road is right near the highway, right? That would be a good selling point."

"Yes, but Beau-Mart would have to arrange with the county to create on- and off-ramps to the highway right there." Mildred frowned. "I'm not sure if that's going to be worth the money for them to do that, and I really need to sell the land."

"You do?"

Mildred gave Anne a quick look, then turned her face away. "I meant, I'd really *like* to sell the land."

But Anne had caught that quick look. Why did Mildred need to sell her land? And why wouldn't she want to talk about it?

Anne also didn't want to push, so she said, "Who are we meeting?"

"His name is Colm Laufey." Mildred might have seemed a little relieved at the change in topic. "He's the Beau-Mart representative who's in charge of the team of land surveyors that will assess all the property in Blue Hill. Mr. Laufey will then make the report and recommendation to the Beau-Mart executives about buying the land chosen and building a store here."

"That's quite a big job. There must have been a lot of people eager to have him look over their land."

"Actually, Beau-Mart must have sent in an advance surveyor to scout out Blue Hill, because they approached me about my farmland perhaps two months ago," Mildred said. "I heard that they did the same for Hugh Zumfelde and Aaron Corrigan. I'm not sure about the other properties that are being considered."

"That would make sense," Anne said. "It would be easier for Mr. Laufey to already know which properties he was interested in, rather than having property owners calling him to make an appointment for land that's obviously not appropriate for Beau-Mart's new store."

"I'm sure some landowners did call him once the news got out," Mildred said. "I think that's how Max Grindell got on the list."

"Max came into the library last week and told me about what happened." Anne sighed. "Such terrible timing." A bunch of reckless boys had done wheelies with their trucks and ruined Max's newly laid gravel the day before he was scheduled to have Mr. Laufey look over his property for Beau-Mart. Max had paid a lot of money to fix up his access road so that Mr. Laufey would even consider looking at his property, and it had been terrible to arrive on the day of the appointment and not be able to drive down his access road because of all the potholes.

"The police haven't mentioned this, because they're still investigating," Mildred said, "but I was talking to Max right after it happened, and he said that those kids went through a lot of trouble to break into his property. They not only cut the heavy chain locking the access gate, they actually broke down some of the fencing around it so that their trucks could fit through."

"That's a lot of effort just for some joyriding," Anne admitted. "Especially because there are other farms that aren't locked down."

"Max wondered if someone paid those kids to deliberately ruin his new access road," Mildred said. "At first I thought he was overreacting, but after I thought about it some more, now I'm beginning to wonder."

"But who would do something like that?"

"Competition *is* pretty fierce," Mildred said.

Anne knew most of the people whose land was being considered by Beau-Mart, and she didn't want to think that one of them would be so underhanded. "Did Max reschedule his appointment?" Anne asked.

"Not yet," Mildred said. "He's trying to fix the potholes in the access road. He can't afford to redo it again, but he doesn't want to give up the chance to show it to Mr. Laufey before he leaves Blue Hill."

"Poor Max," Anne murmured.

Soon they were nearing the highway that arched over the country lane ahead of them, and Anne could clearly see the entry to the access road on the right. She pulled over and parked. The access road cut through fields planted with what Anne guessed were soybeans, and far down the road stood a white and gray two-story house. "Is that where Ray Wilson lives?" Anne asked.

"No, actually that belongs to the Corrigans. Their land is all to this side of the access road." Mildred swept her arm across fields of wheat. "Ray's house is farther down the road. He farms all this area nearest the highway."

"The Corrigans' land is being considered by Beau-Mart too, right?"

"Yes. Their property is bigger than mine, but mine is closer to the highway."

At that moment, a blue sedan pulled up in front of Anne's car and a tall, thin man got out. He had thinning pale brown hair and a large, slightly hooked nose. At the same time, an SUV pulled up in front of the sedan.

Mildred got out of the car. "Hello, Mr. Laufey." She shook hands with him.

"Mrs. Farley." He had a deep voice and a rather grim cast to his face. Anne wondered if something had upset him or if that was his natural expression.

"This is my friend, Anne Gibson," Mildred said.

Anne smiled and held out her hand. Mr. Laufey hesitated, then shook it. He had large hands and a strong grip.

A team of two men and one woman got out of the SUV and approached Mildred and Anne. "Hi, Mrs. Farley," the woman said. She was in her twenties, with dark brown hair done up in a knot at the back of her head. "I'm Kat Lewis. We're the surveyors."

"Chris Portman," said the taller of the two men, with dark blond hair and well-defined muscles beneath his T-shirt.

"And I'm Tam Cain," said the third man with a smile that was wide in his narrow face. His long black hair was held back in a ponytail.

Mr. Laufey had opened a map and was studying the land around them while tracing it on the map in his hand. "Mrs. Farley, your land runs from here toward the ravine?" He pointed toward a point in the distance.

"Yes. I have thirty-five acres total, but Ray Wilson has been farming the ten acres closest to the highway. The rest is lying fallow, but it's pretty flat since it used to all be farmland."

"We wouldn't need all that land," Mr. Laufey said. "But if we were interested, it would be in the acres closest to the highway. Would this upset Mr. Wilson?"

Mildred shook her head. "He wants to give up the lease on the land and retire."

Mr. Laufey nodded in satisfaction. "Well, shall we go look over more of the land?"

They got into their cars and Anne led the way down the access road, with Mildred guiding her. They passed the Corrigans' farmhouse on the right, then continued down a little ways to a second farmhouse on the left, this one painted bright blue. "That's Ray's house," Mildred said. Then she pointed to some barns set some way back from the road, which had a neglected air. "He used to have cows and horses until his knees began giving him too many problems, so that's when he cut back on the number of acres he's leasing."

They drove on a few more yards until the access road turned a corner and ended on a flat expanse of hard-packed dirt in front of a rather dilapidated barn. However, Anne was alarmed to see a haze in the air that seemed to be coming in thin tendrils from the barn.

Then suddenly Ray Wilson came out of the smoking barn and ran toward them, coughing and waving his arms to get their attention.

"Mildred, don't get out!" Anne opened her window and was able to now smell the smoke from the barn. "Ray, are you all right?"

"Get back!" His eyes were red and he stopped to cough, hard. "I've already called the fire department. The barn is on fire!"

A NOTE FROM THE EDITORS

We hope you enjoy Secrets of the Blue Hill Library, created by the Books and Inspirational Media Division of Guideposts, a nonprofit organization that touches millions of lives every day through products and services that inspire, encourage, help you grow in your faith, and celebrate God's love in every aspect of your daily life.

Thank you for making a difference with your purchase of this book, which helps fund our many outreach programs to military personnel, prisons, hospitals, nursing homes, and educational institutions. To learn more, visit GuidepostsFoundation.org.

We also maintain many useful and uplifting online resources. Visit Guideposts.org to read true stories of hope and inspiration, access OurPrayer network, sign up for free newsletters, download free e-books, join our Facebook community, and follow our stimulating blogs.

To learn about other Guideposts publications, including the best-selling devotional *Daily Guideposts*, go to ShopGuideposts.org, call (800) 932-2145, or write to Guideposts, PO Box 5815, Harlan, Iowa 51593.

SIGN UP FOR THE

Guideposts Fiction Newsletter

and stay up-to-date on the Guideposts fiction you love!

You'll get sneak peeks of new releases, hear from authors of your favorite books, receive special offers just for you …

AND IT'S FREE!

Just go to **Guideposts.org/newsletters** *today to sign up.*